TI

A Killer Carriage Collection
By Nancy Lindley-Gauthier
(Cover Image by Lisa Cenis)

THE NEAR WHEELER: A KILLER CARRIAGE COLLECTION

First edition. May 23, 2018.

Written by Nancy Lindley-Gauthier.

Dedication

To Kent, for always

Contents

Chapter 1 The Picture-Perfect Drive

THE CARRIAGE ROAD CURVED along the edge of a sheer drop, though with an ample shoulder, before the sandy track meandered back along a corridor between giant pines.

The stillness of the picture-perfect view imbued the scene with a certain serenity. Sunlight dappled the mirror surface of the pond, leaves shone a healthy green, and the sky above was a perfect, unmarked blue. It might have been a painting.

Thus, the upturned wheels of the antique phaeton carriage at the bottom of the cliff came as a surprise, even though they were searching for that very vehicle.

Alicia Goodwin, stable manager, stood and looked over the faintly surreal scene. Nothing in the immediate environment so much as hinted at what must have been a sudden, violent accident. Only the wish to be thorough had even made her check the edge of the road.

The day had started off as a perfectly ordinary, busily enjoyable day for all her equestrian guests. The stable hosted visiting horse enthusiasts, for trail-riding, wagon rides, and carriage drives throughout the charming state park. Park users shared one huge parking lot: hikers with backpacks arrived with their park-passes all quite correct, having ordered them, incredibly efficiently, online. Dog-walkers and various day-trippers arrived somewhat less prepared, but usually equally enthused.

Alicia had been in the midst of the regular morning mayhem when one very lovely girl groom had reported disaster.

A big pair of bays had returned to the stabling on their own.

Various bits of harness and the carriage pole had arrived with the horses. No carriage, no elderly driver. Alicia had spent the search hours since, hoping against hope.

"My worst nightmare," Alicia muttered, looking down at the wreck. Oh, why hadn't the blasted groom been riding on the carriage like a proper navigator? She'd been off riding her own horse, perfectly sure her boss 'would be fine.'

"This pair are like, bombproof," Belinda Carson had said.

Bombproof. As if any animal were one-hundred percent perfect.

Just like that, disaster.

Alicia sighed again, quite accidentally, as she looked down over the ruined vehicle. She guessed it hid the equally-ruined driver. The long drop, the crash; no doubt about the end result. The whiskery whiskey-sipping driver had reportedly been a pompous ass, but she couldn't help feel regret. He'd been grumpy and given to complaints, yet had appreciated the stylish old stable and the carriage roads. He'd given decent donations in addition to his horses' board, and apparently spent much of his retirement helping with various nonprofits.

She paused a moment there, waiting; for what, she could hardly say. Some sense of life, like a motion, a sound? Hope did not rise from the perfect stillness.

She called out to her search companion. "There it is."

The good sergeant hurried over and began to assess a route down. "How did that happen?"

Alicia shrugged. "Mr. Arbuthnot was supposedly quite a horseman, but accidents happen."

"He was not a professional?" Startled, the sergeant consulted his notebook.

"Oh no. He was something in the city, back before he retired. Still served on various boards and things. This is, was, his hobby. It's not like he was here to give carriage rides or anything."

"Yet, he was out here alone?"

"If it had been later in the day, there would have been people around. I think he often got an early start, so he could do his own drive, at his own pace."

"Fast, you mean? Foolish?" The officer took a long look over the edge of the cliff, and without waiting for Alicia to respond, started to shuffle over the rock ledge.

Alicia seized his arm. "You can't get down there. We'll have to get the wardens to come up that lower access road, to recover the, the remains."

"There's no way down this cliff-face?" The officer scanned the terrain in every direction. "The victim could be, well. I suppose not. It is quite a drop. Incredible that there's no guardrail, no precaution here at all? Hardly sensible." He stepped away from the drop and pulled out his radio.

It did not seem credible that a local officer could be surprised about the park's lack of guardrails.

"Spoil the view?" Alicia quipped. Rails and other safety-additions had been a point of debate among park officials and the local town council, for years. For eons. More than a few accidents had happened within the park. How could he not know?

This was a particularly favorite scenic overlook and folks went out of their way to drive along this stretch of trail. The especially rough and rutted track along this stretch of carriage road attested to its level of use. Several hiking trails lead to gaps in the trees all along here, all for a glimpse of the 'unspoiled' view. Shadows and dapples and distant hills created the sense of a poem in a place. It was a spot Robert Frost would have picked to convey quiet beauty.

"Usually, accidents happen where there's a lot of traffic, bottlenecks, that kind of thing." The officer's brisk words dispelled her reverie.

Alicia did not point out that the road was plenty wide enough, not only for a horse-drawn carriage, but for another to pass.

"It's something of a miracle that the horses weren't injured." Alicia began to explain how the horses might have panicked and galloped off in a blind panic when they parted from the vehicle. "They apparently kept on following the road, until they reached the stable yard. I've gathered they were once wheel-horses for one of the big-time competition drivers, so I guess that speaks to their level of training." In spite of her own explanation, it struck Alicia as odd.

Belinda, the horses' groom, said she caught them as they jogged into the parking area. They were still completely harnessed and apparently not all that upset. The battered swingle trees and torn reins all spoke to disaster, but the horses were unharmed. "Miraculously unharmed," Alicia said aloud, feeling more and more doubtful.

The groom might almost have been watching for them. She'd been riding slow circles in the arena right by the return-trail. Her own horse, another plain bay, looked a perfect match for either of Arbuthnot's imported pair.

"One could hardly blame the groom for watching," Alicia reminded herself, "It is her job take care of the horses when the turnout arrives. She was probably expected to be on hand."

The sergeant was busy reporting in and paid Alicia no mind. Since she had reported the incident, helped with the search, and found the carriage, one would think he'd listen. On the other hand, she'd hardly meant to air doubts. She didn't know anything.

After all, it had all turned out quite fortunate; Oh dear, except for the dead man. She'd heard the gossip. Her own good friend Marigold knew all the gossip, so Mr. Arbuthnot's reputation had indeed preceded him. Alicia had to admit the man had been courteous to her, but apparently he had a whole other side. All she could honestly say, was "It was lucky the horses weren't harmed, that's all."

"Accident," the sergeant said briskly into his radio. Alicia thought of all those crime-scene investigations reported on the television. The sergeant had not so much as looked around, never mind investigated.

Thoughtfully, she began to inspect 'the scene,' as they say.

The dirt road showed the passage of many carriages, as well as innumerable hoof prints. All the marks of travel kept to the main-way. Only one set of wheel tracks had drifted out onto the shoulder of the road, and those lead right to the edge. No hoof prints carried on so far, though. The horses had obviously parted from the vehicle before it left the road.

Alicia followed the tracks. She could see where the vehicle had left the road at the apex of the curve and shot to the right and then off, into space. Exceptionally deep hoof-prints marked the spot.

That doesn't look like driver error, she thought. More like the horses jerked abruptly to the side. Something might have spooked them. "Right there," she said aloud. The carriage had disconnected from the pole and, in so doing, disconnected from the horses, at that sudden jerk.

The officer tapped away at his radio with great focus. Or perhaps it was a GPS? The man had an array of gadgets.

Alicia dismissed him and continued her own investigation. In the midst of the road sat an object rather like a smooth-sided screw. Alicia took two steps closer. It was a metal pin, scuffed and scraped, but recognizable. "The evener pin," she murmured. The pin would connect the carriage pole to the carriage body.

She motioned to the officer.

The policeman clicked something as he muttered "waypoint."

Alicia quietly studied the pin as she mused over the crash. It was an old carriage and several things could have caused it to come apart. This one pin was not the end-all be all, but it was pretty darn important.

It might have simply snapped. On the other hand, it had been built to withstand the pulling power of multiple horses. It didn't appear to have broken, so much as sheered-off from its main attachment point.

She straightened and waved at the officer. Coughed. "An antique carriage expert might be able to tell with more certainty," she began, "but this metal pin might be it. Broke off whole, I think, as it looks solid enough."

"The offending piece?" he raised his eyebrows and – for a second there – looked for all the world like one of those inscrutable English detectives in the old mysteries. "Shame. Broke off in such a dangerous location. Worst spot imaginable."

"Surely if it broke, part of it would have a jagged edge?"

"Now, miss, no need to imagine wrong-doing. Leave all the investigating to us." He scooted the piece into a plastic bag. It didn't look like much; a metal pin.

"Fingerprints." Alicia noted.

The officer chuckled. "Another armchair detective. I know you mean well. No sense looking further here, ma'am. I assure you. We'll take care of the Arbuthnot case."

His cheeks dimpled as he spoke and gave him a suddenly boyish air. He damped down his smile, back to his official demeanor, with haste. If he hadn't been such a smarmy, self-satisfied sort, he might have actually been attractive.

Alicia managed not to stamp at the fool. 'Leave the investigating.' Honestly. Hadn't he said accident? She could tell the officials weren't going to do anything. She quietly looked out over the very famous, picturesque view.

The grand pond overlook would be forever linked in her own mind to this sad affair; sad or ... possibly hateful? She could think of at least one reason for someone to sabotage the carriage. She had only gossip and conjecture, and too-good a grasp of human nature, to suspect that Mr. Arbuthnot's death was no accident.

A tall, slate-blue heron stood in the midst of the distant pond, perfectly at one with the scenery. He looked lovely, although, in truth, he was hunting. With a sharp beak and a keen eye, he was more than capable of becoming nasty. Very deceptive for those not in the know.

'Not every pretty thing is an easy victim.' Alicia did not say the words aloud, for, in fairness, she was only guessing, about the lovely, lovely groom.

Chapter 2 Marathon to Murder

SOCRATES ERUPTED FROM the water hazard and powered up the bank. Slick from sweat and splashing, the chestnut pricked his ears as he passed by the crowd in the snack tent. His speed brought the audience to their feet. A smattering of applause followed as he galloped around to the left, followed by the briefest silence, as his carriage driver did not bring him quite left enough.

Absolute silence reigned as the magnificent horse charged through the out-gate.

"Eliminated." A scrawny woman front-and-center in the patron's tent screeched, "Albert you fool. You fool!"

Not one other spectator affected surprise or shouted. No, as a group the spectators dove into whatever they were doing; checking phones, spreading jam on muffins, or attentively reading over the day's schedule. Mr. Albert Baddinton mimed raising his hat flamboyantly as he trotted off, too far off to hear his wife and plainly oblivious to his mistake.

Silence followed his departure.

Alicia Goodwin, last-minute, fill-in stable manager for the weekend, looked about the tent in surprise. She'd leapt in here when Summer Stables had closed for the season. Barely a 'hop skip and a jump' south along the coast, it was on her way home. She looked on it as a golden, four-day-long opportunity.

Albert's complaints about the original stable manager had gotten that person fired. Plainly, no one else dared to risk his wrath for any reason. No one snickered. No one commented aloud on his silly-ass mistake. Everyone from grooms to competitors, caterers to officials, wanted to keep in his good graces.

His wife did not share their concern. "The fool," she shrieked again as she stormed out. "Eliminated!"

"Oh, surely not," a timid voice offered.

Tipsy Baddinton did not give the comforting soul as much as a glance but bee-lined toward finish line. Every gaze followed her departure. The aging Baddintons, known to all and sundry in the New England carriage world, made their presence felt. They had money; not entirely a help to them, at times. To a horse, it didn't matter what you were, or did, in your other life. They didn't care how you paid the bills. Here, a hairdresser might beat out the top city lawyer, and a teenager might pilot a pony around to put the wealthiest would-be in their place.

A soft titter followed Tipsy's departure. Only then did the comments kick off.

Deviating from the proscribed path or missing markers did indeed result in elimination. A carriage driver, assisted by a navigator, had to drive along the planned course, through 'gates' marked with numbered flags, and through obstacles of various construction. Some of them were elaborate, others tricky.

The water hazard was a favorite among the spectators.

There were ways to correct a mistake, but one had to be paying enough attention to recognize the error. Of course, the pompous driver might try to claim there was no error at all. Indeed, throughout the tent, there were now whispered mutterings about 'blustering his way through it."

Alicia felt certain the officials would not be able to overlook Albert's error. It had happened in the most public of locations, in full view. Disgruntled competitors might worry about Albert Baddinton's sway with the judges, but it would come to nothing.

There were the odd jokes going now. A current of meanness ran through the humor.

Chief donor to a number of equine events; Baddinton's wallet made friends for him everywhere. He was apparently less generous with employees: Lilly, his groom, skulked near the free snacks which were meant for the volunteers and had scarcely glanced up as her boss idiotically eliminated. Another 'E' came as no news to her.

Alicia, guessing it was all part of any competitive scene, got up to pursue coffee. Whether she wanted it or not, she had a ringside seat to all the gossip. She'd been involved in carriage driving most of her life; why she recalled Lilly's mother, who, back in the day, had been known for her particularly spectacular turnout. The poor woman would likely faint dead away if she saw her daughter this morning, in filthy jeans trying to cadge a free breakfast.

For some reason, the groom declined a cup of coffee from another person at the buffet.

The tall woman asked her directly, "Are you Socrates' groom?"

Lilly paused, stuffed her handful of peanut butter crackers into her back pocket, and nodded.

"Well, Sox is turned-out right to the minute. I bred that horse, and I want to tell you, I am thrilled to see him looking so marvelous."

"You bred him?" Lilly leaned toward the woman. "He is marvelous. I mean, he won't win here today but..."

"He's good enough to win, isn't he? Even a big event. Do have the coffee."

Lilly accepted the warm cup with a regretful, "There'll be hell to pay when they tell the boss he got the big 'E' again."

"It wasn't your fault." The woman tucked her front curls more tidily under her stylish, mauve hat, set off with a hatband and equine logo pin. With the weight of her own perfect certainty, she declared, "Driver error. It happens. He'll win next time."

"Don't bet on it." Lilly crammed half a muffin in her mouth, but kept talking. "The mister keeps messing up."

"We all learn from our mistakes." The tall woman shot a quick look around at the other spectators and lowered her voice to continue. "Although I see from the record that they've had inconsistent results."

The teenage groom snorted. "Inconsistent! You mean lousy. It isn't getting any better. No, mister won't blame himself. Oh no. I bet the missus is already blaming the navigator. Horse will be next."

"It wasn't the horse's fault." The tall woman held out her hand "Caitlin Darrow, by the way."

"Nice to meet ya." Lilly had to set the other half of the muffin down to shake hands.

Alicia looked thoughtfully after the pair of them. Loads of people were overhearing this exchange and word of their groom's comments might get back to one of the Baddintons.

"They will blame the horse; got going too fast, not responsive enough, or not paying attention, or something. It's always something." Lilly rolled her eyes. "They'll sack Mike, the navigator, but re-hire him. It happens over and over. They always blame someone."

Mrs. Darrow stood silent for a long moment. Around them, mean-spirited whispers filled the tent. Neither looked around at the others in the tent.

"It's going to be an awful day." Lilly heaved a sigh. "I better get to the finish line. I'll have all the cooling out to do, and then Mrs. B's pony to get ready."

"No one can say that horse doesn't look terrific, and that is the sum total of the groom's responsibility," Mrs. Darrow told her.

Alicia thought it very decent of the woman to speak to the groom so kindly, although her statement was far from true. Grooming was only half the job; the other half was keeping your mouth shut about the boss's business. Once a groom broke that rule, they were likely moving toward departure. Alicia set her coffee cup down and quietly followed after Lilly, hoping to catch her for a private word. A word to the wise, perhaps, about how comments can get around.

Lilly shuffled directly across the parking lot to the vet box, situated not fifty feet from the finish of the marathon. She went quickly and boldly marched straight into the fray.

Tipsy shrieked at her husband, his navigator (the inestimable Mike M.) and at the world in general. Two volunteers and the vet's assistant came in for scathing looks. Tipsy swung around as Lilly marched up, but merely glared as the groom simply set to work on her charge. Albert stood hunched at the horse's head.

Alicia, hanging back, decided against that word of warning. Quite possibly, losing this job might not be the worst thing to happen. The girl would undoubtedly have other opportunities.

Lilly did her job like a pro. She sponged off the big chestnut gelding and led him away from the fracas, although near and far, all were still able to overhear Tipsy shout, "you're sacked, this time for good," at her husband's navigator. People tittered and elbowed one another.

There would be no secrets here. An awful lot of inquisitive eyes sat smugly witness to the lot of it. Alicia did a quick check through stabling on her way back to the main tent.

Unimportant discussions of minor happenings vied with the more important issues related to current standings. Some of the other folks in the singles horse division murmured things on the lines of 'that's too bad about an elimination,' to avoid gloating. Some did gloat, more on the lines of 'who cared what people thought?' Baddinton's own regular drinking buddy gave a great guffaw. He'd taunt Old Albert later, without mercy.

No one really cared, except, perhaps, the other competitors in the single horse division. Chief among them was one Belinda Carson: yes, indeed.

Belinda, the self-same one-time groom to the late Mr. Arbuthnot was entered in this very competition.

What a peculiar coincidence.

Further, with old Baddinton's elimination, it appeared Belinda was in the lead in the singles division. Alicia watched as the woman quietly left the tent, called her groom, and sauntered out on course. Alicia noticed them checking the water hazard from the sidelines, no doubt fearful of a similar mistake. The two were unmistakable in their flamboyant, matching polo shirts and be-ribboned helmet covers.

No one else in the tent failed to notice them, either.

One called out – snidely? Humorously? Alicia couldn't tell, but one squeaky voice declared "Don't stress about your go, Belinda. Albert will make up some excuse and still win." A little ripple of laughter followed the comment.

By the time Albert and his navigator made it to the tent for a quick nip out of a hip flask, Tipsy could be seen driving her pony in the distant warm-up ring, preparing for her own marathon. All back to normal, or so it seemed.

In the stable, Lilly set up the buckets and sponges and a scraper, ready for the pony. She had all of Socrates' harness still to clean. Other grooms were mostly about the same tasks, though a good many, finished for the day, were leading their charges out for some grazing. Mrs. Darrow looked in and then, quite casually, gave Lilly a hand with the barn work.

Alicia had a pretty good view of this side of the stabling tent as well as some of the main parts of the parking lot. Some people had begun painstakingly cleaning and hanging harness. Stuff sat neatly on hooks, ready for tomorrow's cones competition. There was some issue at the main water spigot and she strolled through the back row of a stabling to make sure there wasn't any problem.

Several competitors grazed their horses on the perfect green of the manicured side-lawn. One stocky-looking miniature horse with silver dapples gazed at a tall, pinto mare with a surprisingly dished face, as if love-struck. In the far corner a tanky-looking draft cross yanked tufts out of the lawn that would surely leave bald spots. Alicia suggested he be walked in some less perfectly groomed area and kept an ear out in case the argument over at the water heated up again.

"You'd better get out there to meet that pony," Mrs. Darrow directed Lilly. "Tipsy has already started. You should be waiting right at the finish line for her. Give her no cause for complaint."

Lilly gave the blinkers on Socrates' bridle one more wipe.

Alicia pottered on by, pleased, on the whole. The groom seemed to have landed a new friend, and one with good advice, besides. This Mrs. Caitlin Darrow was plainly a good horsewoman; and a kindly soul to boot.

Lilly slowly, almost resentfully, shot a look out at the marathon finish line. Mrs. Darrow offered to help the groom gather buckets and sponges, to get the groom out there more quickly. With any luck, Lilly would follow her advice.

Alicia slowed a bit, listening, only curious really. Human nature being what it was, and Lilly already having reached the resentful stage, Alicia suspected the groom might very well be ready to throw in the towel.

As if to confirm Alicia's thought, Lilly announced, "I should quit." She reached into her pocket and the big horse popped his head up and looked at her intently through the stall rails.

"He's the reason you stay, isn't he?" This Mrs. Darrow beamed at the chestnut. "He's the spitting image of his sire. Pride of my breeding program, I have to admit. I've been so hopeful Sox would gain us some recognition."

"He's a dream horse, really. My favorite." The big chestnut stuck his nostrils right up to the door and nickered softly. His coat gleamed like copper, attesting to good care – but his eyes attracted the viewer, as they attested to his good character.

"Oh, you." His groom pulled one more treat from her pocket. Sox wiggled his top lip forward to pull the treat gently from her palm. His groom cupped his soft chin in her hand and he stood right there, eyes half shut.

Ah ha, thought Alicia. She stayed for this horse. Her heart horse, plainly, even if he was owned by someone else. Human nature was nothing if not complex.

"But I better get out there." Lilly grabbed the prepared buckets and trundled off, once again, toward the finish.

Mrs. Darrow set the horse's harness a bit more tidily on its hooks.

Alicia noticed the enthusiastic, tank of a grazer was already being led, well, dragged, back toward the stabling tent, so she went back to have a look at how things were running on the marathon course. It was funny how these odd friendships could be struck up so easily at a competition. The two; the teenager and this battle-axe of a middle-aged woman, had nothing really in common. Horses, and this one, exceptional horse, brought them together.

"My Aunty Jane would have loved to analyze these people." Alicia took the opportunity to stroll out to the final hazard on course, set in the far corner of the mown field. This all-posts hazard ran up a hillside and promised a thrilling trip. Alicia joined the little bunch of spectators. She looked out across the great expanse of rolling green field.

Tipsy could be seen, in the distance, going along at a spanking trot. The marked course took her out of view behind a stand of pines. She reappeared after a short gap, noodled around the series of painted posts, and shot triumphantly across the wide field to the last set of flags.

Only Lilly and an official stood there to greet her. Her navigator congratulated her. Tipsy stuck out her lower jaw and glared all around.

No husband, no cheering section, no one worthy of discussing the thrills of marathon watched her triumph at the finish line. She went through to the vet box almost snorting with rage and handed the pony and cart off to Lilly without a word.

The usual flurry seemed to occupy the groom's time; unhitching, sponging down, walking.

Later, Alicia would wish she had remained in the tent. She wished she could put a finger on where, exactly, Lilly had been, during every minute of Tipsy's marathon, and the half hour or so following. Remembering the groom's always-kind mother, Alicia wished she could speak up on behalf of the daughter.

Alicia wasn't thinking that quite yet. She was waiting for the next competitor to demonstrate another thrilling, tight twisty run through the course. This hot driver, Lorenzo, was due next. Every eye strained to see him thunder out of the distant trees.

A shrill scream tore everyone's attention back to the main tents.

Something happening at the stabling.

Alicia ran back across the field, heart-in-mouth. Let a horse not be hurt, let a horse not be: as stable manager she wanted no disasters. No disasters.

The thrills this time were entirely unexpected.

Tipsy Baddinton stood squawking unintelligibly at the corner of the tent. A bystander had already taken over, cell-phone out, assuring people back. "Nothing to be done," he kept repeating, in between explaining to the emergency operator.

"Aged man found dead, appears accidental," he said, or repeated, along with location information. "A blow to the head."

Alicia only realized the extent of the disaster from over-hearing the call, rather than seeing for herself.

Tipsy had discovered her husband, Albert Baddinton flopped over the threshold of his horse's stall, dead. It looked like an accident. Perhaps a kick? He was dead. Quite dead.

The authorities appeared swiftly, and the appearance of uniformed officers awoke even the furthest to the scene.

"Found dead. Perhaps a kick," was repeated here and there until it became a chorus. Ghoulish horror carried the word around the show grounds at light speed. Albert dead. Dead.

The most common response was likely (with a chuckle,) "you don't mean dead drunk?" but gradually, the gravity of the situation got through to all.

Lilly, out grazing the pony, heard the news from Mrs. Darrow. "It's a sad thing, but the fools are saying kicked in the head."

"Never." Lilly marched off to the stabling. "Socrates is the sweetest horse on earth."

All officialdom had already taken over, with yellow tape strung around the barn aisle and then, rather quickly, decently covered then removed the body.

A small crowd gathered, all talking about Albert dead there in the doorway to his own horse's stall. No one had actually seen him kicked. They had all gathered after Tipsy's shriek – mostly after this one sensible fellow had run over and phoned for more official officials. All in all, there was a whole herd of 'near' onlookers in addition to slightly-further off herd made up of 'everyone else.'

No one could claim to have seen much beyond the official vehicles, and various uniformed entities, and so on. Even so, speculation was, as they say, 'rife.'

"The horse, apparently," was an early, yet boring guess, and better, more intriguing ideas followed. "Tipsy looked like to kill, back at the water hazard," was met with a hastily agreed "I'd not cross her for love nor money!"

"If I were the navigator, I'd have killed him myself," was repeated a number of times, and indeed, Mike M. could be seen in the company of uniformed officers. Word had gone around about his doubtful work status, real quick.

"The groom's been complaining all day," was overheard more than once, as well. Everyone felt sure Lilly would also be spoken to. Poor Lilly seemed to feel the many gazes about her, amid waves of doubt.

Tipsy herself was seen struggling to answer officials' questions although she was corralled too far from the crowd to be overheard. Yellow tape set up a privacy perimeter as secure as any fence.

Alicia, as stabling official, was called in to move 'the horse' to an alternate stall, to allow officials to better secure and study the scene. "Be careful now, ma'am. The way it's looking, the animal is dangerous."

She took the opportunity to assure them, "This horse, Socrates, is not the type to kick."

The police officer, with a distant gaze, said, "There'll be a thorough investigation. Now are you all right with this big animal?"

Alicia had all she could do not to roll her eyes. 'All right with this big animal?' She held out his halter to demonstrate his kindness, and Sox obligingly came over and plunked his head into it.

The officer did not look exceptionally impressed.

Alicia led Sox out of 'the scene,' but took a good look around as she went.

Lilly went toward Alicia and stepped away from the officer watching her. "This is not right."

Alicia, paused and Sox obligingly halted. "What isn't right?"

The officer stepped between them. "As this is a person of interest, I'll have to ask you to chat later."

Lilly ignored him and motioned to Socrates' stall door. "Strands of hay spattered down over my freshly cleaned harness. Why would Albert have thrown a flake of hay over the door, anyway?"

"It's likely he went in to remove the horse's studs from his shoes." Mrs. Darrow pointed at the small box next to the stable door.

"He never did that. Why would he do that? And Sox never kicked anyone."

The officer placed a hand on her arm. "I'll have to ask you to wait over there."

"The box of hoof studs out on the floor." Mrs. Darrow insisted, catching the officer's eye.

"I never leave the box outside of the grooming kit," Lilly insisted.

Alicia nodded. "You'd never risk those little studs getting lost, for one thing."

Lilly nodded vigorously.

Alicia believed her. What she said rang true. In spite of her complaints, she was a good groom. Alicia glanced at the policeman, who edged back as she led the horse past. Scared to death, thinks it's another horse accident– he thinks all horses are dangerous. Alicia let Socrates stop at the corner for a mouthful of grass.

Mrs. Darrow said. "The Police will sort it out, though. Do all that forensic stuff."

Socrates took a step forward to reach toward a particularly tasty-looking tuft of grass. His hoof print left several deep imprints in the soft turf.

"I don't suppose they really are considering Mike, the navigator?" Mrs. Darrow looked around at little huddles of people, all still talking. "Folks are saying he more than had reason. Over and over, in fact."

Lilly, still in the barn aisle, said, "They fire him all the time."

"And Tipsy herself. They say she's the one with the money." Mrs. Darrow put her hands on her hips and heaved a sigh. "Accidents do happen."

Alicia tugged on the big chestnut's lead rope. She started to say "C'mon fellow." Paused. The hoof prints in the grass clearly showed the marks of studs. Every stud was still in place.

Mrs. Darrow pointed to the hoof prints. "The most likely answer is, the old man went to check on his horse, and seeing he still had studs in, decided to remove them."

"Mr. Baddinton never did jobs like that himself," Lilly insisted. "Never."

"Did you mean to take out the studs before you went for the pony?" Alicia asked Lilly. "Maybe you left the box out."

"No. I knew I wouldn't have time 'til after. They're hard to do." Lilly was emphatic.

"You've had a lot of distraction today," Mrs. Darrow patted her new friends arm.

"I know how it happened," Lilly responded. "Someone tosses some hay in, over the door. Sox goes to back of his stall to eat it, and then they opened the door and shove Mr. Baddinton's body in the doorway."

"He was already dead," Alicia agreed. "Putting the body there made it easy to explain as an accident."

"I think the box of horse shoe studs explains it perfectly," Mrs. Darrow insisted.

How odd for her to keep offering this explanation, Alicia thought.

Mrs. Darrow prattled on, "Who would even want him dead?"

"You did it," Alicia said, with perfect confidence. "Mrs. Darrow, over a mistake, wasn't it? This latest elimination."

"One mistake! One! Don't be ridiculous." Mrs. Darrow spun away from them. "You are crazy to suspect me. I hardly know those people!"

"You did it? You're actually wanting them to blame Socrates?" Lilly shouted. "How sick is that? You bred him. Took care of him as a foal! What if they think he's dangerous? What if they put him down?"

Mrs. Darrow paled. "They wouldn't. Would they? Look, look how it is! If anyone looks at Socrates' record, it is littered with losses, eliminations, one ridiculous thing after another. Not his fault. I came out here to figure out the problem. When I sold him to them, I thought they had the cash to take him to the top in competition, and instead, they've dragged him down. Socrates could be a champion! He was supposed to be the pride of his sire!"

Her voice, growing louder and louder, put old Tipsy to shame, for indeed, the gathered crowd heard. Not only had the nearest officer heard, they all heard.

"At least, everyone knows, now," Alicia said gently, as the police approached. "Socrates is a great horse."

"No. I didn't mean I did it! These idiot people." Mrs. Darrow protested most vehemently as the police began their questioning. She had all but confessed though; her motive shone clear.

Alicia felt certain they had the culprit. Or nearly certain. Because, no matter what, she could not forget Old Mr. Arbuthnot's death off the edge of a cliff. It was certainly an odd coincidence that his groom, Belinda Carson, happened to be here: Here, in such close proximity to yet another death.

She handed Socrates's lead rope over to Lilly. "Mr. Arbuthnot's end is going to haunt me forever. I wish they'd investigated."

At least this Baddinton case was cut-and-dried.

Chapter 3 Marigold's View

"YOU WANT TO WRITE A scorching tell-all?" Alicia gawked at her friend. "About the world of carriage driving?"

Marigold Johansen, online blogger and star of the national equestrian social media page, leaned back, crossed her arms and smirked like cat. She nodded back toward the competitors' tent and parking beyond. "It'll set them all on their ear."

"I doubt they could be fazed by anything, after yesterday."

They sat ringside, barely dawn, overlooking the cones course.

Marigold sported a cream cashmere sweater set off by an oversized gold-chain, in sharp contrast to Alicia's grubby flannel-over-sweatshirt look. Alicia lolled, eyes half-shut in the plastic chair, blearily reaching around for coffee after being up half the night anxiously checking on the stables. "Bazillion-dollar horses, no budget for security."

Marigold purred, "May I quote you?"

Alicia ignored her. Competitors had to memorize a long, twisty if not downright tricky route, in a wild looping pattern through a course of traffic cones. The official course had yet to be officially approved. The competition itself would start smack on time, so there were no few people waiting to get a look at the course. They waited on the judge's approval.

"And here's the official," Alicia muttered. Bothersome.

The Technical Delegate, 'TD' to all and sundry, strode past, gaze firmly fixed on the starting gate. She did not stop to chat nor did her course deviate by a millimeter from the center of each gate.

"Now that's quite the ensemble." Marigold shot a sidelong look at the woman. "Wide-brimmed hat and a clipboard? More a pleasure show driver? I don't think I've met her."

"She's the show's official. I think she's counting her steps through there. She won't be inclined to stop and chat."

"She looks ready to kill. I could believe her the murderer, any day." Marigold held up her phone to get a quick snap.

"Hush." Alicia shot a look after the TD, Larissa MainWaring. The woman stood apart, both in appearance and in her seriousness. "I bet it's been a nightmare for her to manage. Accommodating the police investigation, sorting out the order of go, checking rules."

Lots of people, show organizer as well as other officials, should have been a help to her. None were about. The TD marched on alone, focused.

A short while after, another official tableau sallied onto the course.

The cones judge slipped on rubber boots and waded out into the dewy dawn grass for a final check. The ringmaster padded after her, eyes half shut, stopped and stroked his beard. Impatience wafted in his direction. He wore a bowler hat like a badge of office and held aloft a measuring wheel.

"The judge wanted to get the official measurement re-checked before everyone was about, and they're late, holding people up." Alicia set her chin on her fist and gazed over the green.

"What fabulous gossip." Marigold pantomimed waving a pen. "I should make note of that. Do you expect it to lead to violence?"

"I don't know what gossip you think you will find among this tame crowd."

Marigold made a face and began swinging one foot back and forth, impatient. "Perhaps I should focus on you then? Divorced, daughter off to college, dilly-dallying around with short-term jobs in the horse industry. What's next?"

Alicia ignored her and fixed her gaze about the action out on the lawn. She did not want to think about her past. She'd focused on moving from temp-job to temp, and was happily contemplating going home to her tiny apartment on the eastern edge of the county, at the finish of this competition. Firmly she said, "Let's watch our intrepid technical delegate in action."

The TD stopped in the midst of her practice walk, hands-on-hips, and surveyed the entire course, before she called to the judge, "We've an error on thirteen."

"An error at cone number thirteen," Alicia repeated. She leaned over the white plastic table, inadvertently dunking her sleeve in the creamer, to dramatically say, "There's a bit of scuttlebutt for you. Is it improper width? Or is it something more scandalous, more like, like," she lowered her voice, "it doesn't match the official diagram?"

"You laugh, but..." Marigold waved a pen.

"But what?"

Marigold jerked her head toward the wide cones-covered lawn course without actually looking. "Look at the human drama playing out right before you."

Alicia shot a look back at the cones lawn. It could have been the dawn of a show day, anywhere. "I see the normal hustle and bustle. What do you see? Mrs. Sutermayer, elderly cones judge, is about to run off with our ringmaster? Our actress look-alike technical-delegate over there actually is a famous actress, working as TD, incognito? There must be something. What, what am I missing?"

Marigold snorted. "That we are carrying on here, with a carriage show for heaven sakes, even with a death amongst us. An unexplained death. The show goes on. Are we so hard-hearted? Or is it that the wife, who is currently winning her division, said, 'Albert would want the competition to go on!' and we all guessed it is mostly because she herself is in position to win the pony division."

Alicia could only gape. "Seriously? Who cares? Best give it up, right now. There's no scorching tell-all to be had from the carriage crowd."

"While I am right here, front and center to a murder investigation?"

Alicia shifted uncomfortably. There was no easy objection there. "I suppose, if you want something to investigate, that Mr. Arbuthnot died in a carriage driving accident, not two months back."

Marigold slapped her hand down on the picnic table. "No one wants to hear about accidents. It's this suspicious death everyone will be talking about for ages. They'll all read whatever is published on this event, I can tell you that much."

"You said there'd be excitement. Something about a scorching tell-all. People don't want old arguments and murder. They want, well I don't know, heaving bosoms and such."

Marigold gave a spluttering laugh. "O.M.G. You are so old fashioned. Murder is big. The biggest! Speculation will be wonderful. For me, I mean. The blog readership will take off. You must promise to tell me whatever you hear. The fact is, you've been involved in carriage driving forever and a day. People tell you stuff. Or, hey, listen," Marigold said. "You could offer your own ideas. Tackle it like a real mystery. People would love to hear your suspicions! You could solve the murder."

Alicia blurted. "It isn't Baddinton's case that needs solving. It's Old Mr. Arbuthnot's!"

Marigold rolled her eyes.

Alicia, horrified, felt caught by the truth. No matter what she told herself, she felt guilty about 'the accident' at the carriage driving park. She had her own suspicions and hadn't really shared them. She could not escape the fact that the man's death had happened on her watch.

"Problems and puzzles reveal so much about people." Marigold gave her a big shark grin. "It's the little details, foibles say, of others that readers so like to hear about. Taking to drink, or second-mortgaging the home to pay for the competition in Connecticut, or what have you. Reveals others' faults."

"Oh good grief," Alicia burst out. "I don't know any details of any interest about anyone!"

Marigold patted her notebook and said, "Let me be the judge of that. No one tells me a thing. But you, you blend."

Alicia set her cup of honest, stiff black coffee back on the table, curled her nose at Meg's leafy, smelly herbal tea. "You are barking up the wrong tree. All I know about carriage driving, I learned from my old aunty, who grew up in Britain at the tail-end of the carriage driving era. I don't know much about the contemporary competition scene."

Their conversation idled along, Marigold insisting, Alicia protesting.

"What do you really want?" Marigold finally demanded. "You can't honestly say you plan to keep finding temporary jobs here on the North Shore."

"What I want?" Alicia flopped back in her chair. "I'd like to be one of those people that pop up to Summer Stables and drive around, enjoying it all with a friend. Spend afternoons at the used bookstore. Goes out to eat with someone who shares my interests." She trailed off, a trifle surprised at her own words. Before Marigold could further interrogate her, she turned the tables. "What do you want, Marigold?"

Marigold laughed. "No fair! But for me, I want to be the modern day princess in a castle."

"You already live in the Johansen's fabulous Hamilton home." Alicia had to think Marigold's mostly absent in-laws owned the closest thing to a castle one could imagine, if you didn't require an actual drawbridge.

"Now I need the social standing to go with it." Marigold leaned forward and tapped the table. "When Steven lands a job with an international company and I land on the board of, well anything, I will have arrived."

"Arrived." Alicia rolled her eyes. "In the horsey realm, you mean?"

"Around here, the horsey crowd is the in crowd."

Beyond, the judge finished measuring and adjusting. Competitors in rubber boots began tramping about the grass.

Various middle-aged ladies in floral pastels brought complaints to the TD's attention.

The TD grimaced as yet another competitor hailed her.

"No wonder she looks so grumpy," Marigold pointed at the woman. "She's worked her ass off and everyone is complaining."

"It is a bit of a thankless position."

Gradually, the day began to take shape. A couple competitors trotted by, aiming for the warm-up arena. The miniature horse division started the day's competition, followed by small ponies. A plain brown pony with spritely trot sped past, pulling a miniscule black-pipe cart. He had a bright look, with his head up and ears pricked. The driver wore a burgundy blazer trimmed in black.

Marigold gave an approving nod. "Smart."

"That woman got her pony for next to nothing because he was a perfect snot to children," Alicia said without thinking, "and she has won all outdoors with him."

"You see? You do know. All these little tidbits."

"Are useless. No one cares," interjected Alicia.

"People like the news. Especially not well-known news. Almost secret stuff, or a trifle nasty, especially. This will be worth reporting on, for sure. It all comes down to human nature," Marigold insisted, and Alicia realized, it did, indeed, it did.

"Human nature," Alicia mused aloud, almost regretfully. She nodded to the classy looking TD there, studying the course so seriously. "Really, she could be the most logical suspect."

Meg leaned back. "What are you talking about?"

"The TD. Larissa Mainwaring. Old Baddinton got the stable manager canned because he wasn't happy with how the event was running. Who's to say the TD wasn't next on the chopping block?" Alicia shrugged. "I still think it was Mrs. Darrow, to be honest, but it could have been the TD."

Marigold raised her eyebrows. "She happens to be in the stable when he gets back from marathon, so she conks him in a fit of rage, then tries to make it look accidental. All the while, overseeing the competitors on the marathon?"

Alicia sighed. "OK, that perhaps isn't it. There is something about her, though."

None other than Mr. 'Leave it to the officials,' drew up to their table. "Ladies?"

"Sergeant Perkins?" Alicia sat up straighter. "I wouldn't have expected to see you here. This can't be your jurisdiction?"

"I was on temporary assignment up in the northern district." The man, for once not staring at some handheld device, continued, "And in fact, am here to follow-up on the death at the carriage driving park up there."

"You are investigating it?" Alicia goggled at the man. Hadn't he said, accident? "At the time, I mean, you seemed to dismiss..."

"There are a number of leads we are following. Quite a number of people here are also visitors there."

"All quite confidential, I would guess?" Marigold leaned toward the man. "Anything you'll commit to, right now? For publication, I mean."

"Police blotter is a matter of public record. We're tying up loose ends, talking to some area people. The victim at the State

Park had been accused of a traffic incident where he had struck and killed a local man's dog."

"Old Gladdie," Alicia supplied. "The little shepherd. Everyone knew her. She always came with the farmer to deliver hay."

"It was apparently an accident, but Arbuthnot never apologized."

Marigold snorted. "Arbuthnot would have run over the farmer without regret, never mind a dog."

"To be clear, you are investigating Mr. Arbuthnot's death, as something other than accident?" Alicia persisted.

"As I mentioned, its matter of tying up loose ends," the officer explained. "But yes, technically, Mr. Arbuthnot's death investigation is still active." He gave Marigold a short nod. "You can certainly quote that."

"How exciting." Marigold fell back in her chair and squinted at the cones field. "Police insist on wasting time on an accident."

Sergeant Perkins wasn't listening. He bent to pick up a multi-colored kerchief, and, without hesitation, handed it to Alicia. "Yours, I think? It suits you."

"It suits me?" she accepted the item, which was comprised of six different colors and looked like it might belong to a circus clown.

"It is yours?"

"It is," she admitted. A guess, or was he surprisingly insightful?

For human nature did tell, when it came down to it. Alicia recalled her great-aunt's stories. Aunt Jane was as great one to 'solve puzzles' as she called them; big and small. 'Human nature will tell,' Aunty Jane often said. Aunt Jane had grown up at the

tail-end of carriage driving time and knew horses, but also, people.

Chapter 4 Ne'er-do-wells and the Road Coach of Old

VISITING 1887

James Emrys-Smith, 'Smithy' to all the world, sorted the leader lines tidily from the wheel-horses' and handed them forward to the coachman. As he sat back on his precarious seat on the top of the venerable old road coach, Smithy straightened the trailing ends over the backrest.

"Ready."

The coachman gave short nod. "Bournemouth, by midday."

"You'll do it, Mr. Edlington." Smithy smirked as he spoke, safely out of the view of either the coachman before him, or of their half-dozen passengers below. They mostly did not know of wagers flying among some of the village gents, though that sharp-eyed niece of Mrs. Grey's had given him quite the look when he had held the door for her.

Smithy's money was on failure. The coach might be able to make it, but the slightest delay would do them in. Smithy felt confident about creating delay.

The coachman glanced at his watch, but still did not send the horses forward. He drove with quite a flourish, as a matter of pride; but then again, he usually had his two stalwart chestnuts in the lead. His usual pompousness had quite disappeared. Finally, he queried, "The near-leader?"

The grey mare, as if she understood, tossed her head-somewhere a step more than impatient and nearer fractious.

"She's a top notch tandem horse and could make the time soul-alone if she needed to."

"I'd have rather had my own." Coachman Edlington did not want to admit the mare seemed like a handful. Gone were the true coaching days, with coachman as skilled as they were elegant. The road-coach run had fallen to a special occasion outing, and it was no usual matter for him to take up the reins on a four. Not anymore. His wheel-horses were dead-honest. Edlington had accomplished this run a fair few times with only the two. It wouldn't do for a coaching event, however. The Bournemouth coach parade required a four, and by gum, Edlington wouldn't let the Mead-to-Bournemouth run fall into disgrace. The big man shifted the reins of the leaders one more time, tugging out any slack.

Smithy knew better to offer to take the box-seat himself, though he styled himself a professional. His ambition was to sit in the coachman's seat, and by hook or by crook, he'd get there eventually. He shot a look at the young man opposite, Geoffrey Grant of Roslingdale House, the only passenger who had opted to ride outside.

Silently, Smithy mouthed, "it was a loose shoe."

Geoffrey shrugged. Pantomimed waving a whip. Plainly, he thought they should get on with it. There was no point to argue.

After a moment, the coachman sang out, "trot on." Sixteen metal-clad hooves rang out on the cobblestones. The coach leapt forward amidst the clatter.

A little ripple went among the men gathered there by the High Street Pub. Every single one, to a man, checked the exact moment the coach set off. Most were 'in the know' and had money on, though they'd all have been careful not to mention to the ladies. A flock of women quacking on about dangerous speed would be no joy to anyone. The Coachman gave the men the barest nod. Bournemouth in three hours was the wager, and the men, as a unit, nodded in return as the horses clattered out of the square.

"Bournemouth. Tourist destination, scoundrels' opportunity, lovers' rendezvous, and likely all at once," Aunt Katherine stated.

"I can't wait," exclaimed young Jane.

Aunt Katherine smiled. "Indeed, you will find many ne'er-do-wells' shenanigans to occupy your busy mind in that city!"

The carriage jerked as the grey mare tossed her head yet again and powered forward. She'd gone lead in a tandem so would be no slouch.

"They are setting off fast, Aunt Katherine." Inside the rocking coach, Jane arched her eyebrows at her companions. "It will be an awfully bumpy ride when we reach the forest."

"If they keep on like that," Claire burst out. "We'll be smack up a tree."

"Girls, I am sure coachman Edlington knows his job." Aunt glared at her two teenage nieces, though they'd said no more than truth.

Aunt Katherine might be forgiven for her terse response, for even now, she gritted her teeth and clutched the handle protruding from the well-worn velvet-covered wall. Remnants of carriage lace still clung to the seat-backs and gilded trim had not faded entirely, but with the advent of the train, these old road-coaches, and their drivers, had become a curiosity. This had been the manner of travel in her day; the only manner, at one point.

The coach lurched around the corner off High Street and onto The Lane, leaving the village of Mead's Mills behind.

"They've borrowed Mr. Armstrong's tandem leader." Jane leaned to look out the window. The fancy grey, owned by the local livery stable, had a smattering of dapples and the reputation of a 'night-mare.'

"Tandem!" Aunt Katherine said the word as if it were scandalous. "I've never approved of driving in such a manner. When I was young, some towns set ordinances against it. There were lads who would take the reins whether they'd skill or no. More than one saved from disaster only by leaders as responsive to voice as to rein."

"This is quite a respectable coach." Jane frowned as she spoke, for the scenery shot by at an unseemly rate for such 're-spectable' vehicle.

The horses settled into a big, steady trot. Edlington reached forward to tug the second rein from the top, held it for the barest moment and eased it forward again. The mare straightened satisfactorily. He held all four reins secure in his left hand, and enjoyed a moment of all four sailing smoothly forward together. It lasted but a moment. The near leader again started to turn toward the inside.

"Smithy, I believe you set the right front rein shorter on the grey." The Coachman again made his slight correction and again, the mare responded nicely. Edlington pursed his lips, his demeanor suddenly jaunty. "Right on the money."

Smithy rolled his eyes. Geoffrey Grant smirked. They two men would have likely shared comments about the coachman, his age, or his want of courage, if they didn't fear him overhearing. Smithy wanted to keep his job, to be sure.

More: Smithy wouldn't mind being coachman. He absolutely believed in his own skill. The skill and the nerve. He'd be one of those coachman, the others referred to, in any discussion of horses and driving. And here he was, sat on the back here like a groom. He shook his head at his boss's back.

The coach jolted off the cobblestones and onto the rutted track through the forest. The grey mare accelerated and her pair-mate, a stalwart character most of the time, sagged, perhaps a bit disgruntled at this sudden, faster effort.

Edlington brought his whip forward with a flourish and tapped the laggard's hip.

It was a marvelously skillful tap, the like of which few could emulate. The great length of lash unfurled and lightly touched its target with impeccable style. Unfortunately, the recoil required a match of skill.

Edlington was undeniably out of practice.

The curl of the lash slapped over to the other, more-sensitive leader and gave her a smart zap high on her croup. She launched into the air and plunged forward. The other horses felt a jerk and scrambled into faster trots.

Those in the passenger compartment, treated to an inexpensive trip to seaside because of Bournemouth's sponsorship of a coaching-day parade, might be forgiven if they had expected a gentle journey there. The coach jolted about suddenly, madly. The passengers fell about the compartment with shrieks.

Snarling, the coachman took an almighty yank on the leaders' inside rein and it snapped below the coupling buckle.

The horses carried forward in disunited mishmash for a stride, then another, as the coach lurched.

Inside the passenger box, Jane retrieved her aunt's crumpled chapeau as that lady clung desperately to the side rail. Cousin Claire gave up entirely and plumped down on the floor, though she nearly sat on another's feet.

Luggage bounced off the top of the compartment and away. The wheel horses sped up, stride for stride, as if mayhem wasn't erupting in front of them.

"The leaders' off side rein!" Edlington gasped.

Smithy leaned forward. "Pull up at once."

Edlington hauled back on the wheelers, but there was naught he could do for the lead; pulling the one lead rein on the grey would send her shooting left into the trees. He sat, frozen, horrified. Yet, the wheelers did slow. His near wheeler, wonderful old Thomas, trotted along as deliberately as if he alone drew the great coach. The stolid fellow ignored the shenanigans around him, and it was but strides before his teammate on the wheel steadied down, as well. With the wheelers setting a more pragmatic pace, more drag on the traces slowed the lead team.

Between the deep ruts of the road and the harness knitting the horses well together, the team held straight. The flamboyant grey still surged into her harness, but it was alright, as the stalwart chestnuts doggedly kept trotting. Thomas, near wheeler, kept dead true to the road, and shouldered his companion straight, besides. The four-in-hand remained, more or less, on course.

Geoffrey Grant, third son of the local great hall, clung on to the roof-rack, shut his eyes, but muttered, "keep on."

Smithy glowered, guessing the young man had wagered on them making the time to Bournemouth.

Edlington took the breath of near relief, but ahead, the track widened and open fields sat temptingly beside the road.

"Nothing for it but to stop, Mr. Edlington," Smithy insisted. "Safety and all that."

"Nothing of the kind," Edlington began to say.

The horses' hooves reached the smoother way. The leaders began to drift left.

Smithy tugged the back of the man's coat. "Pull up! We must bring them to a halt-they will go off the road. There will be a wreck!"

Edlington, bare moments from imagining himself driving jauntily through a crowd of admirers at their destination, cringed at the thought of stumbling to an ignominious stop, in the midst of the woods, with all his passengers witness to his failure. He'd have to stop, certainly, but how to manage it quickly?

"Sir, the danger."

Edlington scarcely managed to glare over his shoulder at his demanding assistant before the grey stumbled over ruts on the far left of the road.

Usurping the coachman's duty, Smithy called "Gee. Gee"

The grey mare at once came to the right.

"Stop shouting. Get back in your place," Edlington snapped. It was out of place for Smithy to command them, but there indeed the mare had swung back as directed. Straight again, for the moment.

Now that the first rush of anxiety had gone, why indeed, the mare come straight, nearly on her own. She was not as dangerous as she seemed. Even with the broken rein, she could be directed by voice.

Behind him, he heard Smithy groan.

The exuberant mare, the broken rein; the facts began to come clear to the coachman. The broken rein was no accident. Was some other disaster planned? He had to assume there was.

The coachman took a loop on the wheelers as they turned off the rutted track and onto the smoother seashore highway. With regret, coachman Edlington called "whoa."

His desire to make the time had run headlong into realizing he'd been sabotaged. What else might be in store? Instead of braving on, he must think of his passengers. "Whoa, there," he repeated.

His gentle, wheedling tone might have spoken to the mare's mare-ish sensibilities, although, and this was more likely, as the wheelers slowed, her own traces tightened and she had to pull much more of the load herself. Whatever the reason, she obeyed. She slowed to walk, and then halted with her fellows. Smithy scrambled down to see about the rein.

Edlington felt sweat trickling down his back. He held the reins with a trembling hand, having had a front-row seat to the decidedly risky dashing in-and-out of the road.

Aunt Katherine poked her head out of the forward window. "Mr. Edlington, I must say." Inside, the two girls scrambled back to their seats and Jane tried to fix the brim of aunt's best felt.

"My apologies, Mrs. Carlisle." The man swept his bowler off his head. "We will stop here a moment, to allow you ladies to recover. Perhaps you would care to admire the view?" It was all lost, anyway; he'd had no more than minutes to spare.

The lone gentleman passenger from inside the compartment checked his watch as he held the door for the ladies. Aunt Katherine frowned as she alighted, gave a sharp look to her young charges, and finally, gave the briefest of nods to Edlington. "No harm done."

Smithy busied himself up front, taking too long to deal with this rein. He smoothed a hand across the fractious grey's neck, and made a bit of a show of checking the traces. Perhaps he should suggest putting her in wheel position? He looked up, about to speak, then hesitated. A dark cloud sat over Mr. Edlington's features. Smithy held his tongue, but took his time about the harness adjustments. It was a good few minutes before he scrambled back to the coach, and held the door himself for the passengers.

Edlington silently rubbed the end of his whip across Thomas' wide croup. The horse, though stock still, raised his head, as if he knew. There was a moment there, between the two. The coachman and the great horse knew one another well. Thomas had come through. The horse could not look back at his driver, because of his blinders, but both ears sagged back, listening.

In a gruff tone, Edlington acknowledged, "Thomas."

The horse straightened, hearing the approval.

Smithy missed the exchange entirely. Later, Aunt Katherine would point out that Smithy was not the type to have understood, anyway. The coachman's assistant knew nothing of the character of horses. He was merely an assistant for a reason.

As Jane set her foot on the beautifully curled iron step, she whispered, "It's a tricky business you're about. You'll come to a bad end if you keep at this sort of thing."

The hairs stood right up on the back of Smithy's neck. He couldn't guess how she knew. Or, then, or what she knew. Finally he hissed, "It's a harmless wager."

Coachman Edlington glanced over the side and down at the pair.

"People might have been hurt." Jane spoke low, but Smithy cringed.

Smithy never did grasp how she knew, but she didn't rat him out to Edlington, that was what mattered. She climbed into the passenger compartment and looked away without another word.

He had his money on the other way, and no one would guess that now, would they? And it would suit his ambitions, too. He climbed aboard with a show of alacrity, knowing full-well they were already too late. He sat smugly, thinking of the pay off.

Edlington recalled the groom calling the 'gee' command and the mare's sudden obedience. An unfamiliar horse, a broken rein, and then, Smithy's clever correction, after he'd let them struggle along for miles. The coachman didn't need to overhear Jane's comment in order to guess.

Edlington glowered down at Smithy. "You're sacked."

Chapter 5 Horse Brasses

"NOW WHAT?"

As a group, people gawked toward the parking lot over where the groom stood about grazing horses. Alicia, lost in memory, found herself dragged back into the contemporary, to her annoyance.

She clambered to her feet. "As it seems to be at the stabling tent, I'd better go check." 'No need for you to come,' she might have added, for all the good it would do. No fear, Marigold grabbed her handheld and followed.

A granite-faced man was painstakingly backing up a massively long trailer into a narrow spot. The front of his truck took up too much road to allow anyone to pass.

A plain pickup truck, sans trailer, sat a hair too close already and edged nearer, as if to harass granite-face out of the way. The person jigged toward the front, with obvious impatience, but her pick-up simply would not fit by.

The bigger rig inched forward again. The other jerked forward a couple inches, too.

It was short of road rage. Still unpleasant.

Alicia plodded over and took up a stance, also in the way. "What seems to be the problem?"

"I need to get going!" The woman in the driver's seat leaned out. "Do you mind?"

"This driver will only be a minute."

"It'll be bumper to bumper on the main road within the hour." The driver took a deep breath and tried again. "I apologize. What's my rush? I can give this guy a couple minutes."

"Mmmm." Alicia noted quite the pile of harness in the back of the truck, along with buckets and assorted other junk. "You're Annie, aren't you? The former barn manager? I was sorry to hear you were let go."

"Oh sure, sure, everyone's sorry." Annie waved her hands above the steering wheel. "All my expenses to get out here, animal care at home, and I end up not paid, not reimbursed a dime. Look, not your fault. No hard feelings. Now, do you mind getting out of the way?"

Marigold held up her phone for photographs.

The woman turned beet red she began to harangue Marigold, too.

"What's the problem?" Sergeant Perkins strode up, the epitome of a calm and calming officer. He glanced at the big rig, laboriously easing backward, then raised his eyebrows at the pick-up. "What's the rush?"

"She's the barn manager old Baddinton got fired," Alicia explained. "In a hurry to depart." Alicia did not, for one minute, consider the former manager a suspect, but...

Perkins announced, "I can't let you drive off without a word with the investigative team. Simply a matter of routine."

The woman barked, "I've stuff to do. I can give you my contact information."

Would she be in a hurry to leave, if she were guilty? Risk causing a stink? Alicia thought not. Better to have departed hours ago, or the opposite, taken up a casual air, hung around, and watched the competition.

People coming down the short drive. A man jogged around the sharp corner from the parking lot, raised a hand and called, "Hey, stop her. Stop her."

Perkins raised his eyebrows. He placed one hand on the driver's side door and leaned back on his heels. "Missing something, sir?"

He'd guessed, Alicia realized. Perkins had delayed the driver on purpose.

The good sergeant was nobody's fool after all.

The man scurried over to them, explaining as he came, "Antique horse brasses, all hanging at the carriage club's display. They were right here, not five minutes ago. I stopped to help load up and when I got back, they were gone."

"And what," asked the sergeant, "is a horse brass?"

Horse brasses! Alicia, startled, recalled an old story of Aunt Jane's about brasses. What an odd coincidence. The pricey, decorative harness pieces didn't crop up all that often, at least, not in competitive driving circles. She peered closer at the back of the lady's pick-up truck. "Sure enough."

Several highly-polished leather straps sat, cleverly hidden in plain sight, in among the rather grubby plastic-type harness dropped atop them. Face down, the decorative brass ornaments attached were not immediately visible, but the quality of the fine leather gave the game away.

The lady tried to bluster. "It's all my ordinary harness, I don't know what you mean!" followed by a hasty "Don't you need a search warrant?"

The sergeant politely explained, "Not for items in plain sight, Ma'am. Afraid I am going to have to ask you to step out of the vehicle."

"Anyone could have that sort of decoration," Annie tried to argue. "There are tons of harnesses here."

The gentleman immediately said, "Officer, these are all individually insured and I can pull up documentation on my phone, with pictures of each. They are quite distinctive."

After discussing the value of the brasses ("Good lord, really?") The arrest, and tears and all, finally, the handsome sergeant offered to see Alicia back to the stables.

Alicia might have been surprised, if she hadn't been focused on the arrest.

"Just because she's a thief, doesn't mean she isn't also a murderer," Alicia couldn't help but point out, "But I don't think she is."

The sergeant said, "Perhaps I could buy you a coffee?"

So attentive, his manner caught Alicia's attention, but she dismissed her interpretation as foolish. Circumstances had brought them but briefly together, a pairing like poet Robert Frost once observed; *She a window flower, and he a winter wind.*

To think of those lines of Frost recalled Aunt Jane again. A fan of Frost as much as a student of human nature, she'd have spotted this thief, at once.

Chapter 6 The Heirloom

BOURNEMOUTH, ENGLAND, 1897

A slight southerly breeze swirled off the ocean as the ladies made their way toward the shoreline. An ancient road-coach rattled to a stop nearly beside them, entirely blocking their view.

"Only this moment did I catch the most enchanting view of sun glinting off waves." Aunt Katherine gestured at the coach. "Then this monstrosity arrived."

Young Jane, not much interested in wave caps, studied the coach directly in front of her. The much-faded 'Tregenwells Folly,' seemed aptly named. Grime and cobwebs spoke of its long incarceration in an old barn somewhere.

Bournemouth's coaching occasion had apparently been a bit too successful attracting entrants; for who wanted this sort of conveyance to appear? The grubby vehicle managed to convey a jaunty air through the addition of bright-colored bunting, tacky sashays and jiggling, poorly-attached door panels. Riders clung to the top amid boxes of luggage, and in the main compartment, children squeezed onto laps to fit everyone. The coachman laughed out loud as his four, unmatched and unwashed, stomped into the square.

"Such a common affair." Aunt nearly pulled her skirts aside, and, had the vehicle tarried, might have been soured, but the coach carried on after a pause. "That man is simply no coach-man, either. Two-handed on the reins." She might have carried on, in the way older folks could, but Bournemouth itself saved the day.

Almost magically, the delights of town were all laid before them; the jetty amid rolling waves to the west, and town square, with its great church, art museum, galleys, taverns and the rather nicer hotels all along the long strip before them.

Several smartly turned out vehicles, flagged as local Dorset coaches, had drawn up by one of the more respectable supper-houses, 'The Albion.'

Aunt all but nodded her appreciation as they strolled by. "Our Mr. Edlington will be hard pressed to impress more than this team of all grey horses." A banner draped at market square announced the upcoming 'Coach Parade,' along with other, inviting diversions: a dramatic reading in the library, a special tea on the Tuesday, cricket on the lawn of the commons. Two days' worth of activities were listed, but Aunt strode by. She passed the dressmaker, a fine-China importer and yet another restaurant.

Her two charges might have paused by the confectioners, if left to their own devices, but Aunt Katherine had set a course for the promenade down beyond the jetty and brooked no di-version. "We'll take in the seaside straightaway," she said. "And have a leisurely tour through the museum during tomorrow's rain."

"What if it's fine tomorrow?" Jane shaded her eyes to gaze toward the city's grandest structure, housing the museum.

"My knee says rain," Aunt Katherine told her charges crisply. "Best to get in our constitutional now."

Claire looked down the long (or as she thought, endless) slope to get to the promenade along the sands. "Even at the museum, we'll still be walking about."

Aunt Katherine affected to ignore her comment and strode along with purposeful vigor. Her charges followed. In truth there was plenty to see, from Bournemouth's various structures to its many inhabitants. Ladies strolled in groups of two or three, or swung along hand-in-hand with their children. Gentlemen ventured in and out of the smoke shop, or stood at the corner with today's newspaper. A fair number strode rather more purposefully toward a tavern luncheon. Boys scurried up or down the street on errands. One vehicle or another clattered by every few minutes.

It was all a good deal busier than their sleepy village. The rather late-season coach-parade and prize attracted a fair number of tourists. The finest of people attended, although, as aunt had pointed out, the less-than fine might also be expected.

Everyone came for their own interest, of course. Claire noticed ladies' fashion, while Aunt Katherine appreciated the views. Jane followed her companions, but it was people that caught her eye.

Down at the end of an alleyway, the shabby coach disgorged its occupants. Jane watched, guessing all those passengers were from the poorer quarters of some city. It was a lifestyle spoken of, but completely alien to her small-village life. The people were not at all as she would have expected; they seemed quite jocular and intent on a good time. Women wore long cotton dresses and their fellows had smart shirts and ties, even if they wore workmen's trousers. The coachman, noticeable for his jacket with a plethora of shiny buttons, scrambled from the top and seemed to be herding all the occupants along. He had left the coach over behind the livery stable.

As Jane gawked, the smartly-attired fellow impatiently summoned a street vender. Something about the coachman recalled Smithy, from their own coach; he hadn't the same narrow face, but he did have the same calculating eyes.

Laughter erupted from the group. They'd all be served jellied eels. They handed little cups around, in determined enjoyment.

Claire followed her cousin's gaze. "No street food for us," she whispered.

Jane nodded, not much concerned. Really, she'd have liked to dawdle right there, just to watch.

Cousin Claire proved correct; they did not enjoy a treat from a vendor, but a bracing walk. The sea air was mentioned, the sea-spray appreciated for its 'poetic value,' the waves declared dramatic. Aunt Katherine kept them among proper society, and when it became appropriate meal time, they strolled back up the promenade to the Albion.

Thinly-sliced bread served with a bland broth made up the starter, though it was followed by a nicely-cooked chop with carrots-Vichy and a few fresh greens. Quite nice, Jane thought it. Aunt Katherine ordered plum tart for dessert, hardly a favorite, but she had not invited preferences.

A bark of complaint broke through the steady rumble of conversation.

Heads turned.

Jane noticed that smartly-jacketed fellow from earlier. His group was hardly the type to eat here at the Albion, yet here he was, in front of a dish of steak, glaring about.

A server scurried to him with a tray of something, and the man nodded. Resolution. Diners turned back to their own conversations.

"How strange that man from the Tregenwell's coach seems here," Jane murmured aloud.

"You will want to notice quite a different sort," Aunt Katherine whispered. "The women in the group by the window are, every one, respectable ladies from our next town over. All councilman's wives, if I am right. Those girls at center table are daughters of the great house at Plumny. They came in by train, I am sure. It's their governess at the end of the table."

The ladies – older or younger – held no attraction for Jane, as they fit perfectly well with the respectable supper place.

The Tregenwell's man was quite other. As she watched, a florid-faced gent swung up beside the fellow, spoke sharp, then set off. "That coachman seems to be dining alone here."

"He's hardly a real coachman." Aunt Katherine, who probably meant to say, 'look at this year's fashionable hats' or direct her charges to other worthwhile considerations, but could not pass by a comment on coaching. "He has neither the clothes nor the flair, nor even proper coaching horses. A farmer who borrowed a clapped out old coach to make a few shillings."

"Yet, he's here."

"What is that, Jane?"

"He's here, spending a good deal more than shillings. He doesn't quite fit."

"My father was a coachman, back when road-coaches had a regular weekly run to the city. They took a certain pride." Aunt Katherine said stiffly. "I can tell you, the skill is not to be found today."

"You said Mr. Edlington was a dab hand," Claire snickered.

"For these times, child. These days don't compare to when I was a girl."

"You are quite good on reins yourself," Jane said absently, thinking how aunt missed the point. Oh, she didn't doubt Aunt Katherine had particular insight into the profession. Certainly, the sharp-eyed man was no coachman even though he'd driven a coach. On the other hand, he did not seem to be working for mere shillings.

He simply did not fit.

She found it curious, but did not belabor the point. She glanced around the room, guessing that most every patron had come in from the country. All but the one fellow.

"The heirloom piece, Jane." Aunt Katherine glared.

Jane stuttered, "er?"

"Do pay attention, Jane. Attend the conversation."

Claire leaned forward. "I like the 'faithful dog' paintings best, Aunt Katherine. I quite admire yours."

"The museum here has several of Landseer's smaller paintings. All are of wildlife subjects. As I was saying Jane, our family heirloom piece was painted in Landseer's tradition. Deer on the heath, quite a common subject for that school." Katherine waited, soup-spoon half raised.

"That odd old coach today had wildlife paintings stuck on it, as door panels," Jane managed to supply. At her aunt's sharp glanced, she gave another try at appropriate dinner conversation. Oh, dear, she'd entirely forgotten that the unkempt coach might be beneath notice. She tried again. "Tomorrow, it will be a treat to see a Landseer original."

Aunt Katherine nodded. "Quite right. And quite a proper comment as well. I'll have no talk of low subjects the like of jellied eels,' She sent barely the flicker of a glance at her other charge. "Human nature being what it is, you must understand how your discourse might make an impression on people. For good or ill."

The girls nodded in unison.

Claire kicked Jane under the table.

Jane guessed her cousin's thoughts, easily. How marvelous Bournemouth would be without their aunt! They would eat pastries at the confectioner's and run down to the boardwalk for ices at midday and go along to watch the singers entertain at Fountain Square far into the evening.

They did none of these things. Instead, they shared a back-room at Tate's Hotel and rose quite early, to fresh linen napkins, small pastries and rain.

"Aunt Katherine, you were right." Claire looked out on the dismal, drizzly day.

"Perfect day for the museum." Jane suspected the museum would prove more interesting, in any case. Perfect for people watching.

They were not the only ones to think so. The 'perfect' evaluation had to be measure against crowds, although the penny-piece for two kept the common sort out. 'The common sort' in the shape of several plump ladies arrived at the front door in their ragged road coach, but bunched up around the doorways and amused themselves looking in the windows.

Aunt Kathryn urged her charges away from the front area entirely, to contemplate paintings that any of the more grandly-dressed ladies chose to study.

Each contemplation took a fair few minutes longer than either Jane or Claire cared for, but some indeed were simply lovely. One otherwise uninteresting watercolor offered particularly bright colors, attracted all of them, and at precisely that moment, came the first shout.

It was in a different room and of course, Aunt Katherine murmured a ladylike "Extraordinary" before shepherding them in the opposite direction. As the fray continued, she thought it best to leave, as a number of other ladies seemed to have decided. Escape for all was quite arrested however, as security guards swung the doors shut.

Word went round: the constable had been called. In a peculiar whispered whirlwind, the ladies heard the gossip: An original Landseer had gone. Stolen.

"Stolen," squealed Claire. "Right while we were here!"

"Improper," snapped Aunt Katherine, who availed herself of a side chair, over by a group of older ladies. She rallied though, apparently thinking this was a 'moment.' "Decorum – decorum is all, speaks to a lady's education, as well as respectability. You must behave. Where you choose to visit, every word you say, reveals something about you." She coughed delicately into her handkerchief, turned an equally delicately shade of pink, and motioned to the girls.

"Water? Can I fetch you a glass?"

"I find the proximity to criminal activity," Aunt Katherine said, pressing her palm to her face, "to untruths and danger, quite undoing. We were nearly witness to reprehensible behavior."

"I think we are all witnesses to such things," Jane said. "Most people don't trouble to much notice them. Intrigue happens every day, and I guess motivations are often similar, whether a person steals to get what they want, or lies, or tells a little fib to get out of a certain dinner party, it's all to get what they want. Even to dress a certain way to impress a person is a kind of deceit. There really isn't much difference in the motivation."

"Or tries to get the world to believe how proper they are," Claire said. Hardly tactful.

"Girls!" Katherine pulled out of her swoon enough to glare at her charges. "Indelicate and unladylike."

Claire murmured 'sorry,' though Jane merely nodded. Interestingly, the Tregenwell's coachman had strolled in here as if he'd come on holiday himself, and stood there among the smart-jacketed holiday crowd. He peered around, hands-in-pockets like the other men. He certainly didn't look like he belonged with the group from the Tregenwell coach.

Jane craned her neck to see if she could see any activity over in the landscapes room. Wildlife, one room over, seemed the source of the trouble.

"Jane," hissed Aunt Katherine. "What did I just say on behavior? You should not gawk around."

"I think the Tregenwell coachman stole a painting. He doesn't look like he's with the group outside, but he is. We saw him bring them. He seized his moment, I suspect. He could have handed the painting off to one of ladies outside, who then fixed it to the coach door. It looks like a door panel. It's another wildlife scene, if you remember. They all look so similar."

"Jane!" Aunt Kathryn began to sound exasperated. Her two nieces seemed a trial to her, on this particular day. "You cannot possibly know."

Jane chirped, "I need a moment." She dashed to the earnest-faced man stationed at the front door. "The painting you seek is on the coach right outside the door. They've replaced the door panels with art."

Before he could respond, she ducked away.

She'd been perfectly sure, though couldn't guess quite how the man had handed the small painting to the waiting ladies, but the curator's exclamation, scarcely a moment later, proved her correct.

"It was all in spotting the person that didn't fit in," Jane mused aloud.

"Theft. Very horrid. You see my point now, about this type of town. Always on your guard my girls, always on your guard."

Aunt Katherine took no further notice of the others in the crowd, or anything to do with fashion, but waited impatiently to depart.

The occurrence had quite ruined the day for her.

Jane pondered human nature. She did not, herself, object to some excitement. She decided against any such admission. Instead, she said, "We should take in the ocean today. We've brought our umbrellas. Think how dramatic the stormy sea will appear."

Chapter 7 Cones Course Insight

MARIGOLD WOULD HARDLY be interested in an almost century-old drama. However, recalling Aunt Jane's run-ins with various unscrupulous types did provide some insight for Alicia. At least, she believed it did. At the picnic-table ringside, she watched the competitors mill before her. Bright orange cones, set exactly, made up a looping pattern across the wide lawn.

A small group of people walked around the course, committing it to memory. Some stopped at various points, talking as if to coach themselves, while others fairly trotted around on their own feet, as quick as they could manage. Each had their own plan of attack.

The batch of people driving the smaller equines in the practice arena began to look impatient. They had not hit official start time, but those first to go wanted to get on with it. Nerves.

Human nature. Alicia looked out over the crowd gathered for this, the final competition of the event. A murder had been committed here, right under her nose. Under all their noses. Most of these people knew one another; some quite well. They had known the victim. They were all laughing and chatting with a sad lack of concern. What would Aunt Jane have thought of sorting a killer out of this crowd? Would she have considered human nature, the vast array of possible motives, or, looked for someone that did not quite fit?

The TD lurked near the finish line, able to see every inch of the course. She carried the mantle of consummate profession-al, yet she must fall prey to her own emotion, at times. The TD was everyone's target, at one time or another. She was known to be remarkably competent. You could certainly imagine her killing someone.

Lovely Belinda swept by, carrying her driving apron over one arm. From groom to the box seat was not such a big leap; for a good horseman. Horsewoman.

Alicia watched as the woman carefully strode through the cones making up the serpentine. She looked like she fit in with the best of the drivers.

But did she really fit in?

Belinda paused at the corner and asked, "as they are flagged 'A' through 'D' can you circle between them? Like the num-bered cones?"

"No. The lettered ones, flagged in order, have to be taken one after the other, without going out of line, as that is seen as off-course." The TD spoke with perfect assurance. "You'll be eliminated if you take them out of order; you have to do one after the next, even if you hit one."

"Ah."

Without a thank-you, Beautiful Belinda slowly paced off the distances between the cone 'gates.' On the sharpest turn, she walked deliberately wide, paused, and then walked back. She marked a wider turn to the corner.

"It'll be a hard turn to negotiate," Alicia murmured.

A moment later a woman in bright blue bobbed through that same furthest corner. She grasped her hat against a sudden gust and said, loud and frustrated, "I'll never get from the 'A' cone to the 'B.'"

Belinda smiled back at her. "You don't have to make a too-tight serpentine. You can make an extra circle, between the cones." Her confidence belied the lie.

Had Belinda explained incorrectly by mistake? It hardly seemed sportsmanlike to misdirect, or did she so wish to win? Exactly how much did she wish to win? Enough to kill? Belinda might have feared Baddinton would win, with the whispers that his mistake might be 'overlooked.'

Belinda. At the scene of two different deaths. Alicia stared uncertainly over the mob of people.

"It's all an elegant façade." Marigold peered over her shoulder at the competitors marching between the array of orange traffic cones. "A façade over a seething pool of deception. That will be a fabulous headline for tonight's blog!"

"Oh my stars, this is not a seething anything. These are nice people!" Hardly were the words out of her mouth, than Alicia recalled Aunt Jane's take on 'nice people.'

Chapter 8 A Society Venture, 1897

LATE IN 1897

The coaching occasion at Bournemouth left Aunt Katherine in the throes of recollection. "In my day," began her every sentence. The clop of even the milk-wagon's horse hooves brought forth a sigh. It marked the start of a boring week, and, sadly, appeared to be carrying on into the following. Aunt sat with her needlepoint and recalled 'society.' Yet 'society' seemed far too far away. For the teenage cousins, Jane and Claire, the road ahead appeared entirely without any foray afar.

Jane knew Mead Mills and all of its, as she believed, very ordinary inhabitants. She'd barely had a glimpse of a person Aunty would term a 'commoner' far less one who might be considered 'society.' Jane was eager to discover the differences in the fine people her aunt spoke about. So far, all she'd gathered involved them eating off fine China and driving fine horses. Were they indeed 'fine,' or nicer than the more ordinary?

Aunt Katherine would be one who knew. After all her years inhabiting Shell Cottage, fourth on the left out of Mead Mills' town square, even with her regular church attendance and quilted-pillow donations to the annual fundraiser, Aunt Katherine was still the one different. She had grown up in the shadow of wealth and education. Her father had been a coach-man, a respected professional attached to a grand estate.

Aunt Katherine understood 'ladylike' to the depth of her being and made it her mission to so direct her nieces. She usually missed no opportunity to introduce them to the finer things.

"Society," Aunt always insisted, "is a whole other world."

And society had become more and more intriguing to Jane. Was it a realm peopled by an entirely different type of person? Did titles come with an uncommon disposition? Her curiosity only grew, but these sorts of questions only made Aunt Katherine cross.

There were no great houses in the area, far less proper mansions with titled inhabitants. Travel alone was unheard of. Jane began to feel she would never get a look at 'proper society.'

When the leaflet arrived announcing Roslingdale Manor's benefit tea, all Aunt did was sigh and turn back to her favorite book of verse. Jane read the obvious signs and sensibly resigned herself to hearing more of 'the old days' as plainly Aunt had no intention of escorting her nieces to the tea. Aunt must, at times, miss the grander lifestyle too much.

Claire was neither resigning type nor willing to miss a party. She skipped sensible requests and went directly to conniving. She plumped down at the wicker table on Aunt's tiny porch and declared, "I've heard a real society lady never drives a horse and trap herself. Unladylike."

No matador ever waved a red cape more effectively.

Aunt sat bolt upright and barked, "I drive with every bit of skill as any lady. Why, in my youth the ladies started with a governess cart and went on to phaetons." She slapped a hand down on the flyer for the tea. "There's not an elder among the

Roslingdale House ladies wouldn't have learnt to drive proper. It's a tradition as much as ever," She thrust out her jaw "I can tell you, in my day, ladies drove."

Claire attempted to assure of her doubtless 'ladylike' ability.

Aunt Katherine got up in a huff. "I do not believe I speak with any undue pride when I claim, it is with as much skill as many a man; in these days, likely better than most. Unladylike! These simpletons of the village. As if they'd know."

"How could they know?" whispered Jane, with a daring, conspirator's air.

"Indeed." Aunt Katherine waved a dismissive hand in the general direction of the village. "With no one to direct their education, they are indeed victims of their small world."

Claire ducked her head, winked at Jane and said, "It was a village lady who said, and I should have paid no attention."

Aunt shook the flyer. "I have quite made up my mind. We shall attend this, Thursday week. Both of you shall wear your best, and I can tell you, we shall be the society there."

"Hosted at the Grant's, Roslingdale House," Claire pointed out.

"Why, they do not even have proper servants, and they are calling this 'a formal tea." Aunt slapped a hand down on the paper. "There's nothing worse than pretending to be above your station, but by heaven, one must not sink below it either! I've half a mind to order a horse and trap from the livery just to show these village types a proper turnout."

It took no effort at all, after that.

They ended up with a nice pony pair from the livery, set to an ordinary 4-wheel trap. The three of them squeezed onto the front seat together. Aunt Katherine sent them off at a spanking trot, reins in one hand, whip held aloft. The chestnut ponies, with their matching blaze faces and snow-white stockings, clattered in unison over the cobblestones. Gents doffed their hat as the trio drove out of the village. At least, Reynolds the Baker and Thomas from the livery did. Aunt Katherine nodded graciously, imagining every eye upon her. Neither of her two charges took much notice of the drive. Their excitement started as they swept up the front staircase and were greeted by the lady of the house.

First of all, no one they knew had 'a front staircase,' to say nothing of the fancy brick front entrance, tall lanterns and a groom at the ready to take one's horses.

The girls fairly floated up the stairs, imagining a proper ball inside.

Mrs. Grant, the lady of the house, wore a dusky blue day dress with decorative satin shawl. Pearls. She was perfect elegance. One of the church committee ladies stood alongside, in a busy pink brocade with too much trim, looking, for all the world, that one step 'lesser.'

Jane guessed her aunt would later giggle about the ridiculousness of an overlarge lady of a certain age in a 'pink frock.'

Bouquets in the foyer were a prelude to a tour of the house and garden. Jane, eager to see 'society,' felt it almost spoilt by the attendance of a quite a few ordinary village ladies. The lady of the house stayed at her post at the door, and various members of the church showed guests about.

They were kindly people but Jane wanted to check on this Grant family and see how they behaved, how they spoke, and if there would be an apparent difference.

She followed the fussy flock of ladies as they stopped by first one room and then another. The older set peeped in the drawing room doorway, every bit as eager as Claire and Jane and some of the other, school-age girls, to get a look at the goodies prepared.

There was a half-hour yet, before it could be considered a decent tea-time, even if one dared hope service would be smartly on time.

The first glance only made the crowd more impatient. An elaborate tea service had been set at the ready. White doilies shone against blue-linen table cloths, each housing a different tray or tureen. Decorative blue-and-white cakes and crystal dishes ready for ices sat amid bouquets and lovely, tapered candles in glowingly polished brass holders.

The ladies could be forgiven for easing in a few steps to better appreciate the fine points. Incongruously, a strap of decorative horse brasses lay on the floor, near a chair leg.

Aunt Katherine accidentally trod on a broken blue taper-style candle on the floor inside the entry way, next to an ornate snuffer. She reached down, paused, and crouched there, arm outstretched, mouth agape.

As one, the village ladies followed her gaze, past the bent brass candelabra half-under the tea table, past the brass ornament and leather strap, to the snow-white hand emerging from under the table's front bunting.

It took a long moment for the ladies to grasp the situation. The hand, scarcely visible, emerged from a black-sleeve arm and...one imagined...under the table...the rest of some gentleman. Such was the paleness and unmoving quality of the hand, death was plainly at hand.

Silence draped the drawing room at Roslingdale. The ladies, each and all, clutched onto something; a couple clung to one another, one placed her hands over her mouth while another seized on her hat. Aunt Katherine stood stock-still with one hand outstretched.

Mrs. Potts, from the upper end of High Street, fainted dead away.

Anyone might have taken charge; the village ladies, after all, ran the gamut from old to young, practical to silly, nervous to pragmatic.

Yet, it took Jane, scarcely a teen, to suggest a sensible route. "We should leave the drawing room and send for a constable."

The various levels of consternation called forth family members. Mrs. Potts was assisted to her feet, though she stood shaking, hand-in-hand with yet another, pale and shaking woman.

Geoffrey, vaguely familiar, ("third son and a mile from any inheritance, never mind title," Aunt hissed) shepherded the ladies from the front hall into a sitting room He looked around as if expecting immediate assistance. "Someone will ah, bring tea."

Not a soul arrived or backed him up. Voices straggled in from the front hall.

"It's the group from The Basingstoke Church running it all." Aunt meant it as disparagement. "Heaven only knows."

Jane took it to mean any sort of chaos might easily be expected from these obviously ordinary organizers? She pondered her aunt's words, but more; she pondered that single, snow-white hand.

They were not speaking of it, yet plainly, each and every person were thinking of it. There was no doubt, none at all, as to what it signified, though of course, none could guess who might be there, under the table and dead, nor yet why.

"Chaos," repeated aunt, at the sound of feet tramping about. Not only in the front rooms and halls, but in the kitchen and free-roaming.

Jane's stomach grumbled, unbecomingly, but Aunt did not seem to notice. Tea time had come and gone, and all of those gathered simply waited.

Aunt took up a casual stance, quite near the door and appeared to be, oh dear, listening.

"The police have arrived," she announced at one point, and "Breeding will tell in these sort of circumstances."

Jane and Claire nudged one another, without any grasp of what Aunt might mean.

At last, officers in uniform stepped in to the room to properly take over. Heaven knew where the family had been closeted. The guests were shepherded into a large sitting room on the opposite side of the house.

A large bobby brooked no argument. "You might have witnessed something quite important. We'll need to ask each of you questions."

Primly, Aunt said, "My dear officer, these younger gals should not be subjected to this discussion."

A muttering of 'decency' followed her comment.

The officer kept a poker face as he nodded to a second: without argument the more junior officer waved the Jane and Claire toward the back stairway. "Surely there's somewhere they can wait."

"Below stairs." The eldest of the church ladies led them to the lovely flagstone kitchen. A few others, dismissed as they had arrived later than the discovery of the body, tagged along.

The Grants had a cook, so (though they fell short to Aunt Katherine's mind), they certainly appeared wealthy enough to the young cousins from the village.

The ladies set about pouring cups of tea for one another. Cook pulled the reserve stock of scones, white cookies, and sugared plums that had been kept back, just in case. She winked at the older women and set an uncorked, half-empty bottle on the table, too.

"For the shock," the pink-frocked lady declared.

Cook, in her wide white apron, settled familiarly at the table with the ladies. She nodded to the two girls. "You set right down an' have a cup-a-tea. Can't have you fainting or swooning, or whatnot. With a death in the house, it's always best to behave sensible."

All the ladies, even in their best Sunday dresses, plumped down at the wide-pine kitchen table and set about their own tea. Upstairs, the earlier guests were corralled in the foyer, but they could hardly be of any use there, could they?

"Dreadful shock for you young things," Cook pushed the scones right over under the girls' noses. "Walked right in and saw it, did you?"

Jane shrank back, feeling every eye turn toward her. After a pause, Claire leaned forward and shot a glance at the door before she whispered, "I am not sure what we should say, really."

"Of course, only sensible," Cook said smartly. "I wondered, you see, I know everyone in the house. You must have seen if it were one of the gentlemen, in tweed that would be, and the master has a beard."

"No," Jane blurted. "I mean, we couldn't see any detail. He was under the table. The table cloth came right down. Only a hand. A white hand. A bit of sleeve, a black-edged sleeve." She trailed off. It had not, in fact, been horrifying. The hand seemed no more real than a doll's. It was now, trying to guess the clothing of the gentleman involved, that the idea of a body attached began to take hold.

Cook did not notice her discomfiture. "Black jacket would only be Smithers. He dresses like a proper butler to 'do' as door-man for our events. He'd been called in for this afternoon."

"Some sort of bad feeling with other servants, perhaps?" Pink Frock mused.

"No other servants. Only me here, and this man Smithers on occasion. He's an old gent. Perhaps he's gone and died."

Claire turned to her cousin. "Go on Jane, you must have seen something more! You said for the police to be called in straightaway."

Jane looked down at her teacup.

"It would only be kindly to clear up any speculation, Jane. If there was some reason to think of, as they say, foul play." Pink Frock patted Jane's hand.

"A candelabra on the floor. Quite mangled. I, I guessed it would be quite near where the person's head must be. And a stain."

A collective "Ah,' or 'ah-ha,' chorused about the table, as the ladies, who had mostly been back from the threshold of the doorway, pictured the scene. The 'ah-ha,' was sadly not regretful but, in Jane's estimation, rather more ghoulish. She regretted sharing. She turned to Claire; the perfectly bright-eyed Clair, who seemed as entertained as any.

Jane could only murmur "It's horrible."

"Certainly, it is," Cook interjected. "But you can see how it is. Anyone would want to know. If it is murder, we could all be in danger."

Pink frock chirped brightly "we could all be in danger."

"Yes indeed," echoed up and down the table as they ladies bit into scones and gossip. "I know this Joshua Smithers. Entirely respectable, I would have said."

"He was in service for a good many years, off London-way."

"Oh, not from around here? Family here, I believe. Came on down to retire, and still takes the odd temporary position."

"Seems unlikely it would be an *affaire d'amour* then?"

"Most unlikely," affirmed Cook.

"Still, you never can tell. Quite smart dress, in his line of work."

"True, true." The ladies launched into 'ever heard of this or that, in connection with their victim, and, though they were all talking so one could hardly sort one conversation from another, they portrayed Smithers, a touch regretfully, as entirely ordinary.

"It was some madman, no doubt." Cook smiled kindly at the two teens. "Not to worry. Police will soon sort it out."

Jane, recalling the scene in the drawing room, simply nodded. As an instrument of death, a brass candelabra seemed an odd choice of weapon.

It was also an unlikely weapon of opportunity, for it was a perfectly sunny afternoon and candles were not required: indeed, no others graced any of the nicely set tables in the room.

A strap of brass jingle bells, a long armed candle snuffer, several horse brasses on a long leather strap. None of them, much like one candelabra, were of everyday use, nor very singular, either, though all were brass, and would fetch a good price. None had business in a drawing room set for afternoon tea.

Theft was the only possibility.

There was all that fine china, and valuable paintings, to say nothing of the silver. Why wouldn't the thief have taken those? There was only one answer: Those finer things would have been missed straightaway. The lesser items, from different rooms and some from the stable, would be missed one at a time, if at all. One might easily believe them misplaced.

"Who is home here today?" Jane asked into the great bubble of conversation, still speculating.

"No one to fear here. Mr. Grant and his wife, and the eldest, Rodney, and then also Geoffrey, the third son."

"But help, surely?"

"There is a man to tend the garden, but he doesn't come into the house. No, it's some stranger, a madman, without doubt."

Jane nodded. She guessed she'd uncovered another example of human nature. She considered some of the 'types' she'd noticed.

The gallery art thief simply wanted to get ahead. He didn't look for any sort of attention, nor yet to hurt a soul. While Smithy, the ne'er-do-well of the village, was quite a different character, wasn't he? Risking everyone when he set the Edlington Coach up for a crash. He hadn't a care who he harmed.

Not so it was with this brass thief. He timed his theft to coincide with the household's guests. If items were missed, how easy to blame some anonymous villager? So he'd not wanted to be caught and had not been too greedy. The thief had started in the harness room and swooped in, arms laden, for the candelabras in the hall closet...and Smithers happened upon him. And sneaky and cautious had become deadly – not carelessly deadly, like Smithy, but deadly nonetheless.

It was all quite plain. Geoffrey, the third son, had no money of his own but easy access to items of value. No doubt the police already had it in hand. Jane nodded, most satisfied, at her own judgment. Human nature was human nature. Society might eat off finer plates but there the difference ended. Young Jane reached for a scone.

Upstairs, eventually they overhead officials painstakingly trying to discover the location of everyone in the house, and the third son, declaring he'd not left Mum a moment, being reminded otherwise.

Jane felt satisfied with her analysis of the case, too.

Chapter 9 The Weathervane

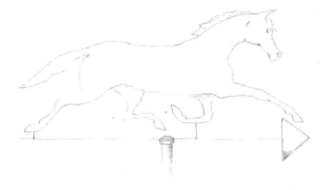

"FRANKLY, I THINK ANNIE the horse-brass thief was the murderer." Marigold rattled out a list of facts; "Annie's here, on the scene. She had it in for old Baddinton, She's been caught red-handed stealing stuff. Probably Baddinton's stuff. Obviously, she's the criminal element."

"Horse brasses are not decoration anyone uses in this kind of competition." Alicia could not believe she had to explain this to Marigold – who, after all – claimed to have all sorts of carriage and horse knowledge. "Horse brasses are for parades, for work horses. They're fun to collect. They are not part of combined driving harness."

Marigold flipped back her perfectly-tinted golden curls and swung one foot impatiently. "I tell you, she's the criminal element. It's a case of people falling into a certain type."

"Poor Annie. They left her with no job and no income quite abruptly, hadn't they? My Aunt Jane would say she's the type for theft. It doesn't make her a murderer."

Educated and elegant did not make one less ambitious. There was one here who did seem 'the type for murder.' Alicia stood abruptly. "I have to make my case."

"Oh, do tell," Marigold chirped.

Alicia marched off after Officer Perkins and started babbling along immediately, before she lost her nerve. "I know you'd like us amateurs to stay strictly out of it."

He smiled down at her. He really did have a nice smile.

Alicia discovered she'd paused there, idiotically staring up at him, so blurted, "I really want you to consider Belinda Carson. She's here, on the scene in both incidences, isn't she?"

"Not exactly conclusive." Perkins clasped his hands together and, in an annoyingly patient tone, said, "I am hoping you don't consider me a suspect. Or Marigold. She was there, as well."

"Marigold had left very early that morning. I waved to her going out the front gate." Alicia found she was waving for her hands for emphasis a purposefully dropped them to her sides. "I can assure you it wasn't me. Belinda is the only one, on both scenes."

"I'll have to consult my notes, but if we go by proximity, there might be quite the list of suspects, what with carriage driving as the common denominator."

Oh, he found himself quite funny, didn't he? Alicia opened her mouth to argue the point, but then, the point proved itself.

If only he had the eyes to see.

In the field beyond, Belinda saluted the cones judge. She drove a single big bay horse, reminiscent of her former boss's horses. Dark dapples gleamed through his shining coat.

The bay trotted smoothly through the starting gate and accelerated through the first cones gate. Belinda's skill shone, as did the horse's training. He was quick and responsive.

She brought the charging bay back to barely a jog to negotiate the 'too-tight turn' with several clever sideways steps.

"That was as near a turn-on-the-haunches as a driven horse can get." Alicia scowled after the horse. Had she not seen Belinda, then groom, trying to ride her horse in that same movement? It was a dressage move Mr. Arbuthnot's fancy, imported and fully trained horses certainly knew. And, Belinda's own horse had been hopeless at it, hadn't he?

"I believe she might be driving Mr. Arbuthnot's near wheeler, right this minute." Alicia looked up at the sergeant. "I am almost certain Belinda killed Mr. Arbuthnot. Maybe Baddinton too."

"It doesn't seem likely."

Distantly, the announcer called 'and a double clear for the overnight leader.'

Belinda had won.

ALICIA GOODWIN'S CONVICTION – about murder – would come back to Perkins later that same day; come sweeping back, in a flurry of intuition or perhaps, instinct.

Sergeant Perkins eased his four-wheel drive vehicle up the dirt lane to return to the completely empty Summer Stables.

Theft, dispatch had reported. Antique weathervane, very valuable, missing from the center roof of the old stable.

A faintly creepy air hung over the whole place, as if, indeed, a murder remained unresolved here. Summer Stables itself seemed gray-drab. Off-season neglect had settled over the charming shed-row stalls, though they'd only sat empty a matter of weeks. Doors shut, grass sprouting unchecked, and one lone car out there in the vast empty field of a parking lot.

A woman scrambled out of the driver's door of the sedan as he drew up. "I'm the one who called. Called about the theft." She hung back, one hand still on the top of the car door, as if she meant to leave straightaway.

Perkins straightened slowly as he took in the area. It was an odd call, out into the middle of nowhere. The park and stables were closed for the season, with gates locked and signs proclaiming 'no admittance.'

The woman must have felt out of place. She sure seemed ready to depart.

He might have taken her for a teen, with her oddly bright clothes and trendy hair, but closer to, he'd guess nearer thirty than twenty.

He stood by his own car door to address her.

"Did you call about a weathervane, ma'am?"

"Yes. It's an old copper one, used to sit up top of the center of the barn there, you see? It was in the shape of a trotting horse." She pointed at the structure behind him.

Perkins didn't glance away. Every sense warned him of watching eyes. He dared not turn his back. Yet, why would there be a worry? He had had to unlock the main entrance to get in. The circumstances struck him as peculiar. "Park's closed. You have some official business here, yourself?"

"Oh. Hiking, you know. Us locals can always get in. We all know. Some hike in, some come up the access roads."

Perkins looked pointedly at her vehicle.

"All right, some of us go mud-bogging. It can be fun to take a rough ride sometimes. Drove up to get some sunrise photos at a couple of scenic spots. And picnic, that kind of thing." Her flurry of hasty statements seemed contrived. "Coming back through, we happened to notice the weather-vane was missing. I thought I'd better report it."

The little sedan did not seem the best choice for either mud-bogging or picnicking. It did have a fair bit of dirt. Perkins saw no picnic accoutrements. He saw no other person, either. "Who is this 'we?'"

"The woman shrugged, but her eyes slid sideways, toward the white-painted paddocks beyond the parking lot.

Perkins did not follow her gaze. The hair on the back of his neck tingled and the soft, soft breeze clattered through dry autumn leaves and sent a shiver up his spine.

Spooked. Unreasonable, instinctive fear welled up. Part of his mind wanted to shake of this weird sense of danger, and part whispered, 'careful, careful.'

"A friend here with you?" He used a flat, calm voice.

"He didn't want to be involved," She said, her voice high. "I told him I'd do the report. He didn't need to stay. That's all right isn't it? I mean, I spotted the weather-vane missing."

"Why did you want to make the report?"

"Why? Well, it's been stolen." She looked puzzled. "I wanted to report it. It's copper or something. Been on these barns here, the carriage barns, since they were first built. It seems like a shame, you know?"

"It does seem a shame," he said. Copper. Odd to have another valuable metal at the center of a crime. He still found the call odd.

The woman could have called in a report anytime or, driving back through town, stopped to make the report at the station. There had been no rush. The park was closed. The weather-vane might well have been missing for some time. Perkins shot a quick look around.

"I didn't check for it, or anything," she said quickly. "They don't like people nosing around the buildings and stuff, and it's all locked up, anyway. I happened to notice it was gone. All set then? I'll be on my way."

"What about your friend?"

"I'll pick him up at the main-gate, on my way out. I mean, it's no big mystery. He didn't want to be involved is all. Thought it was silly to report it. I couldn't leave it, without saying anything though. What with knowing the history, you see." She spoke in a breathless rush. She hadn't moved but stood there, partway inside the car door.

"Pick him up at the main-gate," Perkins mused aloud. "Why wouldn't he assume you would go out the way you came in?" He folded his arms and, in the sternest tone he could muster, snarled, "Is the weather-vane in the barn somewhere, or did you go ahead and take it? Is it in your trunk?"

The woman's mouth sagged open for a long moment, then, she finally managed, "first stall."

Perkins tried to look in every direction. "Why did you call me out here?"

"Locked in," she mumbled.

"Why didn't you simply call and ask to be let out?"

"Danny said they charge people for rescues and stuff and we thought we might have to pay if we called for help."

"How did you get in?"

"The old access road below the overlook. I don't think this car can make the hill to get out again, that way. I didn't expect it to be so rough."

"So you hit on reporting a theft."

In a small voice, the woman said "I figured, if we call in like a police report, someone would come check it out. Leave the main gate unlocked. No charge, you see? It would be like we did a public service kind of thing."

Silly people do silly things, Perkins reflected, though aloud he said, "Probably been up that trail before? Did you say to the overlook?"

"Yes. The overlook at the pond. I didn't realize the access road would be in such rough shape." She looked down at her toes. "It was stupid."

"Did you come in here, intending to steal the weather-vane?"

"We didn't do any damage." She shrugged again, with that side-long look-away that made him want to cringe.

Perkins couldn't help glancing around him. He noted her license plate. He ought to make her wait, while he checked but, no. There'd likely be no charges. He wanted her to depart. He'd feel better alone out here, for some reason.

He jerked his head toward the park road. "Okay, then. I'll let you chalk this one up to experience. Don't be doing anything like it again, though."

She drove off with elaborate caution. Perkins watched her go before he walked over to the end stall in the long row of closed up, bolted stalls. The door swung obligingly open. The weather-vane indeed sat there, unharmed, though some park worker would have to restore it to its usual home in the spring time.

The old, silent building might house anything. Anyone.

In spite of solving the case so easily, Perkins could not dismiss his earlier notion. His ears strained to hear the slightest sound.

He didn't step into the room; one of those cluttered junk rooms, with aged buckets stacked in a corner, and various horse-related implements arrayed along one wall. A pitchfork with a broken tine, hay bags, a few old rain ponchos, spare halters and snaps and metal clips of every description. "Leftover items or stuff meant for guests who forgot some item of their own." He supposed, any of it might prove useful.

The faintly alarmed feeling did not dissipate. He looked well around before he returned to his vehicle. Perhaps it was Arbuthnot's unresolved death. Or murder.

"Access road," he repeated, thoughtful.

Chapter 10 Halloween

MARIGOLD JOHANSEN, far, far removed from origins involving 'Marge from Massachusetts,' heaved the anything-but-common harness over the back of her imported pony.

"Mainly Selle Français," she told the one onlooker, though the pony looked Welsh and the 'imported' came right out of Marigold's own imagination. In point of fact, he could have been imported. Then again, maybe not. His history, like hers, was a bit vague.

"I love that you had this marvelous, old-fashioned harness for me to borrow. All this metalwork is fabulous." Marigold leaned away and held up her cell phone for a quick snap. Post it straightaway? Maybe wait. Get a splashier one, at the start of the carriage parade. Oh, maybe one. She hummed Prince's *'Raspberry Beret'* as she adjusted her own beret; quite her favorite hat, ever, and sent along the selfie before turning back to the pony. Fussily, she settled the hames more tidily around the pony's neck and began adjusting straps. "The collar and hames should really fit very exactly," she noted, "though we aren't honestly having to go all that far."

"It's all about getting these marvelous antiques out and seen." Mrs. May, curator for the local society's big 'Carriage-

Town' parade, display, and educational gathering, seemed to need to oversee every single thing. She pointed to the cart Marigold had left by the doorway. "Your cart is a wonderful spindle-seat gig. Is it a reproduction?"

Marigold scowled. She never used the word 'reproduction,' because of its faint undertones of being less-than-real. It was a good enough imitation to be mistaken for an antique, by most people. Plainly, this curator was not to be fooled.

Marigold brought the pony out to hitch and decided to tackle the facts head-on.

"Most, honestly, wouldn't know the difference between it and an actual antique," she finally said, as she started to back the pony between the shafts. "Stay straight there, Monsieur."

"I know my knock-offs. I suspected as much, I can tell you." This curator-woman gave a snort.

Marigold found the woman completely obnoxious. Knock-offs? Honestly.

If she was all that clever, she wouldn't have needed to ask, would she? Marigold paused before the black-draped, utterly tacky vehicle they had (at the last minute, without warning) provided for her to use.

"I hope you don't mind that we've substituted the museum's caleche. It is so wonderfully macabre! Especially draped in the long black crepe ribbons. You must admit it is vastly more appropriate for Halloween. It's the season for illusion." As she spoke, the woman's gaze wandered upward, as if wondering about Marigold's hair color. Natural? Or straight out of a bottle?

Marigold stepped away abruptly. She admitted to being beyond thirty, but no one needed to speculate on anything else.

"I told the directors, decoration will only add to the interest in vehicles." Mrs. May stepped back, careful of the pony's steel-shod hooves. "I came from the art world, and believe me, there is no group more serious about their displays, and even they embrace Halloween."

"Draw the hoi palloi right in," Marigold snapped. Honestly, how common could this woman be? On the other hand, this curator did have solid connection to the board of trustees. Marigold smiled kindly toward the woman. After all, anyone on a board of trustees would be seen in a certain light, weren't they? And here, 'trustee' was an entirely invited, position. If you wanted to be somebody, or say, establish credential in certain circles, one could hardly do better than become a 'trustee.'

"I imagine your trustees will be delighted with the attendance, today." Marigold, in spite of ambitions relying on nothing more than developing favorite standing with certain people, could not stop herself from adding, "No matter who it is attending."

Mrs. May did not rise to the bait. She fluttered around at the far end of the barn and then gesturing at the carriages lined up across the main lawn. "I put my foot down and made sure the entire lawn display was fully decorated. Absolutely everything in the parade, too. It's been quite a job."

"Set-up alone was quite a job." The pimply self-styled 'curatorial assistant' leaned out of the third stall down, pitchfork in hand. "I've worked double hours this week, easy."

Pony decided to lift his tail as she spoke, which Marigold believed was an editorial comment. Monsieur knew a thing or two about humans.

The curator wrinkled her nose and stepped further away from the pony and his road-apples. She might know all about museums, but she was no horsewoman. Marigold wanted to dismiss her. How unpleasant to have such an individual in a position that could have proved so terribly useful.

Miss curatorial assistant from over in the corner stall, blurted, "I gave a talk last year. Super well-received. I could-a done the same this year."

Mrs. May dismissed her helper's chatter. "We have a real expert coming in to lecture about the hearse."

Did Marigold imagine it, or was there emphasis on 'real expert?' Marigold kept her lip buttoned as she slipped the quick-release trace ends into the collar attachment. She happily diagnosed friction between the chief and her helper. Oh, these little spats were so deliciously intriguing. Perhaps she could stir the pot.

"The museum must push the scholarly aspect, I'm sure." Marigold exchanged a knowing look with Mrs. May, as if saying she too, saw the 'assistant' as no 'real expert.'

The girl leaned against her pitchfork, in a picture that might have made the cover of some sort of 'farmers-r-us' magazine. "It is still Halloween!"

"The lecturer will bring the museum some news coverage. That kind of thing helps with donations." Mrs. May clasped her hands together and leaned forward. "It's a foreign speaker. The big carriage driving club recommended him. We have more than local people planning to attend today's lecture. A bit of a coup."

"Really?" Marigold shot a look up the lawn and the entrance to the museum, beyond.

Giant spider webs draped over a fair number of the centuries-old vehicles. A huge balloon spider hung over the entryway. She had thought this was simply a fun event. She'd only been asked to join the vehicle parade, and for lunch after. Bigwigs in the carriage-driving world coming? Members of the 'big club' expected?

"I had no idea."

"Our Brittany really pushed the fun aspect." Curator lady laughed. "Our wonderful volunteers came in to help decorate everything ghoulish."

"I mostly did it myself," growled her helper.

Marigold ignored the chatter. She'd put real effort into her turnout and would have looked wonderfully stylish, if the curator wasn't insisting she use the museum's old junk vehicle for the parade.

This ugly black-draped caleche had been a surprise.

A tacky, tacky surprise.

The big four wheel vehicle alone might have been acceptable, but the rear-seat scarecrow in bowler hat, the black carnations and plastic Halloween ornaments sunk it all to a different level.

'Big club' members were expected to attend. Oh, dear heaven. This was not the impression she'd planned on making.

She must somehow change this up. "Surely the mannequin is over the top," Marigold began.

"Oh, I think he's wonderful in all the proper livery! Really, your whole turnout will be the star." Mrs. May clasped her hands together and shot a look at pony. "I hope your equine is most well-behaved, the museum's caleche is usually kept under lock and key!"

Oh, if only it had stayed well locked in! Marigold had originally planned on setting off as a turn-of-century Central Park turnout. A grand lady, with a certain measure of class. She'd planned it all to be marvelously historic, with a few touches to add a hint of the macabre.

Poe-inspired black crows lined the dash. Crow earrings and belt-buckle set off her dress. The effect was perfect. Utterly upper-crust.

She'd grudgingly accepted the switch to the black, shining caleche. It did have some measure of grandeur, but she liked the idea of piloting the thing less and less.

"The trustees will be attending." She spoke doubtfully.

"Yes," trilled Mrs. May. "Every one of them."

Every single one of the trustees were the local community's movers and shakers. Suddenly, desperately, Marigold argued, "surely these aren't the correct appointments for the formal turnout. Isn't a groom supposed to wear a beret, not a bowler?" Oh, if only she could get rid of the ugly mannequin, at least she wouldn't look ridiculous.

Mrs. May frowned. "I'd have to consult one of the publications."

"Do you want me to head your pony? No time now to change things up." The assistant, Brittany, barged in and began to rush the hitching along. Marigold grudgingly grasped the near-side shaft to bring the carriage up.

Likely, the weird plastic spiders crinkled or something else made on odd sound as she moved the cart, for 'Monsieur' belted forward, dragging along the twit of a girl, and only stopped when he'd got back into the stable aisle. He snorted and turned half-sideways, glaring back at her.

"Monny, you old fool." Marigold dropped the shaft and sorted the reins - or tried to sort the reins. Her silly black veil fell forward over her eyes. As she stepped forward, the pony, usually the picture of manners, stepped smartly away.

"Idiot," she snapped.

Curator-lady stretched out a hand, from an appreciable distance.

Marigold waved her away. "He's being silly." Happily she had not yet put on the black spike heel shoes. At least she didn't fall down while trying to sort him out. She fumbled with her reins, shoved off the veil and applied herself to some proper horsemanship.

"*L'horrible bete*," she cooed, as if it were a compliment. She stroked one hand down Monsieur's shimmering neck. "Already warm?" She moved her hand to his chest. The pony felt sweaty and tense. "Oh, my poor boy! You don't care for the costumed carriage at all, do you?"

"I can manage him." The assistant, grabbed the pony's bridle and started to shove him backward toward the caleche. "He probably doesn't like this black plume on his head," she said. "He'll get used to it."

Monsieur, with his head snugged up in the vice-like grip, rolled his eye at Marigold. A sensible character, it was unlike him to resist.

Marigold started to take a bit of a dislike to it all, herself. Plastic spiders? Mannequin? This was not a blend of classy and fashionable, her measure for life, was it now?

"Hold on. I'll have a rethink." Darned if she'd set out clad in plastic. Silly. And a disaster if the pony misbehaved, right in front of everyone.

She waved the helper away. "Right you are, my wonderful Monsieur. I shall make some adjustments." She set the pony on cross ties before she went back to the cart. Really, it was all most ridiculous. The Haunted-Hubs Parade might be a *c'est magnifique* fundraiser, but it was beginning to seem a royal pain.

"I think the whole deal is too heavy." Without waiting for argument, she started to push the caleche out of the way. "My gig will have to do."

"Oh, don't ruin it. I'm sure the pony will get used to it." The assistant started to take the pony back over to the other vehicle on her own.

The curator hurriedly said, "You're almost ready to go. It would be such a shame not to have a society-owned vehicle in the parade."

Marigold nearly snorted in irritation. Did it look like she was ready to go, for heaven sakes? With a boggle-eyed pony snorting at her cart from forty feet away? Something about it all felt wrong. Why rush a thing like this? "I guess I won't go."

"There's still time," the helper assured her. "We'll make some adjustments, it would be so disappointing. I am sure the trustees will appreciate your efforts."

Trustees. Marigold stalked back over to the fancy museum vehicle. Darn it. This really would get the trustees to notice her. She eyed the old vehicle and its various decorations. "It would probably be fine if it weren't so completely over-the-top. We can compromise."

The ridiculous mannequin had leaned back in an odd position. He was plainly the problem here. She gave him one quick yank, but the mannequin did not tumble out, lightly, but slumped...oozed... down across the seat.

Marigold couldn't help the tiny shriek. Someone else gasped. This was no mannequin.

She could not bear to notice anything about her gruesome discovery. Marigold ran.

She darted straight up the barn aisle and grabbed Monsieur's bridle and carried straight on and away. They left behind carts and corpse and all. Marigold didn't pull up until they were on half-a-block away.

Her first pause was merely to pull out her cellphone and tap out the three digits cemented into everyone's brain.

Alicia was the next call.

Alicia, at home in her own downtown apartment for the first time in weeks, immediately wished she had not answered the phone. Still, she dragged herself to the scene, if only to be moral support for Marigold.

The faux cemetery provided a macabre gathering spot for officials, the first responders, as well as various museum volunteers and, more distantly, sundry curious spectators.

The bowler-hatted victim, while not immediately identified, did have several stab wounds in his back. So much the police established at first look. That information did not circulate of course, though the news of some disaster did.

Just the delay of the parade itself alerted the gathered crowd – carriage drivers as well as spectators, about something amiss.

The words 'joke' and 'hoax' and 'put-on' circulated around the crowd, although a certain undercurrent belied the comedy.

Without doubt, something was going on.

The small tableau of carriage (and parade) related ladies were in the midst of official questions. "Official" inasmuch as it was, yet again, Sergeant Perkins. Honestly, Alicia's policeman appeared at every incident. How could this even be possible? And, anyone would think he would start getting some horse-sense, but no.

Several times, Marigold explained, "My pony must have known from the start. He simply did not want to go near the carriage. It must have been the scent of death, or something."

In spite of her insistence of Monsieur's greater insight, Officer Perkins did not deign to consider the pony's opinions. Perkins asked if anyone could identify the victim.

Alicia coughed apologetically. "We don't need to identify the victim. We can start with the harness," she said. "It tells us right off, something's rotten here."

"Harness?" Sergeant Perkins said. It was hard to believe he was his department's expert on all things horse-related. Apparently, a nodding acquaintance was all it took.

"This is not, in fact, a valuable antique harness, made to go with a formal, antique caliche," Alicia explained. "This harness has safety-releases. Invented, I assure you, sometime in the twentieth century. Not an antique."

"Possibly not a criminal offense," Perkins pointed out.

"If the harness is not a valuable antique, what else is not a valuable antique? I bet that that hearse up there is a cheap fake."

"Ah?" In spite of himself, Perkins swung around to look at the hearse draped in giant shimmering spider webs, displayed on the front lawn.

"An expert was coming to discuss the gilded, Bavarian hearse, made prior to 1850." Alicia held up the historical society's flier.

Perkins glanced at the covered figure, the victim, over by the stable entrance. "And this is the expert?"

"Betting it is. On a caleche but in a bowler hat!"

Marigold spat, "dolt."

"Discrepancy?" Perkins repeated.

"Yes. It simply isn't correct. Any carriage-enthusiast would know the required livery. Listen, even draped in faux-spider web, an expert would have to look no further than the running gear to know the truth about a vehicle. Most likely, someone sold the valuable antique vehicle and substituted a much newer, American-made hearse, of relatively little value."

"Valuable enough to cover up the theft with a murder?" Perkins looked doubtful.

"The society will have an estimate, somewhere..." Marigold looked toward the curator. "Was there ever an official appraisal?"

"Oh, I think, I do think so," the older woman stuttered. She did not offer a figure, but looked around as if someone else might know.

The clucking around them ceased as the various women, docents and volunteers and nosy-Parkers, leaned in to hear the exchange.

"Insured?"

"Oh, indeed," the curator interjected.

Perkins, far from 'a dolt,' as it turned out, immediately said, "The expert must have been let on the grounds early, by someone here with a key."

Mrs. May pressed her hands to her lips. "Several of us have keys."

"But only you and your assistant were here so early," Marigold pointed out.

"When the expert took a look at his subject, he undoubtedly announced his disappointment in this so-called antique." Perkins continued.

"Someone could not let that bit of news go any further." Alicia added.

"Which lead to four stab wounds," Perkins supplied. "In the back."

"Four tines in a pitch fork." Marigold nodded, as if it were all clear at that point.

"The murderer killed the expert to cover up a much earlier theft. Probably with a pitchfork." Perkins glanced about the narrow stable aisle. "If indeed we discover there was a theft."

Alicia motioned to the caleche. "Have all the harnesses and vehicles checked by an antique expert, follow-up where vehicles might have been sold, check staff bank accounts for unexplained increases."

Sergeant Perkins glared at the curator.

"She's a real curator." Marigold shook her head, feeling as if this fool would never see the obvious. "She takes care of displays and handles fundraising. She's not a horse-n-carriage expert, but she's a professional. She'd know perfectly well that an expert wouldn't be fooled by a bit of drapery and a plastic spider."

"If she'd been guilty, she'd have never invited an expert to comment, in the first place," Alicia agreed.

"So, it was not the curator?" Perkins was obviously struggling to keep up.

"Right. Not. It was the assistant." Marigold knew all about being what you weren't. She adjusted her raspberry beret and shot a look at Alicia. "I believe there will be an assistant's position opening up at the carriage collection here."

Predictably, there were shrieks and protestations. The circumstances could not be ignored. The killer had been on the scene to greet the incoming expert, yet with full access to the collection for some time. Perkins cuffed the assistant. Various crime scene staff took over the stable, caleche, and surrounding area.

"Another case resolved," Alicia spoke lightly.

"The case," snapped Marigold, "has ruined my whole day! The whole point was the trustees meeting. I got invited to one of their scheduled meetings. It's a glorious old-world afternoon tea, for trustees and their guests. I was to be a guest! It was my whole point in getting involved in this irritating, frustrating, wasted day."

"I can't imagine one tea party is important."

"It's my chance to impress them." Marigold pouted.

The two stood at the corner, with pony, and watched the comings and goings at the stable block.

"Drive the pony home and pop back," Alicia suggested, as plainly the temporary stabling was out-of-bounds.

"No transport. I scheduled the truck to pick up Monny-Pony at four-thirty. You know, after the parade and party and all. I've called and badgered and everything. The company isn't about to send the truck over sooner." Marigold clamped a hand to her face. "Do you believe it? I'll have to stand here with Monsieur all afternoon."

"Marigold. You live four miles from here. Just drive him in his carriage back."

"I never take him on the roads."

"He's done whole sections of regular road as part of the club's annual trace pace." Alicia pointed to the dirt drive opposite. "You can take the trail-loop right over to the conserved farm on Beach Street, trot him the quarter-mile to the main road, and land on that sleepy little road that runs behind his barn. All the trail riders that board there take that route, no one will mind."

Marigold gave an elaborate shrug.

"I'd do the drive," Alicia urged. "You'd have him home inside an hour."

"Oh, you, really? You don't mind?" Marigold did not wait for Alicia to clarify her statement, but heaved the harness's saddle onto the pony. "I'd appreciate it. Oh, and of course," She gave a tinkling laugh, "you've not had a horse to drive in ages, have you? Not since yours went off to college with your daughter! I should have thought to offer before. Feel free to drive the old boy." She held up a hand "It's very least I can do. I insist, insist."

Dryly, Alicia remarked, "Oh yes, I've been biding my time." Although, she wouldn't mind the carriage drive through the pleasant dirt roads of 'CarriageTown.' Monsieur had more than demonstrated (over and over) his reliability.

Alicia pottered out to her car and dug through the trunk for her spare helmet. She'd been on the sporting end of driving so long, safety gear was *de rigueur* at this point. Donning the helmet was enough: her fingers itched to grasp those reins. With Marigold heading the pony, she stepped up into the pretty, spindle-back road-cart, grabbed the whip and said, "Walk on."

Marigold smiled. Beamed really. "Have a lovely drive." Alicia had made it halfway down the drive before she thought to ask which stall the pony should go in, and if his halter was there at the barn. Too late – Marigold was already marching up the main stairway.

"Never mind, Monsieur, I'll figure it out." She did wish she'd thought to ask for driving gloves, but possibly Marigold had a pair here in the cricket box. She held the reins one-handed as she opened the floor-level box. Its contents were one large leather spares kit, looking new and never-opened, and a crumpled orange rain poncho. No spare gloves, nor halter, or any of the other recommended 'spares.'

Alicia flipped out the poncho, hoping against hope, but no gloves lurked underneath. The poncho did bear the inked pine tree logo of Summer Stables.

"The one and only practical thing in here and it's not even hers." Alicia rolled her eyes as she spoke. "And when have I ever seen her wear gloves?"

The pony twitched one ear back, then carried on purposefully. This was his kind of place: a dirt road lined with pines and hemlocks. He likely felt he'd stood about those strange environs long enough. Odd people, dead people, and no other horse in the barn? A pony found it unsettling.

Alicia tugged her right rein a trifle shorter, adjusted the whip, and said, 'trot.' It was more of a "T-t-t-t trot."

Monsieur increased his pace before the command was fully out of her mouth, his hoof beats ringing out in a lovely rhythm. Bowling along the country lane, with the sound of birds calling, late blooms and the autumn colors of gold and orange all around, Alicia found a sense of joy. It sped up through the reins and bubbled in her heart. Monsieur perhaps felt it, as he moved with such lightness. Oh, but the empty seat beside her seemed so utterly empty. How lovely it would be to share this moment with another! Still, she did have this wonderful Welsh fellow as companion.

His hoof beats thudded steadily and his mane and tail whipped jauntily along in time. The dusty, grass-edged dirt road recalled the lanes of her youth, and for a moment, she went back to an afternoon on the reins of her wonderful 'Baron.' He'd always moved with a jaunty step, too. These days he was circling in dressage lessons with her daughter, but eventually, she'd claim him back and drive all the picturesque lanes in the old state park. She promised herself she would.

Midday traffic along the main road recalled her to the present. Alicia eased Monsieur back to a walk as they took the shoulder of the hardtop. She turned down onto the first residential street and passed a grand old farm in the midst of fancy new homes. The next turn brought her onto an older lane, toward the pony's home of Glen Green Stables.

The boarding barn sat not four miles from the center and directly off of the oldest street in town. Alicia guided Monsieur along the last mile, though it went far too quickly. By the address, anyone might expect elegant, even a bit grandiose establishments along the historic lane, but 'historic' truly rang through. A charmingly uneven old saltbox home marked the corner and proudly displayed a granite-chiseled *1790*. Its Halloween decor was a tasteful black ribbon wreath. The next house sat well back from the road, its drive lined by maples and its gabled windows glittering in the sun. They'd had a bit more fun; a squashed witch dangled from the first tree, and a plastic street sign claimed 'Salem Circle.'

Two grand old maples marked the end of one drive and a small forest of pine saplings clambered up to the road, having completely surrounded the next house.

Hewn-granite foundations were the norm, with the odd fieldstone. Here a gap in the wall marked a side drive to what must have been a barn. Long gone now. Alicia pictured living on this road in something like 1790.

She could imagine the wheels of the cart jolting in and out of deep ruts. She might have to draw rein as her pony caught up with a wagon load of corn. The driver raised a hand as he turned along a grassy lane. His team, a mismatch of a great black and a slighter bay plodded steadily with slack reins.

Likely, a fancier vehicle, like a covered barouche, sat outside maple house's gate. A groom stood there at the ready, heading a fine-boned chestnut who lipped at his bit and shifted with impatience.

The clapboard house, the ancient stonewall, and likely this very oak, sat there then as now. The squirrels in the trees might be descendants of the little fellows that lived here then.

Oh, it took nothing to see them. The clatter of hooves and felloes over cobblestone, the cart in the dooryard, ready, the bustle of people in an everyday life. Alicia looked down the long, fine leather reins to Monsieur, feeling they held a link to a past few could see.

"Or am I merely fanciful, Monsieur? What do you think?"

A distant neigh greeted them as they reached Glen Green Stable's drive. Monsieur stepped up his pace. Alicia took a better hold of the reins, not much more than to remind him of his manners.

A couple riders hacked along trail at some distance, and in a small paddock sectioned out of a field, two little girls bounced along at trots on tiny ponies, as an instructor repeated, "Up-down, up-down." The line of white fences ran almost up to the next neighbor's house. The farm itself, a leftover from days gone by, appeared incongruous in the residential neighborhood.

"Mostly ridden horses, not driven," Alicia mused. "With all the horse folks boarding here, I bet some ride with the hunt. Marigold no doubt wants an in with the big hunt club. It's probably her next step after winning over the carriage driving gang."

To her own surprise, her heart sank a bit as she drew the pony to a halt by the stable doors. How had she forgotten this joy?

Chapter 11 The Terrible, Terrible Tea

MIRANDA FORTHAM BUSTLED out of the enormously wide stable doors. She did bustle, plump in front and back rather like a well-endowed chicken, and clucked as Alicia drew to a halt.

"Had a lovely drive with Marigold's pony?"

"He has been lovely."

"Of course he has. Not that Marigold would know, as she lets all and sundry borrow the beast. For all her so-called fabulous equine insights, she really hasn't a clue. Do you know, when she first showed up here, she arrived with a Meadowbrook and claimed to be a combined driver! I swear, it was the only model of carriage the woman ever heard of!"

Alicia felt more than a little bemused. Poor Marigold so wanted to be one of the gang, and in this neck of the woods, the 'gang' was entirely equine enthusiasts. And they were not dim: She hadn't fooled anyone.

Alicia stumbled into explaining, "She's honestly busy today, attending this local society's board meeting."

"Blast. Was that today? I left that leaflet in my glovebox, I think. It's somewhere. It's one thing after another these days."

She tapped her fingers together. "No, wait. It's the fund-raising tea, isn't it? Not a real board meeting. No harm in me missing it. Not really."

Alicia felt annoyed with herself for even offering an excuse for poor Marigold, who probably had to contend with this opinionated stable-owner on a regular basis.

Forth-right Fortham didn't notice Alicia's expression but chirped, "the terrible tea party. Our Andreas, such a clever man, came up with it as a fundraising scheme. Invite folks with money, make them feel special, ask them for input as if they mattered, and schmooze some donations out of them. He was quite good at picking out marks. He knew people, you see. Could spot a phony a mile away."

Alicia whispered "not a real board meeting?" Marigold, for once, had been the one duped.

The woman raised a hand. "No time. My groom is holding the pair. You can manage the pony alone? I'll have my girl put the cart away later."

It was all too late if Alicia couldn't manage, as Fortham marched off before she finished speaking.

Alicia determined not to let running into the old battle-axe ruin her afternoon.

She'd had a lovely drive and set about humming John Denver's *Sunshine on My Shoulders* as she unhooked Monsieur and led him into the barn. The scent of hay and leather and pony all wafted about pleasantly. A tiny breeze sent a scattering of crinkly brown leaves into the barn aisle from the far end. It was one of those perfect afternoons. Too bad Marigold had misunderstood about the 'trustees meeting.' She'd had such hopes.

Andreas. Hmmm. Not a name you ran into every day.

There was an angry shout from the far end of the barn. Two horses and carriage and a couple of people, all visible only as one large silhouette through the doorway did not appear to be progressing toward going out for a drive. One human shape, in cartoon fashion, threw her hands in the air and began to scurry around.

"My whip! Antique holly." There was a scattering of discussion Alicia could not understand, then shouting. "I don't care what you say. You!"

And tears, there was no doubting the tears, and one of the figures dashed into the far end of the barn and disappeared.

Alicia drew off Monsieur's halter and slipped the wide oak door shut behind him, all the while listening to the bits of the unhappy exchange from all the length of the barn away.

Horse heads popped up over the open half doors and looked, it seemed with curiosity, toward the commotion.

"Not the first time," rang through perfectly clear.

Surely, there'd been enough awfulness for one day? Sighing, Alicia did not zip for the exit as would have been sensible, but eased quietly toward the action. Perhaps they'd manage to sort themselves out.

The barn cat stretched happily in a spot of sunshine at the corner of the far door. The tubby creature rolled slightly as Alicia approached, and smirked a striped-cat smirk when she bent to pat him.

"This is one time too many." Mrs. Fortham held the left hand horse's rein herself and waved dismissively toward the barn, and presumably at 'my girl.' "I'm notifying the police this time."

Distant spluttering could be heard.

The tall assistant scurried off toward the driveway.

"I'll have you know I intend to check my tack box later, besides, and will be advising the others here to do the same!" Forthright Fortham jutted out her bottom lip and glared, but the girl (who was probably a twenty-something perfectly competent groom on the likes of Lilly) did not look back.

As the offended lady patted the gleaming bay neck before her, a loud car started out in the drive, and then could be heard, turning onto the road much too quickly.

Alicia stepped up to the doorway, unnoticed. Coughed.

"Oh? Oh, Alicia." The woman stood with her lovely pair of horses and shook her head grimly. "I came out to discover my holly whip has gone."

"Gone?"

"It was this ridiculous girl. I know it was her. I've missed other items. I've suspected for ages. I turn my back a moment and she takes something. I'm sure of it. It's hard to believe I've put up with her this long, but there's the end to it."

"Seem quite sure," Alicia offered, a bit doubtful.

"She didn't say a word in her defense, did she?" Old Forthright blasted. "I put the holly whip in the whip socket when I put my gloves on the seat, you see them there. Then I went for a word with you, and here we are. No whip. I keep thinking I am getting forgetful, but I am perfectly sure I carried my whip out with my gloves."

Alicia would have loved to correct the old battle-axe, but could only nod and say, "Seems like you would bring them out together." She did not say, 'who the heck uses a valuable antique whip for an everyday drive?' Because obviously, Mrs. Fortham did. Perhaps she needed the supreme lightness a holly whip offered. Perhaps she'd recently broken her everyday whip.

Alicia stood silent but nodded sympathetically.

"I mean, there has been a wind, but it was secure. The whip holder is a good fit." The lady started to look around, but the off-side horse shifted from foot to foot. 'Been here quite long enough, mum,' he might have said. He was a deep chocolate color, almost black, with that faintly mealy muzzle.

"Orion, stand. You stand." Mrs. Fortham told him.

The horse looked at her with kind, patient eyes. In fact, both horses did. The near horse was a more ordinary bay, with the slightly bony profile, but he shared his companion's large-eyed, kindly expression.

"You could probably use a hand?" Alicia stepped over to head the far horse, 'Orion.' "Pardon an unrelated question, Mrs. Fortham, but you mentioned Andreas earlier. Andreas Arbuthnot? On the board for the carriage historical society?"

"Oh." Mrs. Fortham dropped the rein and brought both hands to her mouth. "Oh, my heavens! My whip is there. There! In those leaves. My word. I must have dropped it."

Alicia followed the woman's gaze. Indeed, the knobby, tan colored whip sat off the edge of the drive, scarcely visible in nearly the same color leaves.

"I am absolutely appalled at myself. I'll, I'll ask you to mind the horses while I go call my girl. I must apologize."

"No."

"Oh?"

"No, I mean, don't apologize." Alicia retrieved the whip, almost-concealed at the edge of the path. "You never dropped your whip, twenty feet from your carriage, in a pile of leaves.

She must have tossed it there. If you hadn't missed it, she'd collect it later. She set it there, hoping you'd forget, and only miss it later."

Mrs. Fortham's eyes narrowed. "I have misplaced a number of things of late. Thought I was becoming forgetful."

"Some of them valuable?"

Mrs. Fortham nodded silently.

"Probably no way to complain officially, as the whip has been found." Alicia placed the delicate, and expensive, item back in its holder. Plainly the helper (Really: 'My Girl?' Had the young woman no name?) had been helping herself for some time. "Can't say you were wrong."

After a few moments hemming and hawing, Mrs. Fortham said, "My dear could I ask you to ride along with me for a brief outing? I hate to put them away, now as I'm all ready. I always bring someone. Not as young as I used to be."

Alicia stood square in front of the two elegant horses and wondered at the weird turns of this day. "Be a wonderful treat for me, to ride along with the pair."

"You'll need to take a hold of the outside rein on Norry."

"Norry?"

"North Star. All mine are named for the heavens."

"I don't run into Standardbreds a lot these days, at least, not in recreational driving."

"My father bred some of the best." Mrs. Fortham scrambled up with the help of an added step on the vehicle, and sorted her reins. "There aren't more reliable horses in harness, for my dough."

It was an odd, old turn of phrase, though, for the most part, Alicia agreed. She could see the honesty shining out of these two. It took their driver several minutes to sort her reins, collect her whip, and survey all the harness.

Orion shifted his back feet but waited, polite. It seemed hard to credit that folks like that elderly Arbuthnot would spend a small fortune to import two expensive warmbloods, when lovely creatures like these were more readily at hand. Alicia shook her head at her own thought. Arbuthnot seemed to be her haunting her these days.

When Mrs. Fortham nodded, Alicia clambered up behind her, and quite casually asked, "You mentioned Andreas. Did you mean Andreas Arbuthnot?"

Sorting her reins, Mrs. Fortham didn't pay much attention, but nodded.

Alicia forced herself to say, "I didn't know he served on the board for the society here."

"Yes. He was valued, very valued. A clever fund-raiser and a clever horseman. Hunt club when he was younger and still enjoyed everything to do with horses. So sad about his accident. We all miss him." The woman tossed the 'we all miss him' over her shoulder quite casually, and trilled out "walk on," to her big shining Standardbreds.

Alicia's heart thudded almost audibly in her chest. She clutched the back of the seat in front of her, and forced out one more question. "And that's left a seat on the board open?"

"Actually, it's added another. We've been needing to fill a couple of empty spots."

"A couple?" Alicia flopped back against the upholstered backseat of the wagonette. Oh, whatever had she let herself imagine? No one killed for a seat on a non-profit's board, for heaven sakes. Why, for a moment there...

"Say, Alicia, would you care to join the board? You've been around forever. Know everyone. Hell's bells, I recall you driving that big chestnut thoroughbred years ago."

"Standardbred," Alicia corrected absentmindedly. "And I appreciate the thought, but I've no idea if I'll be staying in the area. I suspect Marigold might like to help you out."

"Oh, Marigold." The Fortham woman chuckled as she let the reins slide out for the horses to stretch their necks. "She's not one of us."

Chapter 12 Reviewing the Files

ALICIA DIDN'T MUCH want to consider it.

Marigold was tickled pink at the idea.

The assistant curator position was indeed open. It involved everything. Yes. There was absolutely no job description; it encompassed researching, documenting, helping set up exhibits, helping with the various events. Possibly anything, from what Alicia managed to ascertain.

"Documenting our actual collection is the big one," Mrs. May had shared. "We've not had anyone capable."

"Alicia is capable," Marigold had said. "Totally capable."

Alicia suspected that Marigold thought the position would automatically offer wonderful access to gossip.

"Old gossip," Alicia tried to tell her. The records wandered from place to place and year to year, mostly many years back. It hardly detailed the sort of information Marigold could have used. Who would care of tribulations of yesteryear? The desperate business pursuits of carriage builders?

Still, the job put her a comfortable drive from home.

After the kerfuffle died down, Alicia sat down with the curator. The museum, more accurately 'The Ladies Aide and Historical Society Carriage Collection,' had a vast number of vehicles but, thus far, little organization. Mrs. May, though enthused, said, "It's a temporary position until the board can meet, but I can have you start straightaway."

Alicia barely had to nod to land the 'temp' position. She agreed to review and sort documents relating to the collection and make some recommendations. Nothing more was definite, or agreed, as of yet. Thirty days' work and a chance to regroup, in her own little studio apartment, sounded ideal.

She did have another offer. A stable down in Wellington had inquired if she'd be available for their winter operations. It would be a sensible – even a good – position. That wouldn't begin until after the holidays, so somehow, once again, she'd landed on her feet.

She sighed and muttered 'adrift, more like,' lifted an old, handwritten letter from the files, and fell captive to a voice from history.

A handwritten letter?

Well. She set it back down, put on thin white gloves, and carefully lifted the document from its tray. After all, Mrs. May had taken the time to discuss the how-tos of items in their care. Seeing the date was a sharp reminder.

12a. Pink Ice

A fair step from Tamworth Township, 1748

Night time is best left to fiends and such creatures that claim those hours as their own. One dark night I found that out, more surely than I'd have ever cared to.

Hardly can I find the words to warn you proper, but I shall try. Sometimes danger comes to us unbidden, and our choices then make all the difference. I heard an owl call out once, this certain night, and a shadow cast over me. Evil stalked; that was plain. I sat all alone, in an empty house. It felt eerie, though I pushed the thought aside.

I longed for voices, for chatter, for ladies all around stitching on a quilt or the comfort of a good many squeezed into a pew. It had been a time since I felt the comfort of a gathering.

I set foot on the outside stoop and the silver of the moon was plain in the little pond before the house, as perfect and round as a serving dish. T'was not quite spring-time, and it was a better time to be in, than out, if I can speak plain. Yet, I was struck by the reflection of that perfect moon; it tempted me, certain. A promise, it seemed, to light my way, and light my escape.

Dark times is best left to dark creatures. I know better than to fall for their sneaks and trickery. Yet, that moon did some seem to beckon, even though the owl had spoken warning. I should have stepped back, barred the door shut firmly, and gone to my bed.

I can but say that my own thought and will had not a thing to do with it. I simply did what I did, and cannot, with any surety, tell you why.

I stepped along to the lean-to, where our few creatures dwelt. Two goats with the promise of milk and half dozen chickens, my mainstay. The shaggy old pony reached round to nuzzle – he was a gentle creature, born right here to my husband's family. He'd out lived all the family but us. I could see the gleam in his round eyes and guessed he'd like companionship of his own kind, as much as I.

"It's not so very far to town, is it?" Words pushed along the deed. My hands fastened his harness as if of their own will. The pony stepped quiet to the old pung, as when my husband lead him along to collect a forest kill.

It all went along too easily and my mind did not once consider my action. T'was curious, I guess, for I do not recall once deciding to depart, and yet, I did.

Foolishly, I slid onto the cold hard wood of the pung and chirruped to the pony. He plodded off straight and didn't so much as glance at the great shimmering glow of the pond. We progressed into the night and indeed, on into the wee hours of the following morn. The sleigh runners swooshed through the snow and the few dead leaves left to the trees rattled at our passing. The owl gave its low warning, over and over again. You would think I would heed it, yet I didn't. Already far into the depths of the dark forest, as gave the bird no thought at all.

The cold was sharp, biting; almost a long-toothed, nagging creature in its own right. The pung slithered along, up and down and banging between trees, tilting this way and that, until it would be easier to walk. Warmer, besides. Still, well-bundled, I told myself I'd be glad of my travels by dawn's arrival. The pony would quicken as we approached town and recalled friends at the livery stable.

As the night wore on, my courage did some fade. Many hours the pony walked, as I clutched tight to the sides of the pung.

Once, I glanced about me, keenly, almost, may I say, with surprise. I had no clear recollection of deciding on this course. Yet, there grew in me, a greater and greater desire to get to town, and stay no longer in the lonely forest house. Somehow, I felt already there and now more and more determined never to go back; with every step more determined. At no point did

I consider returning to the house I'd so plainly been warned against leaving.

Truthfully, I'd needed little encouragement to go. I'd lived in a busy little village all my life, and found, in the long winter season since my marriage, the lonely cold existence of a hunter's wife, little to my liking. Oh, I mean to say, of course, there were worse. I'd no claim of cruelty to make, nor yet of kindness either. I longed to see a cheery face, and hear the talk of folks, and not just the endless chatter of the pines.

It had been a long year since I'd ridden this narrow path through the forest, with himself leading me on this very pony. The pony knew the way, sure; he'd been back and forth to village before. We took a twisty course, around this great tree to one side and then avoid brambles to the other, but his little hooves guided sure. He seemed to find the path with little effort and I for my part, found I must have expected him to. I believed the Moon shone us along.

In truth our way was lit and guided by some night-time fiend.

Pony settled into a pace I thought good, and I decided that dawn, or not far past dawn, would see me sliding up to the church. I would have sworn to be alone and following a regular route; and yet, there it was, no straight path did we make through the aging forest. Many times, I wondered, or worried, then by some shape of shadow, or the brilliance of a glittering star overhead, would think a certain spot familiar. The fiend allowed as I should trust the good pony, and heaven only knew how he tormented the little fellow's mind.

I never guessed. Landmarks seemed cozily familiar after a bit, and feeling the nearness of the village, I felt less and less alone.

At last, I could feel that hint of sun; you know; that last few seconds of true night, when it is still dark, but you feel the sun's approach. I paused at the brink of a small hillock in time to watch the first bright ray shoot forth over the crest of a distant hill. For a moment, I felt such a surge of joy – for surely daylight and town folk were but a moment away.

Then, the trickery of that night-time fiend was made plain. The sun's ray found its reflection in the lowest dip of a narrow vale below, and I saw the reflection of the pink sunrise in the very ice where I had, hours before, watched the moonrise.

The words of the letter ended, unsigned.

A storage tag noted an 'oak sled' in storage.

Somewhere in the cellar of this old building sat an ancient, handmade pung.

Alicia looked at the darkening late-afternoon out the window. Loneliness swirled up from the manuscript like so much snow. Sergeant Perkins hadn't phoned and she surely wished she had some reason to call him. Had it been in her head all along? She scanned the pages in her hands, back and front, but they were not signed. The author was completely anonymous. Alicia was never to know the woman's name.

She juggled through the chaos of files, to escape the pervading sense of melancholy. Perhaps, a research-based piece might hit the mark.

12b The General's Clever Coach
Looking back, from *mid-nineteenth century*

The old horse drawn coach loomed from a dark corner in the vast barn. Unlike its plain wagon companions, tattered curtains and tarnished brass spoke of grander days.

Annie-bel leaned toward the driver's seat and nodded – again – but her assurance only annoyed her companion. The old coachee had all-brass appointments, apart from its hand-carved whip holder. Annie-bel knew the story of that whip holder.

The august personage of the local expert in 'all things antiquated,' jerked impatiently from dangling cobwebs and stomped toward the door. A chicken squawked indignantly as she had to scurry out of his way. Mrs. Whitson, the historical society lady, squawked in quite a similar fashion as she scurried after him. "We do have the one sure identification."

"An old lady's memories are not proper documentation," the important man did not slow his stride nor lower his voice, as if they weren't right there, as if they couldn't hear him perfectly well.

"I am so sorry; he won't listen." Mrs. Whitson whispered to Annie-bel. "If only he would let me explain it to people as you have described it."

"Never mind. A little mystery can pique interest." Annie-bel Edwards smiled.

"Blast it." The important curator tripped on a piece of old harness before he managed to escape out a side door. "No, no. This is not reliable historical documentation but romantic fancy."

Fancy? Annie-bel nearly laughed out loud.

In fact, it all started with a sudden fancy. It had been a particular cloudy late spring afternoon in 1798 and evening approached swiftly.

It had been particularly fine and people were out and about. Word had come to suggest General Washington himself would attend the discussion. The whisper of his visit swept through their quiet little neighborhood of Perry Point and neighbors, servants and assorted stragglers all lined their cobblestone drive to await the great man.

Annie-bel, in sharp contrast, tarried at the back garden gate.

She did not wish to see him over the heads of the throng. She did not wish to be relegated to peering at him from the far end of a hall. In truth, she didn't much care to see him at all.

It was his horse.

Nelson, the nation's most famous war horse, might well be on his way to her door. Though old now, he was apparently still under saddle occasionally. How she would love to know if all the claims were true! Myth had him as fast as a Pegasus, bold in battle as a bear and, or so they said, his coat glistened like polished copper.

She would wager he could not gleam more than her own chestnut!

The soft clop of hooves on the rutted dirt road warned of their approach. She scurried toward the end of the lane. If her family should see her, why, not a one would doubt she hoped to see the handsome young adjutants to the General. They were the most eligible men in America, weren't they? Her family would twit her about her garden-gate matchmaking, but she didn't fear them catching her out. They, with vastly more dignity, waited by the front entrance to their grand home.

She scrambled onto the bottom rung of the back gate without regard for her Sunday best and peered down the long rutted lane.

A pair of dark-colored horses put to a good sized coach approached. They were little more than silhouettes yet, as the sun had sunk and the whippy pines in the distance were indistinguishable from the nearer elderberry shrubs. She could guess they were very fine horses from their in-step, rhythmic trot.

Surely a whole procession must follow. The neighborhood would be thrilled.

No wealthy household in all of America could hope to claim a greater honor than to entertain the once President Washington, though he'd left his grand title behind and taken up 'General' again, when he left office. It mattered not; his visit was thrilling. Mama and Cook had set to work on a proper dinner and set out the best china. Half the neighborhood already stood by the cobblestone entrance to get a gander at the procession. The more important half of the neighborhood had crammed into the foyer in order to be in all the courtesies of meeting and greeting the man.

Of course, his message had said 'a brief word with the mayor and staff,' with no mention of dinner or a party. Some important precedents would be set with the formation of city ordinances in nearby Baltimore. The details did not interest her – but the horses did!

Annie-bel leaned well out to look down the lane. She wanted to see Nelson close up – and bet the carriage horses would

be the finest in all the land as well. She would get to see each
and every one of them.

The pair of bays drew nearly level with the back garden
gate before she could see past their coachee and down the lane.
Only distantly did she see riders, coming along slow. The horses before her shone with care, though. They each had a fine
white blaze and matching white on their rear fetlocks. Their
manes flowed back in waves at each step. And they stopped,
near enough, mid-step.

"Is the George Manor hence, Miss?" the deep, rolling tones
of the man's voice made her start. She had quite forgotten to
look for the driver.

Her gaze swept up to meet, quite impertinently, the ocean-
blue eyes of the most handsome man she had ever seen. He
grinned and touched his cap with one finger.

She managed a bob of her head.

He smiled widely. "Perhaps, I could trouble you to open
the gate?"

"Of course. They expect your, I mean, the General, around
the front." She managed to point down to where the rutted
road met the cobblestones of the proper entrance. "That's
where they've all assembled."

The off-side bay tossed her mane, impatient to be off, and
the man nearly allowed the horses to start, but paused and
drew rein. "Assembled?"

She started and a blush flew to her cheeks. She had certainly not planned on chatting with the members of the great man's
staff. She had imagined a great procession going by, as if on parade. "Indeed, sir, all the neighborhood has turned out to see
our honored guest and a dinner laid on and all."

"A dinner? Great Stars. I told them brief – I spoke plain. A brief word! The General will have my head, I am to drop these documents he sent and he is coming along later for a brief word, he said. He much wanted to meet Baltimore's Mayor as well as Mr. George."

The mare, irritated at the delay stepped about, restive and fiery. Her partner sighed as if used to her antics.

"Of course if he must rush, why they will still be delighted to have met him."

"He cannot be brief, if he must greet the multitude." The man shook his head. "He would never be so discourteous to not greet them, if once he alighted among them."

He sat silent a moment, before muttering, "Perhaps I will go forward with regrets, before the General arrives. I will tell the General I made a horrible blunder."

"Oh, sir, I know my father much hoped for a word," she burst out. It was likely unseemly.

Certainly, his man looked at her a might curiously.

Hastily, she turned to the gate. "I could let him in the back, when he arrives. A word in the kitchen door, and Cook would run to fetch the mayor and my father."

The fellow ran his fingers over his chin, where a faint beard had started. "If it would not give offense? In truth, it would solve my problem."

The man, dashingly handsome in his uniform and sitting bolt upright in front of the coachee, smiled suddenly and said, "I am much in your debt, Miss. For the General told me, well and clear, it was to be a brief stop." He made a motion as if to stand, there on the driver's seat of the coach. "John Edwards, Lieutenant, and much obliged, Miss."

She could only be glad the fading light hid her blush! She'd never yet been escorted to the local balls or been introduced to grand society. Mama only thought her barely old enough this coming season; and to have a gentleman introduce himself as if at a formal dinner!

"Annie-bel George, that is, Annie, and as you're from the 'Landing,' why you are nigh onto a neighbor. I am perfectly pleased to help."

"If we send him on the back lane, I could still drive round the front and distract the crowd."

Annie-bel giggled. "We should drop the curtains. The crowd will all be pleased to think they saw his procession pass by."

"Truth, it's a clever idea." Edward smiled at her. He had wonderful dimples when he smiled. "After all, no one ever did say the General intended to stop."

"And while all and sundry are watching the coach, the General can slip in and out the back." She held the reins while Edwards clambered around and lowered the heavy leather drapes in the windows of the passenger compartment of the large coachee. The dark material completely hid the interior while adding to the overall splendor of the vehicle.

He smiled at her broadly. "Some will say they could make out his profile against the curtain. This will be a little mystery. Neighborhood wags will discuss whether or not he really visited for a year and day, or longer."

She had to laugh. "They'll enjoy the story all the more."

The man returned to the front, but hesitated before he reached for the reins. "Wait now. I can hardly have you send the General to the back kitchen door to address the cook!"

"Well..." She cast around for some better idea. "You could greet him and go on ahead to the house yourself. Tell Cook you've the papers to deliver, only to Father. I'll drive the coach past the front entrance, and the onlookers will be kept busy."

Distantly, they heard hooves thudding into the soft dirt of the road. Lieutenant Edwards glanced back along the way. "He's only a minute or two off, now."

"I'll put on the driver's wool coat and stay straight on the main road. No one looks at the driver, in any case."

He hesitated. "They're not ladies horses."

She grinned. "I drive the sleighing races every winter. I'd race the roads in summer if it weren't unseemly for a lady. I can drive your fancy team."

"I believe you can, Miss Annie-bel. I believe you can."

"Not a moment to waste." She couldn't wait. Indeed, long since, she'd taken to putting dear Dash together with her brother's fiery mare Celeste and they had become the scourge of the local sleighing races. She didn't give the gentleman a chance to reconsider but hoisted herself onto the box seat.

She took up the reins with a confident hand such that she could see he was much reassured. "A slow walk down around the front and back then, miss. Half hour is all we need."

With a mere softening of the hand, the two horses stepped forward. She eased them left, away from the deeper ruts of the road and aimed them for the turn onto the cobblestone end of the house proper's drive. She could scarcely take a moment to admire beauty of the cream colored coach with the decorated panel and brass trim. She'd heard tell of the decoration on the Washington great coach and guessed this had been painted in like colors. It might be considered more useful than opulent, yet, she could guess it the family favorite. Even over the rutted roads, it proved comfortable. It did not jolt up onto the cobblestone, but glide. The horses strode smoothly together – the offside horse so much like Celeste! She wanted to move along and proved restive if held, but for a soft hand she would glide along at any pace, gracious and powerful. Her pair mate strode smoothly with her, well-practiced.

Annie-bel tipped her hand back just-so and allowed them a trifle more rein. At once, they two-stepped out together and pranced, perfectly in stride, along the loop of road to the front. They trotted by in full view of the front porch. The gathered crowd all pressed forward as one. They seemed to realize from her smart clip that the General would not be stopping, for they, all at once, began waving and cheering. The bays might well have been used to such a reception in their city travels, for neither so much as twisted an ear, but kept on at a smart pace.

Once well by, she eased them to a walk and, with some care, turned them in the dooryard of the mill building. It was all well to claim competence with a team, but for a certainty, the coachee stretched bigger and longer than any vehicle she had ever driven.

She sent them back, more slowly, toward the back garden gate. If Edwards had not yet returned, she decided she would drive on by and turn them in the far barnyard to await the end of the meeting.

A chestnut strode right down the center of her back garden lane, for all the world a real war horse – but small, surely too small to be the famous Nelson.

He drew closer and she realized the horse was not small, but his rider tall. The tall rider made him look small; and the animal did shine, even with the grey on his muzzle.

Then she knew, of course she knew, even in this fading light. She stood the pair aside to make way for the tall man and his grand old mount. She longed to say 'General,' but found herself completely tongue-tied.

She attempted a hasty courtesy while on the box seat. Edwards strode up and climbed directly on the box beside her. She handed over the reins, caught up in this fleeting moment. For Nelson – and his great rider – were stepping past.

She forgot all decorum as she scrambled to the ground.

His horse- his horse! Indeed, now that she stood quite next to him, she saw he was great, indeed. His back was yet a hand's breadth higher than her own head and his shoulders and forearms massive. Yet, now she saw him, she knew she stood at the feet of a great man…a man to match the horse. Statuesque they were, as if the both of them were somewhat above this world. Annie-bel guessed she would remember this moment all her life and maybe the next.

Dashing young Lieutenant Edwards drew rein beside the back garden gate. "A great service you have done for me this day, Miss Anne-bel, and I regret I have no gift for you."

"Quite enough to meet you, and see, and see…" she might have meant to say 'them' but could only motion after the General.

Edwards tapped the top of the whip holder. "For one with such a clever hand on reins, perhaps a small keepsake?" He quickly began to unscrew the fancy brass accessory.

"You cannot remove the whip holder," she chided him.

"Easily replaced. I shall carve another." He winked as he unclipped its keepers and handed it over. "You must have a keepsake. From General Washington's own coachee."

No more than a clever twist of brass, only slightly longer and wider than a finger. It gleamed with polish and proudly displayed a stamped W.

Not terribly long after, at a dinner party down at his aunt's house on Ferry Landing, John Edwards had admitted he had begun carving a replacement whip holder that eve, as it was so annoying to be without.

All their long years together, she and John had laughed about their first meeting at her garden gate, the clever distraction of the cream-colored coach, and the gift of a brass whip holder. He had indeed replaced it with a hand-made one, and so far as he ever admitted, no one had ever commented on the switch.

She leaned in to glance once more at the coachman's seat. The cream had worn off long since and the red trim on the hammer-cloth seats had fared little better, but the hand-hewn whip holder affixed on the right side of the dash was unmistakable. It did not match any of the metalwork, but had done the job well enough, all these years. The hand-hewn whip holder proved the coachee was the General's own, as Young Edwards had given the original fancy brass one to her!

"This is certainly the Washington Family Coachee." She spoke with the fond assurance. "Even from fifty years ago, I know my own husband's hand at carving."

Mrs. Whitson rather unhappily murmured, "We'll put it on display with as much information as we have, and let people debate the issue themselves."

Annie-bel, Mrs. Anibel Edwards really, smiled encouragingly at her. "It won't be the first time this coachee created a little mystery!"

Alicia Goodwin, more than two centuries later, laughed aloud. Oh, how the important little man missed out on the real story! Mrs. Edwards' recollection had been wonderful. The woman's genteel nature called to mind Aunty Jane again, and Alicia found herself adrift in memory, once again with her aunt 'across the pond.'

Chapter 13 Enter the Villain

AUTUMN 1914, ENGLAND

The wishing-well attested to a bit of whimsy quite at odds with the personality of both the structure and its inhabitants. The Buchanan house was scarcely inviting, wishing-well or no.

Jane pulled up and set about inelegantly slithering off the sidesaddle. Grooms were nearly a necessity for ladies in such position. Still, she managed, landed awkwardly, to stand staring up at the door awkwardly.

Olivia Buchanan's stern, strict and stiffly correct outlook on life, people and the world was well-documented. Likewise, the house embodied 'drab gray,' in both actual color and style. The square of yard in front was precise, though entirely bland. Not one flower adorned the border.

Yet, the wishing well sat center-square, fresh painted and brightly attractive.

It only added to the creepy feeling.

Jane placed one hand on the gate. In spite of the well, the front door loomed impossibly tall and gloomily unapproachable. "Proper setting for a ghost story," Jane murmured. "Or a murder. This cannot be the place."

The front door swung open as if on cue.

"Jane!" Her cousin Claire, best friend and confident, waved girlishly. "Here you are riding. Riding! Absolutely no one does these days. A tribute to Aunt Katherine?" Claire bubbled.

Jane hadn't given riding a second thought. Hiring a motor-car was quite an expense, and Thompson's Livery was handy there, in the village. Thompson himself had handed her up, and said, "Miss, you set this mare off a treat. Pair of you right smart," and he'd touched his cap as she set off.

Set off? She'd trotted off onto cloud nine. Cousin Claire might have married a well-to-do Spaniard, but Jane, in one of Aunt Katherine's old riding habits, had achieved 'smart.'

At the hill going past Grant's, the mare had stepped off a bit lively and she had been so carried along with enthusiasm, she'd given forward and let the mare soar up the hillside in a cracking gallop.

"Your cheeks are the most unfashionably pink, Jane," her cousin laughed. "You've been up to something."

"Me? You've been all over the world," Jane walked around the stone pillar to what she hoped would be a stable. She faced another big, plain house. "I'd thought to put the mare up."

"Round here. They've left a hitch ring on a post, in the shade." Claire motioned from the walkway, as her heels were not intended for traipsing about in dirt. She paused there at the corner, her fingers twirling around the single pearl at her throat.

"I suspect your necklace is from afar?" Jane asked.

"From Greece! Oh, I'd have liked a whole string of pearls, but Esteban has simple tastes. He completely failed to take the hint when we window-shopped our way through the streets of Athens."

"You did 'LeGrand Jaut' for your honeymoon." Jane blushed slightly as she said it, thinking of Claire's dashing, foreign husband.

Claire made the slightest moue. "I thought we were. We definitely meant to travel for months. Esteban and I sailed the channel and, well, I planned on Paris, straightaway. We never quite had time for the city. We traveled on to a tiny village in Greece. All very lovely. Small, though. He much prefers to stay at out-of-the-way places. I suspect I could take to city life. We did visit his family in el casa de Madrid. I thought it Esteban's own, but it's a family home." Claire went on, with an odd mix of bragging and complaining. She could claim to have married and traveled in style but, there was this huge 'but.' It was all not quite in the style she would have liked. It was a Villa-Greco and not Athens where she'd stayed. It was single-pearl necklaces. It was baguettes and cheese, not caviar.

"Did you tell him what you prefer?" Jane broke in at last.

"Oh, he's from real money. He's simply oblivious to such things. I'd feel petty."

Jane, since childhood faintly envious of Claire's inheritance, could only guess what 'real money' must mean.

Claire swirled her 'day dress.'

Jane's smart tweed habit suddenly seemed plain brown. Her triangle-hat with its scrap of netting, so very yesterday. Claire, by contrast, wore a shade of pink only a wit darker than scandalous, with heels and clasps and the single black pearl.

Though they were both in the mostly mature realm, Claire managed to look much the younger of the two.

It was Claire though, captive of the dark house.

Jane put such thoughts aside and reached out, thirteen again, if only for a moment. "Found you!" she called, mimicking their girlhood games. "Do you remember?" and they both fell to laughing and chatting; Friends, relatives, expectations, and where are they now? They chatted as if to make up for almost a decade of only letters in the matter of minutes.

"This place," Claire dismissed the dark edifice behind her more than once.

At last, Jane reached out and patted the shelf of the wishing-well. "You'll be changing this place all up, to suit you. Do I see your hand here?"

Claire laughed. "No, no. I suspect the realtor added the well, trying to make the front more inviting! No, none of it is inviting. Esteban thinks it the perfect location. 'Lots of possibilities,' he says. I suppose it is difficult to find many places available these days. Oh. Do come in, I don't know why we are standing out here!"

The mare nickered softly as they left her.

The two marched into the foyer arm-in-arm, as if to confront demons.

Aunt Katherine's portrait, in a gilded frame, graced the front hall.

"Oh," said Jane.

"A bit of a laugh," Claire said. "I mean, not quite sure why I ended up with this painting, but I tossed it up, for lack of anything else really."

"She doted on us."

"She did," affirmed Claire. "I'd have come back to the funeral, if we'd not only just traveled to Greece."

"It was a small affair. I am sure she would not have expected it."

"I am perfectly sure she would have expected it!" Claire gave a bark of laughter. "She did have her firm expectations! Still, I recall her with great fondness, I assure you. We three had wonderful times together."

Jane followed her hostess into the sitting room.

"This is the best room," Claire shoved a thick wooden door open. "We rented this place furnished. It's not exactly fashionable."

Jane perched on the edge of the settee. A musty smell enveloped the room. "I take it that you'll have the place while the Buchanans are away?"

"We've rent-to-own, one of the new schemes. Esteban came up with the idea. Mr. Buchanan works for a solicitor Esteban deals with, in the city. The house came up in conversation, somehow." Claire shrugged. "I suppose I am glad to be close to home, but..."

"An older couple?" Jane looked about the unpleasantly dark room.

"I only met the man once. One of those round-faced, bowler-topped types. Too cheery, really. You know the type. I gathered his wife is somewhat older. He let on she's already moved, wanting to be nearer family."

Jane looked about, for some positive detail to point out. It hardly seemed surprising that the woman wanted to depart the gloomy house, if this, the front sitting room, was the best they had to offer. Any idea of a compliment eluded her.

Claire looked around the room, as if noticing it all for the first time.

Sadness crept around the baseboards along with dust.

"Come out to the kitchen." Claire jumped up. "It's a nice, old fashioned kitchen, great flagstones and all that."

Indeed, at the far-back, they found all the light and air the front so lacked. Claire set the teapot and Jane opened the door onto the kitchen garden. "A bench, a butterfly and a bouquet," she announced.

Claire bobbed up beside her, easily becoming her bouncy self again. "I haven't even looked out this door! Why, it's quite nice." They set up tea out on a handy stump, as if they were girls sent out to play in the garden. Their discussion turned, as it did these days, to talk of war.

"They say Britain's not going to stay out of it long." War was not far from anyone's thoughts. Claire parroted any number of locals, though she was not likely wrong. Danger and espionage and undesirables were words on many, many lips these days. It was all a bit hard for poor Claire to bear, as "after all," as she did admit, "we might have traveled abroad for much longer, otherwise."

Jane murmured, without allowing her expression to betray her thought, "how terribly inconvenient." Indeed, the sunshine, and the few bravely persistent flowers, made it easy to be patient with Claire. She had plainly remained unchanged since girlhood.

Jane leaned forward to reach for her teacup, but hesitated as her eye caught a bit of brightness at the foot of the stump. She reached for it curiously, and lifted a simple white linen table napkin from among the leaves and detritus.

"I think we are not the first to have tea in the garden."

Claire grimaced. She did not again grumble about 'this place,' but nodded. "I can understand why."

"I can't understand why," Jane said. "You've lived here a week and are planning changes. Clearing out, brightening up. Why wouldn't the couple here before have done so? They lived here for years, in the gloom, yet didn't like it?"

Claire rolled her eyes. "I'd guess it was the missus. They say she's the one with money, and pretty tight-fisted about spending a penny or a pound. Probably, Round-bowler husband often brought his tea out here, escaping her and the house."

"You say you never met the wife?" Jane raised both eyebrows.

A clang rang out, sharp and loud.

Claire spilled her tea down her fuchsia frock with a shriek.

Jane shot up, recalling her first look at this house, a look and a thought: setting for murder.

A second clang reverberated from the house. Claire pressed both hands to her chest as if she would collapse on the spot.

Jane, a tad more practically, pointed toward the front. "Is it the door knocker?"

"Really? I suppose I've never heard it."

Together, they made their way to the front...braving yet another assault on their ears. Claire yanked the door open and the two men, there on the step, stumbled back.

They might be forgiven for their surprise, Jane was thinking, as they could hardly have been prepared for the likes of Claire to pop up in front of them.

Two men, in uniform, looked from one to the other of them a moment, plainly in surprise. The one in uniform might have been a shade older than the other, but both had dark, swept-back hair, and the same sharp, green-eyed gaze.

"Is Mrs. Buchanan in?" the slightly taller asked.

"The Buchanans have left. They've not long since gone to live up near Harrogate." Claire still looked pale, from the shock, surprise, or what have you.

The two men, alike as peas in a pod, shot sideways looks at one another. Claire glared. Into the silence, Jane murmured, "Are you gentlemen friends of the Buchanans?"

The one in uniform turned his cap over and over in his hands. An officer, for certain, although possibly only recently.

The one jerked his head at the man in uniform. "This is Lieutenant Sinclair. The service is looking for a house in the district, convenient to the train station you see, where we could house soldiers en-route to their duties. Not more than a few weeks ago, Mrs. Buchanan said she'd rent the back rooms."

The lieutenant glanced at Jane. He almost smiled, coughed, and said, "I'm afraid we've got it wrong."

Claire leaned artfully back against the door frame, a la a movie starlet. "My husband and I have rented it."

Then the non-uniformed man, himself perhaps thirty, said, "Look here. I am Henry Grant, and I'm making the arrangements for civilian support of the war effort. It was not two weeks since I spoke to Mrs. Buchanan. She definitely wanted to rent to the service. Saw it as an act of patriotism."

"I'm afraid she's left." Claire glared at them.

The two men took their leave with somewhat doubtful gentlemanly grace. The one in civilian clothes, looked quite angry, in fact.

"An odd circumstance," Jane reflected. She looked out over the dismal front, with its one bright, if incongruous decoration, the well. "Mrs. Buchanan is expected, but not here. You yourself never met her. Your husband came to an arrangement with the Mister, at some London office. Your Esteban did not come look at the house? He also, did not meet the wife?"

"Why, why no. Esteban said this was the perfect location, and since it was a rental, we could just try it out, over the winter." Claire sank down into a front hall chair, below Aunt Katherine's glimmering gaze.

She barely registered Jane's similar contemplation. She'd told Jane a good deal – a good deal she'd barely considered herself. Jane studied her cousin, and life-long friend, as she ran over the details in her mind.

Claire and her husband had had an inexpensive honeymoon. His gift of jewelry fell short of expectations. His 'house in Madrid' was an older family home, as things turned out. Not his. He'd not found a nice house in London for them on return, but rented an old place, under, well, one must admit it; peculiar circumstance. At the very least, his finances were not what he had led Claire to believe. Claire's husband, though not entirely scrupulous, might be similar to many a man. But, this Buchanan, he was something else again.

"Mr. Buchanan avoided his wife, as was possible. She was the one to control the money, with stern opinions on spending, and as he was reliant on her home and fortune, Mr. Buchanan was captive." Jane made it a statement of fact.

"Yes, I am sure she was no joy to live with," declared Claire. "So, he avoided her."

"And when your husband mentioned looking for a rental, in this area," Jane looked toward the front again, "this house happened to be available. The man who had his tea out in the garden to avoid his wife, was able to set up to rent it out, without so much as discussing it with her."

Claire looked at her oldest friend. "Jane, why do you continue to stare at the front yard?"

"It's one of the two incongruous things about this house. The first is the wishing well, and the second is the missing wife."

Claire moved to the front window to see for herself.

"Think how wonderful life would be for Mr. Cheery-Bowler Hat, if he could leave here with his wife's money and a rental income. No one would miss either of them, if everyone thought they both went off, together." Jane motioned to the front. "Mrs. Buchanan is beneath the new, very pretty wishing well."

A long moment of silence hung between them. Aunt Katherine looked as disapproving in her portrait as she would have, in life. Jane had to imagine, the 'don't be ridiculous' as well as the 'a lady would not involve herself in such unsavory things.'

"Cousin Jane, you have been right before," Claire said faintly.

Jane, far from worried about the Buchanans, wondered what on earth she should say about Esteban de Madrid. There was nothing really, though she continued to consider, as she prepared the mare and went in pursuit of the men. This Mr. Grant – eldest of the family, if she recalled correctly – already had his suspicions. It would take only a word for them to investigate murder...

She had not, even once, considered the lieutenant.

That all changed as she trotted the mare up to them. The military-clad fellow snatched off his cap as if royalty approached. She couldn't help but smile.

Only to be rewarded by his broad grin.

So brash! But he was that handsome.

The other fellow might as well have been invisible. She notified him of 'concerns' in the words she'd carefully planned as she trotted along. Best to let men discover the facts for themselves, as Aunt Katherine always said.

Thus notified, the man stomped off, to bring 'his' suspicions to the authorities. Jane gave him no further thought. Poor Claire would have to have her front yard dug up. Perhaps, Jane considered, she should have invited Claire to stay in the village?

Her thoughts were interrupted.

"I stayed as a guest at Grant's last night."

Jane glanced down to meet the lieutenant's thoughtful gaze. He stepped up and gave the glorious mare a gentle pat.

"A lovely place," Jane acknowledged.

The man looked up at her. "Happened to see a Thoroughbred take the mile hill along there as if she were racing at Ascot."

"Great heavens." Jane felt a bit startled to hear there'd been an audience. She fumbled over words as she asked "Not this morning?"

Lieutenant Sinclair chuckled. "You will forgive me my doubt, but I don't believe you are as demure as you first appear, Miss Jane."

She tried to remind herself of the need for caution.

But the man clapped a hand to the very genuine thorough-bred's gleaming neck as if they were of a kind. Jane's heart leapt.

Their adventure had only started.

Who would have ever guessed their future? Alicia got to her feet and stretched. A chance meeting – it had all started out by chance. She found it hard to turn back to dry documents, with such memories at hand. Still, she wasn't paid to sit here and remember. She glanced down at diagrams for a gypsy wagon, wishing for a bit more whimsy among all this history. Notes along the outer border caught her eye, and the vehicle's story appeared, as if she had conjured it.

Chapter 14 Mare of Mist and Moonlight

AN IRISH EVE OF LONG ago

In a sliver of misty moonlight, a phantom horse strode silently across the fog-strewn moorlands.

"The Moonlight's mare," whispered the tallest boy.

Half a dozen children elbowed one another in the black shadow of their home, a jauntily-painted wagon. Wrapped in darkness, they stifled giggles and tried to be still.

The mare strode closer, her mane damp with dew and shimmering in the thinnest thread of light. Though she approached so near they could hear her breathe, she still seemed a creature from dream, no more substantial than mist and moonlight.

The children pressed their palms over their mouths and shrank low. One or two shut their eyes, as if they couldn't see her, perhaps she would not see them. The one flake of hay, scavenged from scraps around roadways, offered meager bait. Yet, the unshod hooves softly clopped closer.

Four days they'd waited here, since Eolo, the best of spotted cobs in all the world, had stumbled to a stop, inexplicably lame.

The children were tasked with his care as the adults sought towns and day-jobs or the loan of a good working horse. The three families had meant as planned and set off north. They had a week, no more, to catch up with the others. Any of them could have walked to Plumney in time, but all their worldly goods sat in the wagon. "If anyone returns with a beast, take the wagon right on to the meeting place." The adults had agreed. Others could catch up. The good byes to the children had been, to one and all, "Stay out of mischief."

The mare came down from the moors that first night. Eolo had nickered and alerted them.

Estrella had pointed in silence, but her brother had started up too quick, and sent the mare off. Her mane and tail swirled round and round as clouds in storm and her hooves found footing across the steepest stretch.

Eolo had nickered after her and the children, with little more than shared looks, conspired to capture her.

A cob would solve their problems. One good solid cob would take them hence. If they could catch this wandering cob, the adults would return to find them ready to travel.

'Ready to travel,' might prove difficult, for the mare seemed shy, and perhaps, not even real. She might be no more than all their wishes, appearing in silvery form.

Estrella stood watch herself on the next night, her hands clasped around a halter and her breathing soft, for hours and hours and hours. She gave no thought to how her own long hair shimmered in the same gleaming moonlight.

The older teen amongst them noticed how the girl from the southern coast stood like a queen at the helm, determined, fine, as silvery – and as ephemeral – as the wishes of his own heart. Such a lady would not be impressed by failure, but he had the one bit of magic; he knew horses. Even among the people of the horse, even as young as he was, he was a horseman.

He thought to enlist the help of Eolo, the faithful pony, then he announced he had laid an enchantment that could capture the mare made of Moonlight.

Estrella doubted, but time drew short. The various family clans had planned to rendezvous in Plumney. She missed traveling in the large caravans of her own family. There was safety in numbers, as their current predicament showed. Had they been with the family, they could easily have borrowed a spare horse.

There would be no 'borrowing' possible here: often they were barely tolerated to pass. This phantom mare could solve all their problems.

The children collected hay, and bits of grass, and from somewhere, no questions, a handful of corn. They'd pushed the wagon to make a corner, and stood Eolo there out of the wind.

"Moonlight is wild," the tall boy said, "but willing to help, or she'd not come so close to people."

"Lonely," Estrella guessed.

"Yes." His heart did a tiny flip. She had spoken to him...

As evening approached, Eolo turned his huge brown eyes upward toward the moorland. It was all the warning they needed. They all shrank low as the phantom mare clopped near.

The mare seemed more of silver skeins of stars than bone and muscle, and she could see nothing of the knit of magic in a way to catch such a will-o-wisp.

Still, Estralla shrank low, this fourth night, with the others, as the mare strode the closest yet. She held her breath as the old gelding nickered.

The boy tossed the grain onto the hay and then padded over to hand-feed Eolo. He kept his back to the mare

The silver horse clopped closer.

She lowered her head.

The boy caught a rope of shiny silver straight out of the night's darkness and set it, as if every day, over the mare's neck. She reached for the food, as if it were every day

Estrella dared not move for disturbing the magic, dared not breathe, dared not speak. This boy, perhaps he was Lucita's son, from the western clan? Why had she not thought to ask his name? He set about moving Eolo's harness onto the mare, as if confident of his enchantment to hold her.

In the candlelight, she might have been as wild as the stars, yet there she was, docile as Eolo. The children dared creep closer. The mare did not notice.

Without fuss, the boy slipped the collar on, then strap-by-strap, took care to set each adjustment. It was the old, every-day harness, and not one of silver and magic, just ordinary. It did not seem possible. The boy began to whistle low, as if he harnessed their long-tamed pony. He looked tall and lean and scruffy, yet kind and kindly too. He made nothing of capturing Moonlight itself. His power came as no surprise to himself. Estrella wondered if had set out a silver snare for her own heart.

The mare of Moonlight stood as if tame; as harness could not startle her, as if people and their fire and wagons was no surprise at all.

"We'll drive north by night." Lucita's son led the mare over to the wagon. The mare backed into shafts as if long-familiar, as if setting about her day, not tricked nor trapped.

Estella said, "We'll have to wait for the others."

The boy, his hair curled up in from the damp fog, shook his head. "We may only have this one night. I cannot measure the spell. We'll go as far along as we can go, and if we get right the way up the coast, we'll wait at Plumny."

She stood stock still there, wondering if she should tell him her name. As if he might care to know? She hoped he wondered about her.

The boy's own name remained most firmly his own.

"The other's know to meet at Plumney." He stood with reins in his hands but waited for her nod, her blessing.

It was an unexpected power.

She nodded as she scooted up the front of the wagon.

He walked beside the mare, at the start. Estrella set up on the high seat and held the reins and all the younger ones gathered around her. Eolo plodded on a long rope at the back. The wagon, and all the families' goods, and all the children of several houses, slipped along through the night.

Each step closer to Plumny and the gathering.

As the Great Bear dipped his nose toward them from the sky, Estrella gathered her courage and called out the words aloud, "you have a name, you who have tamed Moonlight?"

"We, altogether, are only borrowing the Moonlight." He turned around and strode backward and the darkness could not hide his smile. "I am Caro."

As the first hint of color shot the eastern sky, the boy stopped. "If we are to keep her, we must not let the sunlight touch her."

They all did as he bid, this one from among them, who had tamed Moonlight. Estrella took the mare's head and she stepped up the two steps into the wagon as if she did such things every day. The mare stepped right up to the front and poked her nose out the tiny front window. The children giggled and climbed up on the seat to give her handfuls of grass.

"Roll up the carpet," the boy said. "Drop the curtains."

The children scurried to do his bidding. Had he not caught the creature, in the first place? Who knew what it would take to keep the spell whole?

"The magic might be undone by the Sun's light." The boy warned each of them. He might well have said, "no eye must see her," but might have. If he had, his little band might have guessed this a stolen pony, rather than a magic pony.

The mare stood quiet in there, on the planked floor. They heard her shift occasionally, an ear against the wood could discern her deep breathes. She rested like an ordinary horse.

Estrella did not let herself guess a farmer might have missed a pony. This was not a stolen creature, but one lured from the night, crafted out of moonlight.

They set off the next night, and the next, plodding steadily through darkness.

During the days, day, the magical creature chomped her way through every bit of greenery they could find for her. They rubbed out sweat marks from her coat and untangled the knots in her mane. In utter darkness, she plodded her way northward, drawing their wagon home. Before dawn on the fourth day, they stood outside the gathering town.

Caro set her harness aside, and turned to her to face the south. "She'll gallop and catch up into moonset."

He dropped the bit from her mouth and stepped back. The good mare turned to nuzzle hands a moment- all those hands that had shared clumps of grass. Caro clucked softly and the mare set off, obediently, alone, back the way they had come.

They stood together and listened to her fading hoof beats.

Estrella stood beside the one who had brought them to the doorstep of all the family.

When they asked, "how did you get here? Where is your pony?" She would tell them it had been a creature enchanted from the night itself. Caro's mama, Lucita, should be proud.

Caro, himself, spoke no word. He stood back, confident: he had enchanted more than the horse.

Chapter 15 Three at Post Time

PERKINS AT THE DOOR.

Alicia rubbed her eyes. "Sergeant?"

"I hope you don't mind." He lifted a manila envelope. "I happened on this the other day. An old file. A few cases. Referred on to me, as I've now had experience in the horse industry."

"Oh?"

"Which I don't have, not much, as you know." He stood awkwardly on the step, but carried on, as if making everyday conversation. "You were right about the assistant over at the Halloween display. I thought I might ask you to take a look?"

"Come in." Alicia poured coffee and rubbed her eyes. She'd been reading, so much reading! These last few days. Her eyes felt tired. She'd been thinking of going out for a walk along the beach to clear her mind. She needed to feel the air and hear some gull's cry to come back to the present.

Her mind was full of old-time horse-drawn vehicles, and the sense of how each connected to various lives. The past was enthralling. She could hardly say, "I don't much feel like returning to the current era," could she?

"Two I believe are resolved, but one is not." He pulled out files of documents, photographs and reports. "All involve untimely deaths. Uniformed officers took thorough note of circumstances at the times. I've added potential incriminating details, researched persons of interest, and included descriptions along with photographs of the scene."

He placed a hand on yet another folder. "I can show you some details."

"No. I mean, sorry, but if you don't mind, I'll have a look at all the info myself." Alicia's mind was awhirl. Real police cases! Brought here for her to solve. She could hardly share that her method involved imagining the mind and motive of the players in each case. "I'll give you a call. Is that ok?"

"Perhaps we could discuss the cases over dinner?"

She nodded, tongue-tied. Dinner? Dinner. She hadn't expected an invitation. She'd been looking out this very window, feeling lonely and wishing for some distraction. Out of the blue, this handsome distraction arrived.

She showed him out, her mind half curious about the cases, and more curious about 'dinner.'

"For heaven sakes," she said aloud, more than once, in an effort to put aside school-girlish fancies. It took ages to settle down, but eventually she applied her mind to the contents of the first file.

15A POST TIME ONE
   Police Report:
   Location: Buckram Downs, County Fairgrounds Road
   Middle-aged male collapsed in restricted area. Many witnesses. Call for assistance was immediate. Paramedics, already on scene for race safety, responded, started CPR in under two minutes. On the advice of bystanders, they applied the antidote for drug overdose.
   Victim, Bernard McDermitt. Died on scene. Appeared to be natural causes.
   Coroner subsequently determined death due to poison: Poison typically used for Domestic vermin (rat poison.) Likely ingested within fifteen minutes of death.
   Those in the immediate area were interviewed at the time of death: since the finding of possible homicide, review recommended.
   Alicia leaned forward with interest. Buckham Downs, a well-known Standardbred racetrack, sat alongside the famous old fairgrounds on the western edge of the county. A good number of racehorses actually stabled right there on the grounds, year-round. Any sort of conflicts might arise between the racehorse owners and various staff.

At first look, it seemed like the possible number of suspects would be huge, it was not the case. "Its 'murder in a locked room," she murmured.

The paddock area was restricted to those involved in the pre-race presentation of the horses due in the next race: Owners, trainers, sulky drivers, grooms. Most would be busy with their own horse, harness, or sulky, in those few, pre-race moments. Anyone not busy might easily be noticed as out of place.

McDermitt, an assistant recently promoted to full trainer, had lead the favorite 'Another Hope.' A groom assisted him. His jockey was still to be cleared on weight, so was not yet in the enclosure. As 'Another Hope' was owned by a syndicate, no owner representative was present.

The victim was observed to be sipping coffee, while waiting for jockeys to weigh-in.

There was no coffee available in the enclosure: No coffee available in the stables. Someone must have handed the victim a coffee from an outside vendor.

Alicia flipped through the notes. No one admitted seeing anyone handing McDermitt a coffee.

Harnessing had begun; horses had been in paddock for an estimated 20 minutes.

Third race of the day: well-known stakes race. As a crime was not established at time, the race was delayed but not abandoned. Most interviews were not immediate. All present, within in the restricted area at the relevant time were interviewed, although in some cases, it was hours later and perfunctory.

"Still," Alicia leaned forward over the file. "Every suspect there, on the spot. Intriguing. The police must have spoken to the killer."

In addition to interviewing each person present, the police had gone to great effort to find any connection between each and the victim, or any other hint of motive.

The first interviewed, Mike Lee, was actually immediately available as his horse "Princeton" had been pulled from the race. When asked if he knew the victim, Mr. Lee said he had not been to this racecourse in ten years. As 'Princeton' was owner-trained, only a groom had also been present to help harness him.

Groom, Denise Mack, said she had never traveled to the races before and did not know the victim. She noted Lee's brother had died at a racecourse and the family had avoided racing for some time. "I was distracted and didn't notice anything else in the enclosure."

"What distracted you?"

"I forgot the Prince's shadow-roll and thought there'd be hell to pay. He's never even jogged without it, because he's seriously spooky, but Mike didn't seem to care." Further questions ascertained the item was part of the animal's headgear. "Prince wasn't gonna win, anyway, I guess."

As the groom admitted she had no race experience, Alicia doubted that her assessment of the horse's chances were based on any real knowledge.

The next to be interviewed was also a groom: Groom to the second favorite, Jade Lion. He went to great length to assure police officers that winnings in this race weren't 'enough to have a heart attack over.' He was described as a racetrack 'regular,' and stated that, "First off, that 'Another Hope' shouldn't have been favorite. There was no need for anyone to meddle with that horse, as, as the groom put it, there was "no way he could make the distance."

'Jade Lion' had indeed won. James Smith, owner, assured police he did not know or at any point speak to, the trainer of the favorite. Smith's financials were subsequently viewed and they established he had no immediate need for the race winnings. A financial motive seemed doubtful. Jade Lion's driver had weighed in and then been thoroughly busy with his horse's preparations throughout their time in 'the paddock.' Witnesses supported that. As the second-favorite, the horse and all those associated with Jade Lion had been under scrutiny throughout.

Mr. Smith himself pointed out that the victim had only recently moved up to trainer from assistant, and that the timing was a shame.

Alicia scanned the list of those interviewed. Several whole groups were present with an individual horse: One, 'Hanover's High Miler,' had its two owners present, along with a trainer, assistant and groom. Each had been interviewed separately.

Alicia doubted any one of them could possibly be above suspicion, as each would vouch for the others. A conspiracy?

There were ten horses in the race. The paddock area had to be seriously crowded. She pictured the various handlers trying to keep the horses from crowding each other, all the while harnessing. The horses would have been keyed-up for the coming race. One or two might have been quite fractious. Trainers would have been bellowing last minute instructions at the drivers. Grooms double-checked the equipment. Officials checked the horses, the equipment, and watched for any irregularities. It was surely mayhem and though some offered details of the scene, none could claim to have seen anything untoward.

"Always complaining, always trying to put others at a disadvantage. That McDermitt would tattle on anyone, like a rat," said Noreen Roger, groom of Silver Stream. "He went an' tried to get us blocked. Said old Silver here wasn't fit to race. Tried to say he'd been blistered! Sheesh, you can see his legs are good."

"I dreaded working for the dude," his own jockey had said. "He always blamed the guy on the reins. He's canned practically every jockey here at one time or another."

Most noted his argumentative personality. Some version of "I didn't have it in for the guy, but loads hated him," appeared routinely in the notes.

"Super popular," contradicted a Mr. Jones (yet another groom.) "Always a good time for everybody at the end of the day."

As Jones had suggested a drug antidote be attempted, he was further asked if he had reason to suspect McDermitt used drugs. "Nah, he might frequent parties. Yeah, for an older guy, he was popular with the party crowd. So, I was guessing. That antidote don't hurt anything to try. And if it didn't help, so it's not like he'd taken anything."

Pressed if he recalled any event with victim used drugs Jones insisted 'everything is hearsay.'

Several horses were being prepared on the far side of the enclosure, and their support staff were interviewed, but none of them were ever within arm's length of the victim.

"The assistant trainer of 'Seventh Heaven' said, "He was super ambitious to get to full trainer status himself. A bit of a jerk. He'd shove anybody out of the way."

Another owner shrugged and said "unsavory."

That sort of comment seemed common. McDermitt, new-ly a trainer, often rubbed people the wrong way.

Alicia frowned at the interview list. Hopeless. It didn't help to have 'murder in a locked room' when there were so many possible suspects. Some didn't like him, but neither motive nor opportunity shone out from the various discussions. She went to the sheet of attached documentation on the horses.

Eight of the ten horses declared for the race actually raced: the favorite (trained by the victim) and one other, Princeton, were withdrawn before post time.

The placings were not entirely predictable. Only the sec-ond favorite, 'Jade Lion,' had obviously benefited by the fa-vorite being pulled.

Alicia looked at the list of horses. The field had three po-tential winners, and two relative unknowns, as well as one that appeared to have needed the outing. The other four would have been hard to predict, as none had much experience at the dis-tance. She thought to look up Princeton's record. He, in spite of his groom's lack of faith, was well qualified. Yet, he'd been a real outsider as far as the betting public was concerned. She dug for more information online. Princeton had old issues with a bowed tendon. Horses might well recover from such an in-jury...but he'd been pulled before the race. The trainer didn't care about a missing piece of equipment – a very necessary piece of equipment, for those that relied on it. She nodded. For whatever reason, the trainer had never intended to race the horse Princeton.

She texted Perkins. "Was it Mr. Lee?"

"How did you know?" shot back at once.

"A guess. No one thought the horse stood a chance in the race. Is there other info?'

"Lee's brother died of an overdose, on that very track. So I followed up on that lead, and McDermitt had been the suspected supplier. No proof." The sergeant said. "And you arrive at the same conclusion, but with nothing that could be used as evidence, either."

"Payback." Alicia couldn't help but wish for a more conclusive conclusion.

She turned her attention to the second case, with greater determination.

15B POST TIME TWO

Location: Buckram County Fairgrounds Road

Theft of items: Laptop, electronics, some cash, 1 winning horse 'fleece cooler' and other.

Report at 2:15 on the first day of the fair, Thursday: various items, including a laptop, backpack, and radio stolen from the secure vehicles in the secure car park. A money can was taken from the race-horse workers break room. A winner's fleece cooler (blanket) in royal blue was also taken, from a fence rail, near where the winning equine was being unharnessed.

The backstretch area is fairly secure from fair-goers, for the safety of the horses. Security watches the main access points, so only those directly involved with the horse care or day's racing were permitted in. That said, there were some few that were not part of the usual backstretch crowd.

A steward had led a tour of a visiting contingent of race officials through the main stabling during the afternoon. Some fair attendees accessed the stable area as friends of specific horse owners. These were relatively few.

The party involved with the winning horse were interviewed, as any of them might have caught a glimpse of the person(s) removing the cooler from the nearby fence.

"Someone got some nerve," was the most common response among them, although some chose to word that statement a bit more coarsely.

"Wouldn't you know it was during the one time there was actually a Steward shepherding a group around back here?" was a direct quote from Speedy Stan's groom. He suggested the official giving the tour be interviewed. "I mean, no one wants to believe it was one of us, and today there were more than few people around that really shouldn't a been here, behind the gates and in the enclosure."

Speedy Stan's owner was notably upset over the loss of the cooler. "I can provide a photo of it. It was on him at the finish." A photograph of the horse wearing a long cape over his harness, there at the finish, was duly included. The tote board sat squarely behind him, his groom stood at his head, and the owner and trainer stood smiling broadly around the driver in his sulky.

'Cooler/blanket' missing at same time as other items, was noted underneath.

The sense of the officer on scene was, the perpetrator was likely one of the 'backstretch' group, which included an unsavory lot, thieves and convicted whatnots among them. There were a number of fairgoers in the general vicinity, although the main crowd tended to hang out near the rides and food vendors.

"Hmm..." Alicia looked over the facts one more time. Having enjoyed more than one trip above the scene on the famous Buckram Ferris Wheel, she had a good idea of the general layout. The raceway was most securely fenced away from the fair-area.

The perpetrator might have hoped to avoid blame because so many 'unofficial' people were allowed behind the scenes on this particular day. However, it would have taken some time to break into half a dozen different cars, and insider knowledge to grab the money can. Also, grabbing the cooler could not have been easy.

She phoned Perkins, sure of her analysis.

"Speedy Sam's groom."

Over the phone, she heard a shuffle of papers, as Perkins muttered, "What? He was never suspected. Why do you think?"

"It might well have started out as spite. Speedy Sam's groom likely has some gripe with the owner.

"In the photo, the official race photo, they are grouped around this famous horse, with the groom right at his head," Perkins pointed out. "Looking like part of the team."

Alicia snorted. "He looks like the only one in the bunch that can manage the horse. And probably only feeling somewhat under-appreciated."

"Ok, I give up. How did you hit on the groom?"

"How would he have known 'right then?' if he weren't there? He grabbed that cooler himself, as the noisy group wandered by, and who would even notice?"

"It's possible," the sergeant conceded.

"He did," Alicia insisted. "I know that sort and he wouldn't be happy unless he came out ahead somehow. He took it out of spite, but wouldn't mind benefiting too. So, I searched it online and the fool is trying to sell the thing. Picked off the letters and trying to get a hundred bucks for a 'nice, blue fleece cooler.'"

Perkins said, "I'll call my counterpart out there. Get back to you later."

Alicia clicked the phone off with satisfaction. Knowing a little something about human nature might just pay off after all.

Before she had time to gloat (even secretly to herself) a familiar trill echoed from the upper hall.

"Marigold!"

Madame Equestrienne Socialite-blogger herself bustled in with two shopping bags under one arm and dragging a space heater under the other.

"What on earth?"

"I totally got you into this, for my own ends, I freely admit. So I thought I best make this dungeon habitable." Marigold swung the bigger bag onto the desk. "A desk lamp, a space heater, a cushion for your chair. Just stopped myself from buying you an expresso maker."

Laughing, Alicia shoved the police reports to one side. "I needed an in-between job, as it was, so I can't say I hold you accountable."

"I hope to convince you to stay." Marigold raised one hand. "I know, I know. You must fight the allure of a nice warm Wellington winter. Look at all you can do for me, right here. Include me in the museum events. Pass along all sorts of information. And, I could use a feel-good story for my blog. Keep me in mind, as you are dusting off these ancient wheels. Say, what are these?"

Alicia eased the police files out from under Marigold's inquisitive eyes. "Mind puzzlers. You know, the odd case out at the racetrack. A theft. That sort."

"Not the 'in' crowd." Marigold stood. "Although if any celebrities are involved, I'd make an exception."

"I'll keep that in mind," Alicia assured her.

15C: A FAMILY AFFAIR

Location: Buckram County Racetrack

The third case report stated boldly: Likely suicide.

Report: Buckram Country Raceway Chief Executive Ethelridge found dead in the racetrack skybox. Appeared to be result of substance abuse.

Later determined to be overdose of sleeping pills.

Alicia needed no more to recall the event. It had been the day of the big East Coast Pacing Championships. The 'Hollywood' entanglement had added to the intrigue and even landed the story in Marigold's blog.

It had been all about the romance, at the start. Hardly anyone realized the real importance of the day's race.

Marigold's page had exuded enthusiasm: *everyone expects to see a star launched. Tomorrow, will the Montvey Cup become a household name? And shall a certain celebrity appear? Curious eyes are watching.*

Indeed, the rumored romance overshadowed the actual race; for people expected Ethelridge's girlfriend, starlet Erika Montvey to appear.

Then the romance ended. The end was publicly paraded on blogs and social pages amid more nasty giggles than warranted. Ethelridge tried to paddle above it all: he announced he would name the great race after himself and add a bonus payout besides. He hinted he might have been seeing some other actress, too. He sent whispers out like red herrings, but who could say which were real?

Afterward, the police investigated and reported on every possibility: The celebrity link, the potential for a love triangle, the possibility of foul-play having to do with such a strong favorite in the famous race, all were considered, studied, and finally abandoned.

Marigold had speculated on much the same points, very publicly, on her blog.

No one considered the famous race, itself.

Alicia remembered years back. She'd got her own too-slow Standardbred from an off, off-track stable. The gent in charge had proudly shown her one of his finer animals, with a booming 'This horse qualified for the MacLain Cup Race.'

The MacLain. Alicia pictured the family, and a certain woman: (call her 'Mira,' Alicia decided.) Of more than mature age, she likely appeared a spectator, with a fancy wide-brimmed hat and a fresh perm. Alicia motioned to push all those curls back, as if she stood, herself, on the stands.

Years back, Mira reflected, she'd been right out there, and now, relegated to the stands of spectators.

Well, she needed to blend.

Fools.

Even fooled her own family.

'Constellation' was a son of the mighty 'Lone Star,' by 'Starry Night.' He would be going to the post, and was expected to win. The MacLain cup would be awarded, possibly for the last time, if the track chief director had his way. Next year, the Ethelridge Cup would grace the winner of the big one: his name celebrated for all the world to see, but only if the Mr. CEO could get the Board of Directors to agree.

It had been shared around, hot news.

Things were always happening in the paddock. Grooms prepping horses for the following race shouted at one another, trainers held tense discussions, owners waddled into the fray for selfies. In the midst of melee, people got stepped on, buckets overturned, arguments ran rife. It was the regular hubbub.

Mira thumped her grandson on the head and pointed out a brilliant chestnut sauntering by. "Breezy," she said succinctly. "Not a horse to take lightly. He might well take it. Breezy is the dark horse here, for certain."

No one with eyes to see, could argue. Breezy sauntered along with an immensely long stride, even at a slow pace. He towered over most of the field, including the favorite, and he had the 'look.' He was a contender, for certain. Constellation might have won the pacing series but was by no means a shoe in. Mira smiled softly. It didn't matter which horse won.

"Constellation is set in stone and soon to be set in history," her grandson said. "Right?"

He'd said her own words back to her. He might be the one to take up the family legacy. If there was a family legacy to keep. She leaned down to tell him, "Fifty years back, almost exactly now, I led my Dad's first real hopeful out onto this very course. Not in a big race, but it ended up as Daddy's first win at a real race course."

"Mac MacLain driving the Little Dipper," her grandson supplied, without prompting.

"You remember." She beamed down at him. "Your Great Grandad would have thought you wonderful."

The boy might not have heard her clearly, for there truly was something going on behind them-people were clearing out of the way of official vehicles.

Mostly, everyone focused on the horses.

Six gleaming racer horses made their way out on to the track. A couple anxiously jigging, one with two grooms in attendance and then the famous fellow, strolling, head-high. The set off, one after the other, going the wrong-way, to warm up. Sweat already gleamed on the necks of the perfectly groomed ensemble.

Ladies wore big hats as if it were a certain weekend in May. The small touches gave away the significance of the race.

"He started all this," Mira said aloud, though to no one.

Her son, and his son, my stars and garters, how had she got so old? Leaned over the rail, echoing her posture exactly.

They had no idea, not really. Standardbred racing hadn't stayed 'in the family.'

"Got you here to watch 'Constellation' go in person," Brian said, self-satisfied, but he had no idea. He thought they were there for the race. "The horse is odds-on."

'The horse,' was Constellation, whose blood carried that distant link to The Little Dipper. Dippy, the little bay, gone now, these last three decades. It was this horse 'Constellation,' her son Brian thought she was here to see. Brian remembered the lineage, of course, but who among the betting public recalled pedigrees three or four generations back? No one. No one at all.

Mira excused herself for a moment, circled the grandstand, marched through the clubhouse and then went straight on into the private box. Who argued with an old lady?

She had never quite believed she'd pull it off.

Ethelridge stood twirling a glass of champagne, before the race even, telling some trainer about track conditions, as if he were a race guy, as if he had the faintest idea, and not only a big money CEO without any actual horse sense.

He wasn't a horseman, was he? A businessman. She pulled out a hip flask and waved it under his nose. "Man upstairs said you deserved a shot." She had nodded toward the grandstand and didn't tell him she considered she'd be sending him on, further than upstairs, with this one drink.

She waited for this Mr. Fancy-CEO Ethelridge to decline. He didn't know her, did he? Even if security had let her in. She hadn't said some name. 'Upstairs' he might think of anyone on the board, but it would be more likely he'd be suspicious.

He had beamed at her, the fool. He didn't want to be caught failing to recognize an old hand in the game, did he? And here she was, in the clubhouse. She could see his thought process, plain as plain. She must be one of these eccentric race horse owners, whom he ought to remember, was what he was thinking. He'd taken a quick nip, looked surprised, and then said, "It's an older name whiskey? A hint?"

She smiled. What an idiot. "Best have another taste."

He'd given her a grin, and had another sip, though the one had probably been enough.

She reached for his champagne glass. "Shall I set this down for you?"

He didn't so much as sway, for even that load of sleeping pills would take some time, "Constellation," he said, and started to describe the eventual winner.

"I'll be a minute," she told him, and left. One lie after another. The first to get extra pills from her doctor (people were so ridiculously gullible with people they expected to be harmless. Plump, seventy-something with a grey perm, and out of the blue, couldn't sleep?) Oh well, it opened doors.

Then she got Brian to drive her all the way here, to "see Constellation."

It was all one tangled web, but she'd done it.

No sense missing a minute, now she was here. She descended to the track and took a spot on the railing next to her grandson.

CEO Mike Ethelridge, once-tied to the well-known celebrity Erika Montvey, was currently slumped dead in the back of his fancy box seat.

Mira's business with him was done.

She stood in the midst of the crowd, though she might as well be alone. She hadn't known what she would feel, but come to it, not much of anything. He didn't matter. Standing here again, standing at the Buckram Raceway with the hubbub of the people behind her and the famous oval in front of her; that mattered. History and memory entwined in a certain joy.

Constellation, representation of another generation, was a privilege to watch, certain, but he wasn't her 'Little Dippy.' The racing itself, the big name at the gateway, that was what mattered. The horses, about to go off in the big race, 'The MacLain,' on everyone's lips; that mattered. This race attracted the very best of pacers. The legacy mattered.

Lots of folks were getting last minute bets in or struggling for a great seat with view in the stands, the club house folks gathered by the windows as the drivers in sleek silks started to make the turn on the backstretch. The truck carrying the automatic starting gate glided out on the track and began to accelerate.

The first lap of the MacLain Cup was underway.

The favorite won, though the race was overshadowed. Momentarily, the death of the track manager leapt to the top of the news, but likely only because of the celebrity entanglement. The MacLain was discussed and the famous horse affixed to history.

Marigold had blogged about the winner's payoff and the sad celebrity entanglement.

She had missed the real news.

The MacLain would run again next year. Pacer enthusiasts would remember.

Alicia could imagine the bugle call for the next post-time. Life goes on.

Alicia didn't need to read the police report further. She needed only memory. Mrs. Fortham's pair, named for the heavens, recalled a certain family link: an equine family as well as a human one. Miranda Fortham's dad, Mac MacLain, had bred Standardbreds. He'd got that race championship going himself and had meant it to last. All these years later, his daughter was not about to let his memory die.

Alicia set the police report aside. She wouldn't have anything to say on that one. She could imagine it as if she were Miranda MacLain Fortham, but she had no facts.

Pacers would vie for the MacLain next year.

Chapter 16 The Photographer's Case

DECEPTIVE DRESSAGE? headed Marigold's weekly blog, accompanied by a dramatic photograph of the handsome Hanoverian 'Malibu,' at the precise moment he turned off of the rail at H. *Trust your favorite equine-investigator to check the facts! According to one expert, resistance can make a horse look deceptively uplifted in front; uninformed viewers might believe the horse is properly collected. The giveaway of this error is the fact that the horse's face is behind the vertical.*

Of course, Marigold had named neither the horse nor his driver.

Everyone could identify the big chestnut, even so.

He'd won the top division of the big local horse driving trial, by a country mile.

Is this sort of force actually cruel? Marigold carried on.

The driver, his name made by his remarkable horse, had a clinic scheduled the same day: a dressage driving clinic of course, aimed at helping drivers get their horse on-the-bit. How ironic, Alicia shook her head. Marigold's timing was not by accident.

Should we talk about judges? Marigold snarked. *Should the real inquiry here be about so-called professionals rewarding this sort of driving? Or about trumped-up clinicians?*

Alicia wanted to bang her head on her computer screen. Aloud, she said, "Should we ask if this photo actually shows over-bending, or is it a matter of the photograph's angle?"

She shook her head and looked for the photographer's signature, not wanting to believe anyone had supplied this very deceiving image as an illustration of fault.

No Signature. It was undoubtedly a professional's shot, but with part of the image cut off, there was no acknowledgment. The image caught the big Hanoverian as he was turning onto the diagonal to cross a dressage arena. He appeared to shoulder slightly into the left hand shaft, as he was still at a slight angle to the two-wheeled gig he drew. The driver's hands, in all honesty, might be considered a trifle high.

The clever angle of the photograph gave it a certain dramatic flair. It caught perhaps the very first step of the horse's extension. His head did appear behind the vertical. It might have been the angle, or a bit of tension but it did seem to exhibit the fault. It all might have been the result of a certain angular awkwardness to the shot.

If only the next step or two were also shown! Then the horse's balance and overall happiness might have been clearer.

And you-know-who won/can that be right? Marigold whipped up her readers.

Plainly hyperflexion/cruel/cruel/cruel roared back, along with more realistic *possibly a trifle too much force used.*

Alicia could not help looking down the list of comments. Already this morning, the blog had been shared a ton. Comments were all over, from damning the driver to calling out the judges. No doubt, everyone planning to attend the clinic would have seen it. They'd be talking of nothing else, to the embarrassment of their teacher.

This is completely unfair, Marigold. Alicia did not type that in the comments, but in a text directly to the 'favorite equine investigator.' *And it's not accurate. Not the photo, and not about this horse and driver. I've seen Lorenzo drive this horse, many times!*

Marigold flashed back, *Doesn't matter! Got a discussion rolling and it's being shared! If my count goes over a thousand I'll land the hoof-boot advertising!!*

Alicia stopped short of responding publicly. It would only add to the argumentative fodder.

Already, more than a dozen people were taking up arms on either side: either big 'Mal' was victim of a nasty bit or rough hands, or the so-call expert hadn't got a clue.

The photographer, whichever unlucky soul that happened to be, hadn't commented.

Probably prefers anonymity on this one.

In the dog-eat-dog world of specialized photography, operating a successful company came down to quality. Style, catching the perfect moments, advertising and clever branding all played a part, but producing excellent photographs was pretty nearly the end-all, be-all. This photograph had captured so many elements from the impulsion of the horse and the total concentration of the driver, all at a moment combining speed and grace.

Any action photographer would be thrilled to have captured this moment. Recognition meant a lot to their ongoing business...but in this case, recognition might not be a good thing.

What if people blamed the photographer for this deceiving image? Would the popularity of Lorenzo and his lovely Malibu drum up ill feeling toward Marigold – and this very innocent photographer?

Alicia scanned the list. No photographer had, as yet, commented.

Malibu's driver hadn't left any comment either.

It was early yet.

Perhaps he hadn't seen.

The blog was making the rounds though. Shared and shared and commented and discussed.

An embarrassment, for certain.

Alicia shook her head, mainly at the ill-feeling generated. The blog itself was deceptive, but even people who realized that felt the need to get in on the argument. She decided against looking at any further social media and shut down the laptop. And, quite honestly, forgot all about it.

Until the noontime call from Sergeant Perkins.

His query sent her scurrying back to her computer.

Those who thrive on ever-topping the next vicious statement had carried it too far, and it was out there, for all to see.

Jealousy, spectacular mover, naturally athletic. What started as a complaint about correct or incorrect judging turned into an opinion free-for-all. Blamed spewed in all directions.

The driver caught some blame – but more nastiness was aimed at the judges, sort of universally, for 'rewarding mean driving techniques.'

Larisa MainWaring weighed in at one point. She sensibly pointed out the mismatch of complaint and the exhibited photograph, but the hue and cry did not die down. Alicia groaned, guessing that Marigold was pleased she had gotten an official to comment.

Commenting trolls went on to discuss the failures of the show regulatory board: why obviously they ought to be ashamed, too, as a matter of course, according to some. The 'regulatory board' had no personal names attached and seemed less fun to attack. Nastiness switched back to the poor driver pictured, pretty quickly.

Did everyone in the northeast have to say something?

Apparently, the only one without a voice was Malibu, the star.

And the only one not blamed was Marigold, who'd kicked the hornet's nest at the start.

Sergeant Perkins pointed at the computer and said, "What are they all talking about?"

"It has to do with carriage: the horse's carriage, I mean." Before Alicia managed to get out her question, the obvious question; why would the police be involved?

Perkins said, "A man's been shot and killed at the Kilkenny Photography Studio downtown His wife says this blog is the cause of it."

Alicia, very unofficially joined the police as 'a consultant' downtown. Alicia was late on scene. It was a narrow studio, with one high window right on the street. Several soft, half-height office walls offered room for the display of photographs. One hid the scene; though only a polite white line outlined the victim's space. An empty coffee cup sat on the desk, next to the laptop computer. Several cameras sat at the ready, along with a travel case.

Alicia needed one glance, but then, took a moment further to look around.

Photographs filled the studio. A sun-lit dappled grey horse grazed in a picturesque field, a lone rider plodded over sand dunes. All sorts of dogs sat in all sorts of poses. Carriage drivers posed with ribbons dangling from the end of their whips. Riders stood their horses up in front of dramatic backgrounds. Brilliant work, really.

By far, this photographer's work featured still portraits. Adults and children posed, or animals posed... Casual, almost dreamy moments were a specialty of this particular photographer, and Alicia guessed he made loads of individual sales to people who found themselves attractively depicted with their favorite equine.

Perkins explained briskly, "Must have happened fairly late morning."

Wife went out to pick up lunch. Perkins pointed out the unopened, untouched box, which sat on a counter in the backroom. "Says she picked it up at from the *'Sprouts and Such Sandwichery'* at 11. Came back to find him down."

"A vegetarian lunch?"

"Yes, very strict."

"A jogger, I think."

"Yes, always went for his mid-morning run."

"Yet, found here dead at 11:30?"

"Yes. Wife says he was following the blog, not his usual routine. He feared the local horse folks would be horrified. The wife thinks the killer might have been the horse's driver, incensed by this recent scandal."

"Likely the wife." Alicia shrugged. "I'm sure when you check her story, there'll be discrepancies in the timing."

"What makes you think it's not one of the carriage driving clan?"

"He's displayed portraits and stills by the ton. Dreamy images out on the sand dunes of the beach. Horses grazing. Not one competition photograph. No action. He didn't take that photograph, and wouldn't have been worried about reaction. He was probably shot before he got ready for his morning run."

"The photographer in this morning's blog was not identified."

"Well, I guess the wife didn't know it, but anyone who knows horses can identify the work of specific photographers, signature or no. It is easy to see that this man specialized in portraits. There isn't one competition shot here."

Perkins muttered, "She shoots him, then dashes to the sandwich shop for an alibi."

Although it wasn't really a result of the blog, Alicia could not help taking Marigold to task for stirring up a completely fabricated controversy.

Marigold's response text read:

Everyone likes to snipe at the successful.

Chapter 17 A Blue Ribbon at Amesbury

"NOW THIS HISTORICAL society application," Marigold began.

Alicia slid into the booth's opposite seat and made a show of lifting the diner menu. "I have by no means decided on applying for the permanent post. What's good to eat here?"

"This is a blue-ribbon position," Marigold enthused.

"A blue ribbon at Amesbury meant something, once." A querulous voice interjected. A woman peered over the back of her booth at them. Her frost-tipped hair attested to her chief qualification – age, and her sharp eyes left them in no doubt she'd speak her mind. "A blue ribbon at Amesbury," she repeated. "At the fair, or the parade. A matter of pride for anyone, young or old, to come here and compete successfully. It was a way for the ambitious to get ahead. Home-built vied with commercial, in the good old days, and a win."

"Meant something. Yes. Thank-you." Marigold gave her a scowl and turned very deliberately back to Alicia. She tapped the device in front of her. "Besides knowing all these wealthy carriage drivers around here, you know carriages, and old-time carriages made this town."

"Wasn't only carriages," the lady carried on. "Woolen mills and leather workers. Plumes and jingle bells. Patents alone, from umbrellas to gears and the famous fifth-wheel, brought a fortune to this town. Horse-training. My father was a wheel-wright for a big shop, but he designed a dray of his own. His own patent."

Alicia smiled past grumpy Marigold at the lady. "I'd not even thought of all the accessories."

"Paints and decals, too. It was everything, everything. They advertised on the commercial vehicles back then. Are you look-ing into Amesbury's vehicles?"

"Gathering information on a historical society's collec-tions." Alicia began to explain.

"I have plenty of information right here." Marigold jerked her hand-held up. "I found a reprint of an actual, historic issue of *The Clarion*. Local paper, turn-of-the-century. All the infor-mation you will need, Alicia and," she paused for effect, before she said "Properly documented, too."

The old lady pursed her lips but sat silent.

Ignoring her, Marigold told Alicia, "The carriage trade here made the place one huge, close-knit community. Sort of heart-warming. Mention something like that to the curator. It's the kind of stuff they love. You are a shoe-in for the job. When they make it permanent, I mean."

The older lady, easing to her feet, tittered. "Competition and close-knit do not go hand-in-hand. As my father would say, a tandem may be two, but is not the same as a pair." She leaned forward and said, "And he went overseas to learn tan-dem. Those craftsmen were perfectionists."

Marigold rolled her eyes. Alicia had to stifle a giggle.

The lady paused at the end of their booth. "Don't bother with heartwarming claptrap. If you are researching, ask instead, who built it and how did they get the job? Or the patent? And what about the person that didn't? You look into that. You look into Mike Taskey's tandem dray. There's more than one story like his."

"Gram." A young man strode over and held out his arm. As 'Gram' struggled to her feet, she muttered 'Taskey' one last time.

Marigold twirled a finger at her temple. "Seriously."

"She's probably not wrong." Alicia tapped a finger on the old magazine. "You keep insisting this historical society position is so 'important and valuable,' but then you ignore a person with a window to that world."

"Ancient history is not going to do us any good. You want the job, you have to present information the way people want it. Heartwarming claptrap. Smarten up."

Alicia looked at the magazine, and too late, thought she should have asked introduced herself. If she was going to bother to research, a real memory would make it all worthwhile. "What did she mean about 'the nature of competition?'"

"Someone wins, someone loses," Marigold declared. She shoved the copy of the old magazine across the table and reached for the menu. "Craftsmen's secrets, patents. You don't get ahead in this world without serious conniving."

In spite of Marigold's encouragement, Alicia decided to make some effort at applying. Yes; in spite. She had to laugh. She'd known Marigold through her online equine blog for ages, but had only actually met her a year back. Marigold was a bit too 'Aunt Katherine' perhaps; a determined perfectionist, but funny, as well.

Alicia had to admit it would not be entirely unpleasant to stay in the area, keep her current apartment, and not have to pack again. Not as Marigold recommended, though. "None of the 'heartwarming' claptrap. I'll do some actual research."

She wanted to do up an essay on a locally made vehicle, and cast about for options. The fanciful surrey with the fringe on top seemed a bit obvious, so she went looking for one of those specialty patents the lady had mentioned.

The wealth of them made for no easy selection, from cut-under innovations, the development of the fifth wheel, the patented carriage umbrella, to even the resins used to protect the wood and glue for the decals.

There were patents upon patents.

Taskey's Tandem Dray seemed a bit unique, and she kept the name in the back of her mind as she searched. Tandem driving had not been locally popular, but she supposed it might have fit a niche somewhere.

A black-and-white photograph, ancient and grainy, exhibited Shoreline Breweries' workhorse tandem, and its long, narrow delivery wagon.

Could this be Taskey's? Alicia took a moment to envision it. Tandem driving wasn't only the realm of rakes and rascals. There had been at least one practical application: Breweries, in the old cities, had to make deliveries via some narrow old back alleys. Tandem allowed the power of two, without needing the width.

She could imagine how a local man might sell the idea of a specialty dray and a tandem to a local ale merchant. "It

would be eye-catching and very old world. Make a statement."
Mike Taskey might have said "Make your name and logo mem-
orable." Likely, he meant to take out a patent on his dray design
and sell that, on the side. He'd hardly tell that to this local ale
merchant though, would he?

Tandem had a certain appeal. Alicia decided to look into
information on this dray. It might well be the heartwarming
claptrap called for – and researching it might provide some so-
lace to a certain 'Gram.'

.

Chapter 18 Sooty Snow

THE CLARION's summer, 1897 issue provided the first bit of evidence. It was all there, the sooty snow scattered over the cobblestones, the great chimney at city center, all as backdrop to the pride of Shoreside Ale. Two great horses stood proudly in line, with a bowler hatted gent 'on the ribbons.' Taskey, no doubt. Another gentleman stood by the great casks loaded in the back of the long, peculiarly narrow brewery dray. Tandem. A long fancy ribbon dangled off the bridle of the lead horse. A blue-ribbon affaire, to be certain, and smack here in the midst of town. They must have been photographed at a parade.

Fine print stated *Shoreside's new delivery conveyance.* There was no mention of patent. Well, of course, Taskey would own the patent, himself.

The proprietor was quoted "This very singular turnout is a wonderful advertising investment."

Alicia decided to do her essay on that one, an apparently forgotten trade vehicle with interesting history, in a town known for vehicles. She set off to find Shoreside, somewhere along Seaside Boulevard.

"Are you lost, Ms. Goodwin?" Perkins, so often about, materialized on the corner.

"Oh, you!" She laughed. "You always seem to turn-up. Why are you wandering the streets? Are you out directing traffic now?"

He smiled. I was on my way to the historical club. I have a question or two for you."

"I am not lost but looking for this brewery-the Shoreside. Their old address was along here."

"The company is gone now," he informed her. "Sold out to a NYC firm some time back."

"Darnitall. It would have been perfect, if I could have located the vehicle. I wanted to see if they'd kept one of the vehicles from their horse-drawn days."

"Ah. Horse and buggy." He turned to stroll along with her quite casually. "I wanted to ask you if you know anything about the businesses some of your carriage driving friends are involved in."

Alicia glanced up at him. "Are you still investigating Mr. Arbuthnot's death?"

"It's still an open case," he answered. He studied the narrow store front at the corner, glanced up at the old-time iron lamppost at the street with the cobblestones. He didn't seem inclined to explain what he was still investigating.

"It should be open. I know there have to be suspects: I mean, the man made his money in some sort of international business, so perhaps there were enemies I could not even guess at, but I still suspect Belinda Carson."

Officer Perkins nodded, though he did not meet her eye. "I understand you've taken a position at the historical society?"

Alicia wished he'd at least discuss the Arbuthnot case. She might not be at fault, but she hated to think such a thing could happen on her watch. If only he would share some details. She glanced up at him, but he stared away, out at the crashing surf. Plainly, he didn't plan on discussing Arbuthnot. It was the historical society thing or nothing, apparently. She waved a hand back toward the renovated Victorian building that housed the offices. "A temporary position. That's why I wanted to see this brewer's dray. I'd like to make a proposal for a new display."

"Would it have gone to another local company?"

"Possibly. I wonder if there are companies still here, that are about as old? We're talking turn of the century.

"You could check a list of companies at the Chamber of Commerce records. Quite likely it's something you can access at the city's site." Pursuing dry old records became a mini-adventure, the two guessing at where and how data had been stored, and checking related businesses, brainstorming in thesaurus-mode, to find any companies that did business with the brewery. Shipping, packaging, imported hops, farm supplies...you name it. They produced their product from basic materials."

They did find lots of related businesses. Shoreside itself warranted scarcely a footnote. The dray got no mention at all. Alicia tooled up and down the screen, featuring far too much irrelevant information. "This Taskey's commercial dray would have been special, so the question isn't so much what happened to Taskey, but more like, why isn't the vehicle famous?"

"The ingenious wagon was made only once?" the good officer guessed.

"It's possible. It's quite the trick to drive tandem, and it might not have been seen as practical, for this area."

Finally they went in search of the origins of that one photograph, from the '*Clarion*.'

In thumbing through, they spotted an advertisement for the sale of 'two imported Percheron Horses.'

In an issue only days after, they happened on the sad obituary for Mr. Michael Taskey. Misadventure was mentioned. It wasn't the realm of polite remembrances to admit to the falling of the fallen, but a letter to the editor in the same paper, lamenting the misfortune of the innocently inebriated walking along the dangerous shore, alluded to the man's demise.

Taskey's dray will be displayed as the logo of a local brewery, was noted among the man's achievements.

Alicia hesitated. "Curious."

"One could easily imagine murder," Perkins said.

"I could easily imagine anything," Alicia admitted.

"Taskey convinced the Shoreside proprietor to go all in for this unique wagon and configuration of horses. The Shoreside guy paid for the vehicle, he paid for specially trained horses, he paid for Taskey to go abroad for training, and then, Mike sets up to sell his plans for the dray, to all and sundry. After all, he owned the patent, himself. Anyone could have emulated this so-called 'singular' turnout."

"Exactly what I would have imagined," Alicia blurted. How had this police officer conjured up such a story, from such spare facts?

"Mike Taskey then met with an untimely, and unlikely end, in the sea," finished the good sergeant.

"I bet that you have uncovered a murder."

"No proof. And no real relevance to today."

Alicia followed Perkins out onto the walkway, so much like yesteryear-and the old chimney, at the head of the mill yard still dominated the landscape this end of town.

I bet it's relevant to that woman at the diner. What had she said? "A blue ribbon at Amesbury meant something."

"A blue ribbon here was not one win, but a sign or symbol of something extraordinary."

"Taskey did manage something extraordinary," she murmured. "Though he never got a chance for fame. I might see about getting this photograph reproduced for display."

"I don't think we could prove a crime." Perkins smiled down at her.

Alicia thought of the old woman from the diner, wanting to recall her father's 'blue ribbon at Amesbury.' A framed photograph from yesteryear gracing the entrance of the local museum might do it. "I think that remembering Mr. Taskey's prize-winning tandem might be enough to please some parties."

The sound of the surf followed them on this grey day, with a hint the salt-sea air. The great chimney still loomed over all, from greying sky to sooty snow, and hardly a house or vehicle sat untainted. The surf rolled on in. Relentless.

"You are quite an astonishingly good detective." She told her companion. "I would not have found those links."

Perkins stood hands clasped behind his back, again facing the sea. "It took your intuition."

Alicia could only wish he'd consider her intuition in the Arbuthnot case.

Chapter 19 The Swan-Body Cutter at Christmas Time

THE SIGN READ, 'HISTORICAL Christmas on the North Shore.' The society's stagecoach sat in the one vast window, whimsically hitched to eight tiny reindeer. The music of '*Silver Bells*,' serenaded the main gallery. Cinnamon scent wafted purposefully through the air.

Over by the children's gallery, with things like pony sleighs and governess carts, inflatable candy canes offered a measure of tacky charm.

Alicia stood a long moment, wanting to be charmed. Music, lights, candy. It certainly seemed a smashing place to work. Imbued with cheer and all that. Then she slithered through the side door marched 'Archives' and left the glittery Christmas display behind.

Dark as it was, even her own realm had its appeal. She ruled these endless shelves, the file cabinets, boxes, and vehicles. The vehicles, all with their own secret stories, awaited first her own discovery, then recognition, authentication, and finally, fabulous celebration upstairs in one of the climate-controlled galleries. Of course, unless some sort of endowment drifted in on the tide, there would never be display space for all. A shame, for most vehicles here offered insight into the craftsmanship and made no little contribution to the understanding of artistic decoration in times past.

Once a busy factory dedicated to creating freight wagons, it now held the still silent remnants of all sorts of vehicles, as well as dust and cobwebs.

She'd been here a week already. Am I still on a trial? She thought to wonder. Showing up to work here still felt a bit surreal. The Mrs. Museum Curator had waved a vague hand at the parked and piled collection and said, "These old vehicles have been donated over years. The groups seems to accept any sort of junk! At least half of it has no documentation at all. It's more than I want to tackle."

Alicia paused there, remembering how the woman had set her hook.

"It'll be a methodical job. Well, I might as well say it. Boring. That reproduction of a Concord Coach up top is the absolute best of the collection. I love the color. People want to see fun vehicles, that's what I say. A surrey with a fringe on top. A surrey is always super, but our display one is great. The ladies re-upholstered the thing, came up with in-action photos, everyone loves it. Most of the rest are some sort of historical something. Drab. Some simply junk. They collected anything. Oh, How I wish we had a half-a-dozen of surreys, all in different colors! Believe me."

"Oh, I believe you." Alicia had stood there, trying not to say, 'Good Grief." Had the woman have no feeling for history? Here were wheel-making machines, next to a stack of felloes. Steaming equipment for bending wood. Beyond, vehicles crowded cheek-by-jowl, all drab-gray in the unlit space.

"Someone has to go through it. Determine what to toss."

As the woman said 'toss,' Alicia all but shuddered. 'Irreplaceable' occurred to her.

Alicia noticed the unmistakable curled dash of a sleigh. She had eased between a stout hay wagon and a bedraggled old governess cart until she could make out the lines of a magnificent old Albany cutter, the classic 'swan-body sleigh' squeezed tight against the far wall.

A very practical-looking mountain wagon with jaunty scrollwork sat next to a European-styled barouche, and beyond that was certainly a London cab? Metal makers' plates were mostly obscured by grime; here she saw 'Brewster,' and there "Studebaker." A Kimball sleigh sat in a far corner and more than one Concord Coach plate turned up, as well.

"It's certainly all worthy of review," she had found herself saying, as if rescuing unloved horse-drawn stuff had suddenly become a passion.

She pointed an accusing finger at the Albany Cutter. "It was you who got me into this. I could be down south, grooming some fancy dressage horse in the Wellington sunshine." The cutter itself was more than deserving of sunshine. She felt pretty sure it had once been someone's pride and joy. Perhaps she'd work on the sleigh's history next. Might land the stylish thing a space upstairs. Too much to do.

Alicia finished printing a museum placard for the governor's ugly old freight wagon, while the faint strains of 'Silver Bells' started yet again. She was puzzled by the lack of a surrey, as Mrs. May had mentioned one, specifically. A locally-made surrey would surely be a bit of a treasure, regardless of its condition.

She let her chin thump into her palm as she waited on the ancient printer.

"Soon it will be Christmas Day,' lyrics echoed from above. Alicia could feel herself nodding off. '*Christmas Day.*'

"Fabulous." Someone spoke.

Alicia tip-toed around an ice-crusted snowbank, blown almost to her door. In the manner of dreams, she did not think to wonder at her magically changed location, but simply went along with it.

Ice crusted the edges of the stairs up to the old brownstone and twirled, quite artistically, around the reproduction nineteenth-century era finials decorating the banisters. The wrought-iron lanterns looked appropriately nineteenth century, as did the cobblestones of the street.

A little puzzled, Alicia muttered "Fabulous" again.

She was transported to a dream world.

Snow tidily trimmed the edge of the sidewalk. Wreaths and ribbons bedecked lamp-posts, doors, and way down on the left, one even hung on the 'Snow Lane' street sign.

Alicia ignored the snow-globe enchantment of it all, but sing-songed "I hate my job' to the tune of '*Silver Bells.*'

"Alicia. You never!"

"I love my job, oh love my job," Alicia trilled in response to her neighbor's rebuke.

Was no one else on this street remotely in tune with reality? It could not be Christmas every day. Except here, of course; The Christmas Factory.

Alicia tucked her tin of utterly perfect fruitcake tighter under her arm and marched toward city-center.

The neighbor, Charlotte Rousse tsk-tsked after her. How could that one be so disagreeable? There Alicia went, with the best of holiday goodies. Charlotte made sure every single person on this street had the finest of treats, as befit this era in 'the Christmas Factory.' Yet, Alicia had to be the crabbiest Christmas-worker in the whole factory. How did the woman keep her job? Okay, so 'naughty-list manager' might lend one to a rather querulous outlook, but she added nothing to the atmosphere. Someone ought to complain.

Charlotte decided to take a charitable view. Today, she would not complain about anyone. Today was to be her day.

She flipped her long cinnamon locks over her shoulder, checked that her long gown swooshed satisfactorily, and began dancing down her own front steps. She hummed *it's Christmas time in the city...*

Charlotte, sometimes known as Marigold, had been in 'Desserts' forever. It was a good job, of course. She distributed goodies to every corner of the factory. From peppermints to gingerbread, she oversaw it all. 'Desserts' was not without prestige, but, for every moment there, every twist of candy cane, she had been dreaming of this day. She had finally landed her role in the coveted 'Holiday Nostalgia Department: nineteenth century.' She got the *Currier and Ives* golden satin party gown, she had the ribbons and glitter and, as the faint and distant jingling grew louder, she announced, "I landed the sleigh ride!"

The fancy swell-body cutter would be drawing up, momentarily.

Charlotte swept down the last stair and paused, one hand on the banister, like a model. All those days - weeks and years - of ignoring the fudge, refusing even a crumb of the molasses cookies, of pretending she didn't care for candy canes, meant, when the moment finally arrived, she had fit. She had literally fit. She had slipped into the ball gown and could step right into the Christmas-postcard image.

A pair of chestnut ponies trotted around the corner and drew up with an old-time bob sleigh, in navy blue, with a pretty painted-on trim. They were lovely ponies, but not precisely matched. The near one had a thick flaxen mane and tail while the other's darker chestnut color included his mane. They had wide chests and thick necks, and looked powerful.

"Bob sleigh," she muttered. Oh, it was nice. Lovely really. It was a squared front two seater, in classic style. It had that faint hint of 'rural' about it, though. It probably came from over the way, in 'Farm Christmas.'

She ought not say anything, but one might have (quite reasonably) expected some version of a stylish city sleigh. In her mind's eye, she's seen it as a deep green, swan-body Albany cutter, decked out with brass appointments, rein rail, with plumes as trim. The ponies would step along as fancy as hackneys and match one another like twins. The coachman, forward of the passengers, ought to look dashing and wear a high top-hat. Most definitely a fine, raspberry crème-filled petit four sort of character.

The chimes stilled as the driver drew rein almost at her feet. He was not the top-hat type. In fact, she recognized him as the toothless old geezer that typically drove the farm horse, a big Belgian to an enormous box sleigh.

That corner of the company existed on all pulled-taffy and hard peppermints, as befit those years.

The driver (one could hardly call him a coachman) leapt out and, all in one motion, shook out a vast woolen robe for her.

The music stopped.

The vision sagged.

Aghast, the street awaited.

Who in their right mind would wrap up in horrible scratchy wool? It would hide her dress. The hood would flatten her hair. She was to ride, so bundled, to the party? She, the crowning touch to the Christmas Factory's Christmas-postcard image?

Well, she could do nothing about the conveyance, but drew the line at this. She held up a hand. "No, thank-you."

The driver, as dour as her stinker of a neighbor Alicia, for goodness sakes, scowled.

Why would anyone who worked at the Christmas Factory be so gloomy? She refused to be defeated or diminished. She would be the shining touch to the factory's perfect picture-postcard image.

She settled into the rear seat as the driver returned to his. He scarcely touched a rein, but clucked, and the ponies stepped off into a lively trot. Snow sparkled all around them.

Chimes rang out as the sleigh runners slipped silently through the snow.

"Shake the snow-globe." She laughed out loud. Joy bubbled around her. She rose above all the little challenges. This moment had filled her daydreams, all those ages of frosting sugar cookies.

Snowflakes shimmered in the air all around her. They lit on her nose and eyelashes. They began to feel a bit cold. In fact, they stung.

The ponies trotted faster and faster. As freezing air swirled about her, she gave a moment's thought to the robe.

But, no: there, her first admirers! A group of carolers waved from the edge of the road. She half raised a hand. She'd forgotten her white gloves, but her hand looked snow-white anyway.

Heavenly voices rang out around her.

The sleigh turned off Snow Lane onto 'Sugar and Spice' Street as they sped on toward city center. Children threw snowballs back and forth at the first little park. More than one shot over or into the sleigh.

Charlotte cringed low. Was this part of 'the scene?' Those brats. If she'd known, they'd have gotten nothing but stale oatmeal cookies. Oh, dear. Perhaps; perhaps she should wave. She lifted a cold hand, but they were already beyond the children. Did it always take ages to make the rounds? Surely she'd not meant to freeze?

As she straightened, she spotted a square of fruitcake encased in dark-green wrapping. Surely, they overdid the green here. Oh, perhaps they hadn't thrown a snowball, they'd tried to share a goody! It appeared to have survived a snowball direct hit. It was not the sort of fruitcake she'd be proud to label as from the Dessert Department. It didn't have a proper tin nor yet a lovely bow, but it might prove warming. She picked it out from under a bit of snowball, broke off a large crumb and bit...

She absolutely never ate fruitcake. It was sweet but dry and crumbly. She leaned forward to keep crumbs off her dress.

The dress might well have been her final concern.

There was no 'Final Department' at the Christmas Factory. No one knew who to call. There it was though: Miss Charlotte Rousse laid undeniably dead in the authentic 1870's blue bob sleigh stopped by the ice skating rink.

Alicia, naughty list manager, stomped up in a most un-picturesque way and glared at all and sundry.

Christmas Factory workers, in various costumes stared back, wide-eyed.

'*Silver Bells,*' had looped around and was playing again, as it did, every few minutes.

Old Dagen, the sleigh driver, shook his head, side to side, very slowly. "She wouldn't wear the cape."

Alicia said, "Is there a robe?"

"She wouldn't have it," he repeated, and lifted the article from the seat beside him.

"She'll have it now. Cover her over. Wait now - what's that on the seat?"

He shrugged, without looking. "A bit of snow."

"Snowball," she corrected.

Dagen said, "I drove right through the park, like always."

"And fruitcake. There's a clump of fruitcake, and leaves."

Dagen shrugged again.

"There, by that broken bit of snowball."

Dagen didn't bother to shrug this time, but looked around at the growing crowd.

"Who was throwing snowballs?"

No one answered.

Alicia snapped, "Will someone shut that music off?"

The crowd started at her tone. One shot that way, another went this, and someone tripped and another gasped.

"Be still." Alicia glanced at her watch, at the crowd, at the snowball, and finally, back at Dagen.

She reached into the sleigh to touch the leaves of mistletoe wrapped around the remnants of fruitcake.

"A mistake?" One of the carolers whispered. "Indeed, Miss Charlotte ought to have known, what with being in Desserts so long."

"Ought to have known," the sleigh driver barked. "If she'd paid attention to her own four corners instead of complaining about everyone else."

"She did fuss about how things looked. She wanted everything to look perfectly authentic." Alicia leaned back and peered at the outside of the sleigh. "This is not the sleigh one would ride to a nineteenth-century ball."

"It's the right era," said one of the carolers. The rest nodded.

"But not the right application. A family would have ridden this to town, perhaps, everyone bundled in wool. This is not the city-party sleigh."

The driver pursed his lips. "I offered her a cape."

"And fruitcake? All wrapped in leaves of mistletoe." Alicia touched the crumbled treat on the sleigh cushion. "No proper sweets for you, all these years, coachman?"

"Proper sweets? I never got no fancy sweets. I weren't pretty enough to suit, I guess. Not Charlotte's idea of a gentleman."

"You should have been pleased enough with doing your job well, even if you weren't a favorite." Alicia glared at the man. "You've proved her opinion now, haven't you?"

"What's this then?" asked the carolers, in well-planned harmony.

"Mistletoe is poisonous. It's around the fruitcake. Maybe even in it. Dagen here came up with a ruse to do in Charlotte."

Law enforcement had to step in. A tall officer, particularly reminiscent of Perkins, but in top hat and tails, arrived. He offered Alicia a bouquet of roses before he clapped handcuffs on the sleigh driver.

Alicia, enveloped in the scent of roses, thought to mutter "how strange."

One of the chorus nodded sadly. "Nothing but hard taffy, all these years."

A snowy silence fell.

Alicia lifted her face from her desk and contemplated the plate of frosted Christmas cookies before her. '*It's Christmas time...*' crooned incessantly around her. It took her a long moment - maybe two. Then she clapped a hand to her head. "What a dream."

She pushed her chair back, aware of the faint strains of *Silver Bells* still playing. Aloud she said, "No more of that darned eggnog."

Chapter 20 A Star of Stage and Screen

RECORDS OF A SURREY turned up. Not the fancy, nearly-new ultra-favorite surrey the ladies had decorated for upstairs. No, an original-condition, locally-made surrey, with a proper fringed top, wide hubs, and correct accoutrements was supposed to be stored with the rest of the collection.

It did not sit in its assigned location, nor anywhere near, although its official documentation insisted it existed.

At length, Mrs. May, this celebrated professional collection curator, admitted the local theater group, "an honest to goodness not-for-profit, so no doubt it's fine," had borrowed it. Some time back. "Not exactly in condition to worry over," she had said, vaguely. Mrs. May had been pursuing the 'real' hearse, sold on by her criminal ex-assistant, and was not much concerned with vehicles of lesser dollar value.

Alicia added 'pursuit of missing vehicles' to her job description and hiked to the local playhouse.

She was puzzling outside the 'playhouse' which looked like an old garage, when she was interrupted.

"You're a fan?"

Alicia startled, looked up at none other than Perkins. Officer Perkins, always investigating crime.

"A fan of Frost are you? Or do you, like I, admire the works of Ms. Crescendo?"

Frost? Crescendo? Alicia's mind was firmly set on locating the historical society's locally made surrey; a real artifact, and could only look at the man, puzzled.

"Not that I don't admire Frost," he assured her.

"Frost?" Alicia repeated.

"Yes, this week's play is about one of his poems."

Amid the signs and schedules, sure enough, one line listed *'The Witch of Coos County.'* Alicia had not thought about the place being a playhouse. Her own mission involved finding this surrey.

'The surrey with a fringe on top,' the ridiculous curator had, at length, made a call (I'm sure it's just a matter of checking...')

But it was the midst of a busy show season, wasn't' it? And when no one returned the call, Alicia marched off to find someone, anyone, who knew.

She'd stalked right by Perkins at the entranceway to the playhouse.

He handed her a leaflet.

She frowned. "Heavens above, is there an investigation going on here?"

Perkins chuckled. Actually chuckled. "I am strictly off-duty, ma'am. Volunteering as usher. Great to see you here, the various arts supporting one another. Let me show you in."

She always suspected there was a human under that policeman's facade. She followed him through the main door to the box office. The box office had purplish drapes bunched on either side of a window and artfully over whatever little office space housed the box office. A clerk leaned down to them with a ticket.

Perkins ushered her, rather proudly, inside. Although it was all one level, and there was no raised 'stage,' more artfully hung purple drapes gave the theater its shape. A narrow antique lamp stuck out right there. A balcony painted in *trompe l'oeil* style graced one wall, and they'd put up actual seating and wonderful old brass wall sconces for lighting.

"This place is a treasure."

Perkins beamed. "It used to be a grange hall. Perfectly plain." He swept a hand toward the side. "I recommend row six, not too close, but easy to hear. I wish I could watch with you- come find me at the end? I really only have usher duties and will be free after the show. Er. Perhaps dinner?"

"Dinner after the show." She repeated, trying not to sound surprised.

In gentlemanly fashion, he touched the back of one of the freezing metal chairs as she settled in.

The lights went down and her original mission was entirely forgotten. The play did a credible job, especially if one already knew the poem. When the son claimed his mother could make a table 'gallop,' it did indeed give a shudder. Creepy sound effects warned of the march of the skeleton. Throughout, she kept thinking about this latest invitation. Impulsive, or...?

It was a tale she'd never have imagined as a play, which was the first thing she shared with Perkins on the way out. In fact, she'd prepared some commentary, as she watched, so as to not be so idiotically tongue tied.

It had been decades since she'd dated.

"Call me Al." He offered her his arm and set a course for the diner on the opposite corner. "Our Madam Crescendo always manages to drum up some original take on things for our plays, so it's often not what you'd expect, and not what's going around' at other playhouses."

Madam Crescendo?

"Incredible mind. Very dedicated. A real star of stage and screen. Can't tell you some of the events she has planned for us - her creativity brings a wealth of enjoyment to the community. I so admire her."

Hmmm. Alicia did not say aloud. So Admire. Make a mental note there. This was plainly a friendly 'dinner after show.' He admired this miss super star, obviously.

Allen stopped in the doorway of the diner. "You know, I often pop in here, after a show- I didn't even give it a thought. We could certainly go somewhere nicer."

"Nicer than a diner?" Alicia smiled. No sense making a big deal out of the chance meeting.

"A woman after my own heart! I agree. And I'll tell you what, the hot corn fritters in here are the best in the world."

Amid giggles, the two of them both ordered fritters. So decadent, in the middle of the evening! "Hot syrup," Alicia suggested, and her date laughed.

"Oh, and reminds me," She hesitated, but what the heck. "I'm looking for a surrey that was on loan to the playhouse."

"They offered '*Oklahoma!*' ages ago." He pulled out his phone. "I can look up the date. Wait...no, not listed. Last year maybe?"

"Would it be in prop storage?"

"We don't really have storage."

"What a wonderful hobby. Helping plan and do the shows."

"I'd likely have thought the same about your horse and carriage bit, if I'd not first met it due to a mysterious death."

Alicia said, "They are mostly gentle creatures."

"And bring you, very quietly, into the most beautiful places."

"I have a wonderful horse for driving, but he's boarded this year near my daughter's college. Perhaps next summer I could drive you around one of our scenic carriage parks." She stopped abruptly, as her words suddenly seemed like she was awkwardly suggesting too much. After all, the man kept saying how he admired this Madam C – probably an off-Broadway blue-eyed beauty, who started her career as a dancer in the big NYC music halls?

"I'd love to go on a carriage tour."

She smiled at him, searched for words, and then they were interrupted.

A gypsy fortune teller of some advanced years, complete with bright, flowing clothes, shiny black, obviously-dyed hair, and an assortment of beads and bangles, leaned over their table. "A grand show tonight, Al. Thank you again. Your galloping table was a wonder! So unexpected! The audience gasped."

Perkins stood and formally motioned to Alicia. So glad you liked it! Mrs. Crescendo, my friend, Alicia, and I believe, if I may say so, a new fan of our playhouse."

The rotund dimpled doll held out her hand. "It's Cranmore, really, but Crescendo is so much more theatrical."

"Yes, it is." Alicia took in the older, much older, oh, so much older woman's hand. "I am glad to meet you."

"My public awaits," the woman gestured to blow them each a kiss, then toddled off, a grand duchess.

Allen, sat down saying "I so admire her. Really has brought something to the community here. I expect you'll help the Historical Gallery in much the same way."

Alicia grinned at him, mostly thinking how lovely he simply admired Mrs. C's efforts, and her talents, as he'd said, and it was not more.

She realized she'd entirely forgotten about the surrey. It was nothing to forget about. Yet she hated now to mention it.

He leaned forward. "I can see your mind is far away. Have I overstayed my welcome?"

Would he think she was only looking for the surrey? "I remembered my mission is all. Trying to locate this antique vehicle." She waved a hand. "I'll contact the staff at the playhouse tomorrow."

His eyebrows drew down. He was much less guarded about his expression when he was out of uniform.

"I'm afraid there are no regular staff."

"Someone in charge of props?"

He shrugged. "Not so much any one job. People go look for, dig out, make or borrow whatever we need."

"It's quite large, really. I mean, more movable but easily the size of a piano."

He spread his hands on the table. "I'm as 'staff' as anyone. We can go take a look for props right now."

"I didn't mean to bother you."

"No bother. It's your business to locate the item." He got up and paid as they went out the door.

Keys, lights; he was as staff as anyone. He showed her down the half-lit hall to the prop closet

"A surrey wouldn't even fit in the door."

"Cellar," he said.

She shuddered. "Lord no. The damp."

He soldiered on ahead, all business.

"I wish I'd left the surrey-hunt for another day," Alicia reflected as she slunk along after him. It kind of ruined the evening. They'd had such lovely moments, then it had gone wrong, or had it? Perhaps it was no more than casual, in the first place. She had perhaps read too much into a simple invitation. The man wanted to chat about the play. He wanted someone to admire his galloping table contraption.

She stifled a sigh as she followed him down a back stairway.

He flipped on the lights at the bottom of the stair; furnace, pipes, cans of paint, signboards and other odd leftover items met their gaze.

"There isn't a door big enough to fit the surrey in here." Alicia reached out and placed a hand firmly on his arm. "Let's call it a night. The play was wonderful, dinner super. I've enjoyed it all, but this surrey hunt is part of my job. I'll start again tomorrow."

Allen stood slightly stooped under the low-ceiling and she could not read his expression.

"I'll see you home," he said, his voice oddly deep.

"I've got my car right down at the society lot. Although it's a nice little walk to there."

"I'll see you there."

The walk was nowhere near long enough, although evening lights made it pretty. After, Alicia wished she'd thought to make some sort of clever conversation: What was next for the playhouse, how he had made the dancing table contraption, what was next. Anything!

The quiet stroll answered nothing that mattered.

At home, sleepless, she pondered the surrey's info.

It was awful they'd lost track of it. Per the museum acquisition documents in the files, it had the original top still attached, the cut-under design that had been hugely popular at one time, and although it wasn't rare, and had been locally made, so fit the society's mission to a T.

She consulted the copy of the vehicle's documents she'd brought home from the office. Description, sales agreement; details were readily at hand. She could authenticate it easily enough, when she found it. "If I find it," she said aloud.

It should sport a maker's label, and in the provenance information, there was included a photograph of the vehicle in the local '*Clarion,*' with a write-up about the Ladies' Aide Society outing.

Rectangular in general shape, with a round bracket and square cornered seats, and nice wood molding along the sides. Its elliptic springs would likely be found on any vehicle of the type, so were little help.

The documentation described the colors as deep blue and striped in silver. The seats were blue cloth with two cushions trimmed in lace. The lace color precisely matched the fringe surrounding the canopy top. The upholstery was not much worth noting, because any of that could have changed or been replaced, but the squared-edge of the seats would still be correct, as were the tall flange lamps and their mountings.

She guessed she would know it when she saw it. Digging online finally landed her a playbill for the 'Songs of' nearly a year prior. 2 a.m. She decided to turn in, but all she did was turn over, retracing the vehicle's route in her mid. It had been in the lower storage at the society, and sent to the playhouse. Movers took it, as neither organization could move it, and it would have been pushed through the single wide door at the front entrance to the playhouse, and at the same floor level as the stage, pushed right there. It would have had to be removed the same way; pushed from the 'stage' end of the building to the front again, where the box office sat. They'd have had to move that box office, roll it perhaps... roll it. The box office with the purple drapes? Acres of purple drapes. She sat bolt upright. There isn't a box office at all; the ticket window was part of the surrey. The clerk sat on the back seat and handed tickets out the window. Likely, neither organization wanted to pay for its transport home, so there it sat. It gave shape to the whole front, separating a 'lobby' area from the seating.

The surrey itself had become a star of the stage, for heaven sakes.

Chapter 21 Party Invitation

"YOU'LL BE ANOTHER FROZEN Charlotte," Alicia declared, almost before her friend made it through the museum's back entry door.

"I have no idea what you mean." Marigold flipped her flimsy turquoise scarf back over her shoulder.

"Have you never heard of Charlotte? She froze to death because of her terrible vanity. Wouldn't wear a woolen cape, went out in a sleigh in her ball gown. Some wit even named a dessert after her. Gelatin, I think. I had a dream about her."

"Blame a gal for being stylish. This is my little black dress. Trying to decide if I wear it for the party." Marigold struck a pose. "Add any color accessory, and it's a new outfit. Very New York."

"You are very north of New York. It is twenty-two degrees out, right now."

"It is a party. And, your outfit won't do."

Alicia shrank down in the plushy seat and did not admit she had never intended to go.

Marigold leaned over the desk, the papers, the documents, and glared straight into Alicia's eyes. "You are coming, aren't you?"

"Only have this temp job for the thirty days and I'd like to get through this stuff here, at least."

"They pay you for evening hours?"

"Well, no. But I don't have anything to wear, anyway."

Marigold silently lifted her right hand, revealing a deep green velvet frock-like thing. "For you."

"What are the odds it'll fit?" Alicia knew it was a lost cause. She was clinging to her chair now like a cat getting ousted out of its comfortable spot.

Marigold smiled. "It'll fit. I bought it for you. You-you-you. Green suits your eyes and it's your favorite material and you will look stunning."

"It might be a little over-the-top."

"This party is a very big deal. It's like, my debutante ball. They'll see I am a somebody. I'm going to announce Steven's foreign job. I have arrived. We'll set out for Paris first and then I don't care. Somewhere. Abroad, wealthy, and when we get back, I'll be asked to every stinking club, gathering or tea. That's me. I shall be the center of the whole North Shore circle."

"He got it then."

"They said the letters would be out today. It's why I planned the party for today. A Thursday. Not waiting another minute."

"Congratulations to Steven." Alicia slipped her reading glasses back on. "It'll be kind of a more formal affair than I do. And listen, I want to go through some of this, as I am still deciding if want to stay on permanently."

Marigold cut her off, as she turned as if to stalk away. "Just be there. I would take it as a great favor. This once."

Alicia pretended not to be irritated. Plainly, Marigold wanted her 'around.' Marigold, in her desperation to impress, had plainly invited people she didn't even know. She wanted it to seem she just so happened to include the horse-enthusiast crowd.

"I could call and let Mrs. Fortham know about the party. She knows all the ones that board horses here in town."

"Don't bother. She's already invited. And I asked Belinda Carson, old Arbuthnot's groom. She's a useful connection."

Alicia, startled, repeated, "Belinda? I've still half a mind to think Belinda a murderess."

"If you are concerned about her, come check her out at the party. It would have been useful for us to have introductions back when I first asked you."

"To Mrs. Fortham, you mean? Because of her political interest?" Alicia mused, a bit startled at the thought. In fact, half the ladies in the club were movers and shakers in some realm, business or political, some both. "Is this to help Steven's ambitions? I thought you wanted to be included on local events."

Marigold snorted. "Show up tonight. Half of the people I invited I have barely met. It will be so awkward."

"Without me, you mean."

Marigold held the shimmery velvet frock aloft.

Alicia held out a hand. One evening, what would it hurt? "I'll pop in for maybe an hour," she warned, as Marigold marched, triumphant, to the door.

Alicia sighed as she wove her way through the collection, back to her office. The dress must have cost a mint. It had been a nice gesture. Nice to be invited. She propped her toes up on the small space heater and remembered it was a gift, too.

The vehicles, and the ghosts of their people gathered around her, waiting patiently. How was it she could imagine the people associated with these various wagons, carriages and buggies, yet could not begin to fathom this friendship she had with Marigold? Oh well, Aunt Jane often said much the same about her own cousin, Claire. She was always interesting.

Actually, Claire was never described as 'interesting.' She was 'not sensible.'

'Not sensible,' might be a good deal more accurate about Marigold, as well.

Alicia stared down at her plain loafers. They wouldn't do. She sighed. She had to go, there was no getting around it. She had the afternoon, so could zip to a shoe-store, do something with her hair; part of her hated the distraction. She'd just read about the Wentworth Legend: the one-time Governor Wentworth, who escaped 'the colonies' prior to the Revolutionary War, and left a vast treasure buried somewhere between Portsmouth, New Hampshire and Lake Wentworth.

No doubt he'd meant to return for it. He never got the chance.

The Duty Officer's Log, open on her desk, drew her in. April 19...

19th April, 1775. Portsmouth, New Hampshire

Tension stilled the air, as if they all waited; listened and waited.

"Governor Wentworth?"

John Wentworth turned from the tall window overlooking the harbor. His aide paused, scarcely inside the door. "They've confirmed this riot in Boston Harbor, sir. Word is spreading."

The governor clapped his hands together. "Right then, Thomas. I think we should convene a meeting of..."

"No, sir." His aide interrupted. "You must remove your family, straightaway, sir. Secure your property and prepare."

"The tide of politics can ebb, as easily as rise." John Wentworth shifted uneasily, for, even though he'd spoken up for the working men of the city more than once, his favor here had sunk. They knew him though, the people of town here, they knew him as a good governor. Surely the danger would not gallop upon Portsmouth?

Truly, the governor did not want to admit their danger, nor depart. The grey clad house, the eastern view, the wonders of the rural lands beyond city limits, all were home to him. "It will all pass."

"But the situation, sir..."

"An abrupt departure has political implications, Thomas." The governor clasped his hands behind his back. "Still, some lesser measure might be considered."

"You are here at His Majesty's pleasure and may not survive the wait. Sir, I beg you. For your own safety, retire to the fort at New Castle." His aide had never spoken so plainly, so urgently. Had he further word, or some sense of the townsfolk's mood?

Governor John Wentworth turned back toward the sea. The gently rolling waves grew to a swell here, and then there, with a certain suddenness. The threat of revolution seemed much the same. Calmer seas would surely return, as the points of contention were addressed?

Most issues were at some distance. They heard little, and late, and it was not the sort of operation a once-soldier tolerated with patience. The governor shook his head.

"Very well, Thomas. We will prepare. I'll take one last ride out to the lake property, make sure all is secure."

"With a full escort of men."

"However many you can have ready within the hour. I will have Florence pack ready for a move by end of week. Will that suit?"

The good aide noted the decision in the official log. He did not, of course, include the full discussion. Alicia conjured that, entirely, in her mind. She could see the preparations, the half-dozen King's soldiers, draft horses and the freight wagon requisitioned as part of the governor's party.

How terribly peculiar.

Journey particulars: They traveled the Strafford county road, through Durham Township and northwesterly toward Wolfeboro and the hundred acres of wood along the lake. The freight wagon must have slowed them, when surely they could carry all they needed on a pack horse or two?

Of course, one and all saw the point of the freight wagon. Governor Wentworth must have taken his riches to his property and buried it there. In the years since, not an inch along the shore of the lake went unturned, and so one and all turned to think it buried somewhere along the way. Ever after, folks looked for gold coins buried along the road, and re-checked the lake property.

Nothing had ever been found.

The legend, tied so closely with the Wentworth vehicles long enshrouded in the society's cellar, compelled Alicia to action.

She turned to the archives, to maps and small details until finally, she stood. "It's no good. I must see it. Start with

Portsmouth, then travel west." She could not even guess what had transpired. Usually, her imagination was so much more accommodating.

She checked her watch as she made for the stairs. She might make a quick round trip of it, to get a sense of the area. She could still hit Marigold's party. Most likely. Find party shoes along the way.

Done for the night? The Sergeant texted, before she'd hit the stairs.

Her heart did a little flip.

Off to solve a mystery, she responded.

Solving sounds too good to miss, he answered.

She flipped a response about watching the action, giggling. She'd not mind this fellow, not so much at all.

Those flip remarks can get you into trouble, she did not say aloud, as she slipped into the passenger seat of the slick-looking SUV, minutes later. "It's a treasure hunt," she told him, as she gave him a run-down of the legend.

"And you took this up, because...?"

"The historical folks have got the freight wagon stored away in the stone-lined cellar of the old building. Cracked wood, steel shod wheels. It's rough but sturdy, and honestly, given its condition, it must have been stored away almost when the governor departed."

"Definitely his?"

"From what I can tell from documents. It's crammed in next to another vehicle also listed at Wentworth's. Those fanciful spoked wheels sure spoke of a European maker."

"So find the treasure, to go along with the vehicles."

"I suspect no one took that freight wagon, heavy as it is, on a speed-drive over barely-passable dirt roads. No, I think that was a diversion. I mean, why take extra men and a freight wagon, unless you want people to talk about where your riches have gone. My dear old Aunt Jane, famous for solving mysteries, would say start by evaluating human nature." Alicia nodded.

Allen smiled. "A more professional approach, if you will forgive my saying so, starts by evaluating the facts."

"The facts we have are mostly hearsay." She could scarcely admit she could see the governor in her mind's eye. "There is information noted about the governor. Very strong, great stamina. Family man. That sort of thing."

"Maybe we should start with a topographical map of area." Allen pulled out his handheld. He patted another pocket, muttering about a GPS.

Alicia did not point out that she'd looked at maps. Historical maps, current maps. "I thought I'd start with the house and see if I could sort out the oldest route west."

Allen stopped to click from one map to another. "Nineteenth century New Hampshire roads are not a common search," he grumbled as he showed her the screen. Irritatingly, he shot right along to another map. "Say, you are right. The freight wagon was subterfuge. Look at this: Portsmouth is almost on the mouth of the great Piscataqua River. It was a stone's throw from New Castle, and the revolutionary-era fort, then held by the Brits."

Allen traced the waterway on the map.

"Hmmm."

"The Piscataqua ran past his doorstep. Why would he not set off by boat? He could have traveled upstream, selected any tributary, and moving any amount of gold easily, on a small ship or even fishing vessel. The river would support a fair-sized vessel as far inland as he needed to go."

"Maybe he did, and the freight-wagon trip was a diversion."

"Where would he go?

"I would say, here. Oyster River, to the millwork. It is on the way to his properties – he might well be acquainted with the village. Knew people, knew the area, knew he'd be able to return to wherever he left his wealth."

"The legends say he went by horseback, escorting a freight wagon." Alicia pondered the map.

"I can't explain the legend. I say we make our way to Durham, first off."

It made sense, though the idea failed to grab her imagination. She nodded and they traveled to Durham Point, to a pretty park overlooking the tidal river, which was fed by a quiet millstream. Seagulls and cormorants attested to the nearness of saltwater. A brief flurry of snowflakes set a smattering of white over tree limbs and freshened the snow shoveled around the edges of walkways.

Silently, Allen offered his elbow and they strode over the threshold into what might be this winter garden. The stone lined path brought them below the great white Victorian-style house, with its historic marker.

"Docks and houses, any might have been build atop treasure. The old mill and wheel - the pond, the overlook. Lots of places for a hidden treasure." Allen spoke with the enthusiasm of a treasure hunter. Possibilities abounded.

Alicia wandered over to the frosted grass to read the historic marker. She looked up at the ancient saltbox weathering gently into the ground. "All wrong.'

Allen stopped short. "Wrong?"

She blushed, but put forth her point. "There was a village here, even then. See that square place with the center chimney? Those front windows look right down the river. There was likely a tavern. I mean, there's nowhere secret here, and they were on the doorstep of open rebellion. The governor could not have known who among his own soldiers he could trust."

He looked down at her as if to argue, but said, "You have snowflakes on your eyelashes."

She'd expected some logical point and a giggle escaped before she thought.

"I think we had best stop for some sort of frothy latte or cocoa. You'll be frozen."

"Back then it was a hot toddy or an egg nog," murmured Alicia. "I can smell the nutmeg."

"In keeping with the times, we shall find a toddy." He offered his arm again.

"You might be right," she said.

Allen dismissed the millpond with a glance. "I guess you're right, again. The governor might have squirreled his wealth away along a deserted stretch of shoreline, but he likely never got the chance to travel alone, once the threat of war loomed."

"We don't know if the treasure was too large to move and unload himself."

"Oh." Allen stopped. "What if he never unloaded?"

They chorused, "The freight wagon."

The return drive was filled with anticipation, and doubt, and sprinkled with laughter. "Facts and psychology," Allen swirled a finger in the air. "I am convinced we could be quite the old-fashioned sleuthing team."

"A combination of Agatha's Miss Jane and Arther C-D.'s gentleman from Baker Street," Alicia agreed.

"No Poirot?" her escort chuckled. So they shared a love of old mysteries...

The freight wagon, roughly made and unlovely, sat on great, iron-shod wheels in the dimmest, deepest corner of the cellar.

They confronted it, hopeful, doubtful, and before long, exhausted. The ancient vehicle sat wide and plain and strong, with its enclosed box in front and a narrow space below its plank floor. No secret drawers emerged and no space offered anything up but empty space. Not a coin, not a paper dollar, not an intriguing map.

"Someone thought of this long ago," Alicia finally said. "If it had ever been here to find. It would have made sense for the governor to take the treasure along to the safety of the fort. And then safer for those there, his family and all, if the revolutionaries were convinced he'd hidden it all somewhere else."

"Yes." Allen pointed out. "So maybe the legend was a set-up. Talk of a hidden treasure out by Lake Wentworth was always a goose chase. It made sense the treasure would be here."

"We could check Wentworth's other vehicles." Alicia said.

"Other vehicles?"

"I noticed the Wentworth name attached to a couple of other artifacts. The unrestored road coach over in the corner must have been imported, so worth something in itself."

"Perhaps the fortune was entirely a myth. I mean, if he had a liking for finer living."

Actually. Alicia paused, one hand outstretched. "The sleigh collection features one of his, too. Ordered from Bavaria. I read somewhere about raising funds to have it conserved. It's supposedly decorated with gold leaf."

"Gold leaf." Allen gave her a sidelong look. "Gold leaf. Literally made of gold?"

She marched over to the corner and pulled a cloth off the first vehicle she came to. The green vis-à-vis style sleigh, with separate seat for the coachman, leaped right out of her dreams.

"The varnishes have darkened it so the exterior looks plain. But the gold is there." she whispered. "I mean, the whole vehicle is priceless."

He nodded. "The clever governor invested his funds in a sleigh?"

"In vehicles." She shone a flashlight at the front of the coach. "If I am not much mistaken, this decorative seat cloth covering the coach's front seat is hammer cloth." She careful opened the narrow door to the passenger compartment. "The interior cushions look like real Melton cloth. We've got carriage lace. There's a case for a gentleman's card, made into the door. Silver fittings, silver trim, and under all this grime, these tall lamps are silver." She wiped the middle door panel with a tissue, and beneath the darkened varnish could discern a shape. "Sure enough, a family crest graced the door."

"The old coach might well have been valuable, too?"

"It was worth a king's ransom in its own time." She clapped a hand to her head. "Two hundred years, these vehicles have been squirreled away here, and no one has ever guessed?"

"And if you now bring it to light?"

"It will be up to the society."

The officer might be forgiven for looking doubtful. The vehicles did not look remarkably different from many of the other, dust-covered wagons and whatnot squashed into the storage area. Still, he clasped his hands together and said, "A celebratory dinner then, since you've solved this centuries-old mystery?" The big officer, usually so confident, appeared suddenly much taken with the wildlife scene painted on the door panel of the old stagecoach.

"Are you sure we've solved it?" She challenged, laughing. "Well. I'd like to say yes. But..."

He glanced down at the handrail and stepped away quietly. "No worries."

"I've got this darn party. Oh blast, and I still haven't any shoes." Alicia had thought she might bring the man; somehow, it didn't feel right.

Not to Marigold's. She didn't want him to see her being phony, as part of some masterplan of Marigold's.

"Tomorrow?" She put out a hand to touch his sleeve, but he mistook and caught her hand.

The stood awkwardly in the doorway, like schoolkids.

"Tomorrow," he said.

She watched him stride off down the lane, with snowflakes still flitting about. It was as picturesque as 'Snow Lane' in her dream. "Only better."

Chapter 22 Uninvited

ALICIA SCRAMBLED TO get to the party, a touch late, not bad; not bad, but with passable shoes on to set off the green dress.

She tagged onto the Merriwethers as they strolled up to the front door, to be greeted by Steven, amid the crush in the Johansen family's fancy foyer.

"Your house looks lovely," she beamed at him. She didn't know him well, but Marigold's husband seemed like a good egg.

"Oh Alicia. Glad it's you." He ignored the wide open door, the cold swirling right in and around his guests, and the Merriwethers, as he leaned forward to whisper, "Marigold. Fit to be tied. She's in the dining room. Go have a word?"

"Of course," she said, a tad too-warmly. Alicia hoped Marigold wasn't mad at her, maybe thinking she wouldn't show? It wasn't all that late. She scooted around a couple and on through the next doorway.

Marigold stood by the threshold, stone-faced, nodding silently as her guests tried to strike up conversation.

Alicia gave the fancy green frock a bit of a flounce. "Magical matchmaking must be your thing. Guess who has a date tomorrow night?"

Marigold stared straight at her, nodding as if in greeting, but utterly blank.

"Marigold. What on Earth is wrong?" Alicia shook her friend's arm.

"It's a disaster."

"What? It's lovely. The party's hardly begun and there must be a hundred people here."

Marigold blanched. "A hundred? A hundred. I will look a fool. A laughing stock. I've been made a fool, I'll look a fool, and I am a fool."

"Marigold. For heaven sakes."

"He's made a fool of me. A laughing stock. All these people here for a big announcement. My big announcement," she repeated bitterly.

Alicia squashed Marigold toward the corner and whispered. "What are you talking about? "It's a party. Go around, be a nice hostess. These are all carriage driving folks that we both know. There's no problem."

"Carriage folks." Marigold grabbed at Alicia's hand. "Carriages? Did you take the job with the damn carriage society? Did you decide to stay?"

"Well it's not mine to just claim, but, I find I am suddenly very interested in staying." Normally a broad hint like that would have elicited twenty questions, but no.

Marigold chattered away as if in some whole other conversation. "Oh Alicia. Thank God. Your new position."

Marigold strode away, suddenly energized.

She posed below the gilt chandelier in the center of the foyer and shouted "good news, here is my good news. Our wonderful Alicia Goodwin is the new assistant for the historical society! She's taken charge of the carriages. I know we are all excited to keep her, and the news was far too good to post it in an ordinary way on my blog."

There was a smattering of applause. People glanced around, as if wondering if this were, indeed, the news.

"Hardly momentous," someone said, very audibly.

Alicia sank back into the thick drapes and wished she could disappear altogether.

Steven stepped forward, holding aloft a glass he'd already been drinking. "A toast to Alicia. Very exciting."

People followed suit, a touch hastily, amid murmurings of 'congratulations.'

Alicia could only stand and stare. What craziness was this? She stood there, barely nodding, as people smiled and said pleasant things at her that she could scarcely understand.

The foyer bell rang.

More people? The house bulged at the seams. Alicia eased around toward the door, set on escape. She tried to dismiss her irritation with Marigold.

For a few minutes there, Alicia had been about to share that she might have one better reason to stay around these parts. Thank heaven she'd not got to that, what would Marigold have shared with the crowd?

This was absolutely it.

People kept looking at her, as they continued their own conversations, in little groups here and there. What were they saying? Laughing about this 'big announcement' about a middle aged woman attaining a part-time job a kid had been doing. Alicia did not want to guess at what they were saying. And yes, yes she did not want to look a fool in front of all these people, so perhaps she could understand Marigold a tad; but she'd not gone to all crazy lengths to impress them, either. And, for none of that was she willing to use those friends. None was such a desperate ambition that she'd trick or lie or twist the truth.

The bell rang, yet again. Honestly. She thought to make a dash for the door, around behind these three ladies who were sorting out their own coats. Suddenly Allen Perkins materialized in the midst of all.

Alicia stopped dead. The man looked around the room in a businesslike manner, then leaned back to look at the up the stairs, as well.

Somehow, she untangled thoughts enough to move her feet. He spotted her at once, and spoke to someone on his handheld before he stepped over to her.

She stepped forward. "Allen?"

"Alicia." He stood a long moment, silent. "I regret this. The timing. But you see."

"Did you forget something?"

"I'm going to ask you to step back. I regret the timing, but in the course of reviewing evidence, it occurred to me, you, at hand during certain recent events, might be in danger. I decided not to delay."

As he spoke, two uniformed officers stepped around him, into the crowd. He directed them up the stairs with a wave.

"Danger." Alicia repeated, only more puzzled.

"Arbuthnot's untimely death."

"I thought you were going to say Mr. Baddinton. Did you mean Baddinton? Were you talking about the man who was killed in his horse, Socrates' stall?"

Allen, brusquely, shook his head. "Arbuthnot. The man's death was no accident. I am afraid we have received the forensic reports. Fingerprints. Purposeful damage to the vehicle's undercarriage."

The other officers did not stop and Allen swept off after them, up the stairs. Oddly, their entrance was scarcely noticed. They might have been a few extra waiters hired on for the eve, for the crowd showed scarce interest.

Conversation had already left Alicia, and the historical society, and (had she but known it) scarcely touched on 'this Marigold woman.' Most of the gathered crowd were focused on next season's calendar, not yet published, but generally fraught with contention. Everyone wanted to be assured the dates for their favorite events would not conflict with others. Many premium dates were claimed by long-established tradition. "Others don't have a chance!" was a popular argument. Volume in the room increased as if one could, by shouting, show prior claim on the best weekends.

Steven emerged from the middle of the room to touch Alicia's elbow. "Was that the police? Has something happened?"

"It's to do with that old investigation."

"Thank God it's nothing to do with us." Steven shook his head. "I've had enough drama for one night."

"I don't understand." Alicia looked around, but Marigold was nowhere in sight. "I haven't even had the job offered. I mean it's likely but, why did she say that?"

"Marigold thought she'd be announcing my new position." He shrugged. "I didn't even apply to the consulate's office. I did look at the position, but they touched the one applicant they actually wanted long ago. Jerome was getting it."

"You didn't apply?"

"No. I let it go. They had the one they wanted. The consulate did send out a note, saying they'd make an official announcement today. I guess, I let Marigold think I had applied, to get her off my back. I didn't know she'd find out there'd only been one applicant. She assumed they had picked me. All of a sudden this surprise party, out of the blue, and she's asking me for the acceptance letter to read."

"You never applied," Alicia repeated.

"Exactly what she said." He snorted, exasperated. "I never said I would apply. I let it go."

"I need to powder my nose," she managed to squeak. Then she darted off down the stairs, her mind fairly spinning.

The green velvet dress was impossibly hot and she wasn't used to these heels and one earing had snagged on her hair. She leaned over the sink to cope with that, thinking it was no wonder Marigold was having a breakdown. Poor Marigold! No wonder she'd been desperate for an announcement. She'd probably hinted to dozens of people about this big event.

Exasperated, she gave her earing a twist and managed to wrench the post right out of the back.

"Dammit." She glared down at the tiny post in her hand.

The metal rod on Arbuthnot's phaeton had sheered exactly the same. It had come cleanly off its mooring. She could picture it. One twist of a wrench and it had simply let go. A glob of glue would fix it back on, for a short while. But it would have been insecure.

She stood there, frozen before the mirror, staring down at the tiny metal rod in her hand. Belinda was here at the party.

She shook her head. Aloud, she said, "It did not break, it was set to let go." She could see it. It had been cut. Belinda, his groom, the lovely, lovely groom...had to be.

It had been easy to look away when Belinda had seemed the victim of this lecherous old fool. Still.

Alicia looked up at her reflection. The good sergeant had come to arrest Belinda Carson for murder. She should have seen this coming. Without hesitation she shot out of the room and down the hall. She had to be there, wanted desperately to hear what the woman said when they slapped the handcuffs on.

Something about it sat wrong, and she guessed she felt a bit of guilt. Truth was, she'd not done enough to get Belinda charged, right at the start. She'd let her own suspicions go, on purpose, because she guessed Belinda had been something of a victim.

And that had been completely wrong. Obviously, it had been a mean, premeditated murder, motivated by ambition. She remembered Belinda riding her young gelding in turn-on-the haunches, over and over again. Determined to get it right. Plainly, he didn't get it right. Belinda had killed her employer and taken his fabulous near wheeler, all in an effort to win. She likely planned it all along.

"Show them all." A shrill voice cut through the crowd and conversation from upstairs.

Alicia felt her heart racing.

She knew that voice.

That voice was not Belinda.

They were escorting Marigold down the front stairs of her own home.

The party attendees took a new interest in their hostess.

Marigold jerked her arm from the one officer with a sharp "Arbuthnot was nothing to me."

"He was on the society board," someone offered.

"He knew you," another giggled.

The giggle worked like a trigger.

"Arbuthnot!" Marigold snapped. "Stalked around the damned stables singing 'Lynn, Lynn, city-of-sin!' So he knew where I came from. So what? He was long gone before that next board meeting. He never got to tell anyone a thing."

Mrs. Fortham, in her usual, slightly-throaty, North-Shore voice proclaimed "as if we needed to be told."

Alicia crept backward, away from the action, as her friend was handed off to uniformed officers.

Alicia could only stare. "She's another Smithy, isn't she?"

Smithy. If Aunt Jane had been here, she'd have known from the start. She'd have nodded and said, "Charming. Ruthless, but charming."

"I realize you'd hardly want things to go this way." Perkins hesitated by Alicia's side. "However, we've turned up Marigold's fingerprints on the framework of the vehicle. She used a battery-powered supersaw to shave that pin off the vehicle, and a simple glue to reset it. Of course, the glue didn't have the strength to withstand a sudden jerk. She simply drove up the access road on the morning of the accident, startled the horses somehow, and the pin she'd already damaged let go."

Alicia thought of the yellow poncho borrowed from the stables. A flapping poncho would have startled the horses. She thought of Marigold's continual dismissal of Mr. Arbuthnot's death as accident.

Was Allen's continued attention, because he knew she was a friend of his suspect?

"Yet another motive I missed," she said sadly, more to herself than anything. Alicia pushed her way toward the door, unable to stop rambling. "I thought she was a Cousin Claire. Not sensible, but fun you know. Wanting popularity. Not this ruthless ambition."

"I don't want you to think I'd stopped by tonight to gain entry here. Chance." Perkins followed after her as he rambled on into a long explanation. They'd waited for fingerprints...traces of the glue had turned up at once, but he had not shared every fact.

He had spoken as if facts were all, but had not shared all the facts.

She had relied on her great sense of human nature. Failure. Alicia couldn't make sense of his words. All her insights had utterly failed, as evidenced by her standing here. The evening took on a dream-like quality. She focused on the door to get her bearings and headed that way. Perkins disappeared, like people do in dreams. Others swam up, or by, and she barely took notice.

Steven departed, seeking a lawyer. The horde, largely oblivious, chatted, laughed even, as they set to depart. None hurried to part from their cocktails, either.

Alicia located her coat and bumped into Belinda at the same time. She gulped back all sorts of guilt and tried to greet her pleasantly.

"Wonderful about your job, I mean, in spite of all this." Belinda enthused. "I bet you are already transforming the whole place."

"Transforming?"

"Oh yes. Like you did at the Summer Stables. You pay attention to what people want. Customer service, I guess. Everyone has such a wonderful time there now. I have no doubt you'll work your magic with the historical society's collection."

Alicia stuttered out, "You worked magic yourself this season, bringing on that young horse. I couldn't believe how well he went in that last event."

"Secret weapon." Belinda winked. "My big bay has come on leaps and bounds since I started training lateral work under saddle. It was all thanks to Mr. Arbuthnot. He suggested ridden dressage lessons at the start of the summer. He really was a brilliant horseman."

Alicia could only nod. She'd been wrong about him and wrong about his killer. All because of something Marigold had said. She'd assumed he'd been a horrible old guy because Marigold had said so. "I was wrong, so wrong about Mr. Arbuthnot," she said to Belinda. Alicia realized she'd also been wrong about Marigold. All along, fooled into friendship. Plainly, she had also been wrong, wrong, wrong about Allen Perkins, who used her to get a handle on the case.

Belinda gabbled on about a horsey get-together.

Alicia didn't listen. "Clearly I am no Aunt Jane." Alicia didn't so much let her mind drift back toward a more comforting past, but actually race there.

Chapter 23 Cucumber Sandwiches

A 1950S TRIP 'ACROSS the pond'

Aunt Jane's arrival had been entirely unexpected, although it should not have been. She had, after all, announced her intention to travel, duly accepted the invitation to stay, and inquired as to convenient meeting locale.

Alicia, barely a teen at the time, had been both excited and anxious.

"She's spoke of visiting off and on for ages. I'm sure she'd like to, but don't be disappointed if she doesn't come," Alicia's Mum predicted. "When it comes to it, I don't see her hopping on a plane."

"Her letter said." Alicia remained focused on her task: cutting white bread into triangles. A simple-sounding goal that kept resulting in squashed-looking blobs. An English style tea, for lunch, looked doomed.

Aunt Jane's most recent missive for Alicia had been "I look forward to finally meeting in person." Since Alicia was a tot, aunt had included short notes at the bottom of family letters, just for Alicia.

"She said she made all the arrangements."

Her mother nodded. "You keep on ruining that whole loaf of bread then. We can use it for bread-pudding, I guess, in the long run."

Alicia wanted to ignore her, but there was this nagging doubt. Mum had already run through the list, several times: Aunt Jane was quite the old lady now, and hardly known to travel. If she'd been on the train line, it might have been different, but fly across the Atlantic? Spend a weeks away from her quiet garden? And all to stay with distant relatives, she'd hardly met? Not likely was the upshot.

"She knows me, we write all the time." Although Alicia felt quite sure, or wanted to feel sure, doubt nibbled away at her as she butchered the hapless bread.

She'd never actually met Aunt Jane, who was not even an aunt, but something more like a distant cousin, on Uncle Edmund's side. Even so, the short notes had grown and now that Alicia had reached teen-years, the two had kept up a lively correspondence for some time.

"I'm making proper English tea, so she'll feel at home when she arrives."

"Grilled cheese and tomato would have been more sensible. And I don't think we have any tea in the house." Mum yanked off her apron and checked her watch. Indeed, she'd go along to the bus stop, due at one. "I expect a message; a call or a note or a wire or something, momentarily. The old lady will send polite regrets. No doubt she'd let the idea get this far, just to show her best intentions. Perhaps she's sent a gift package, with a note. We'll hear, you mark my words."

Alicia did not voice doubt, but moved on to setting a pretty, and in her mind, "English-style' table. She listed the items over and over again; table cloth, linen napkins, and actual tea cups with saucers. The sandwiches would not go right, but she had plain biscuits, butter and jam. She wondered about cheese, or if she should make the grilled sandwiches her mother mentioned? Surely they were plain fare for a proper tea? The cucumber sandwiches would be perfect. Would be, if only they would go right! She focused on her task and barely noticed Mum's departure.

Smearing cream cheese as gently as possible only further mangled the soft white bread and it was only as she gave up, literally, stood up and said, "I give up," that the back kitchen door opened to reveal the expected person.

"My Alicia." Somehow, the voice was entirely as imagined, as was Aunt Jane, from top to toe. Awash in wintergreen and grey, such was her perfection to her role, the lady might have been a store-bought aunt. Her slight-brimmed hat embodied practicality, as did her simple green travel suit, adorned by a cream-colored scarf. Quite correctly, though somehow still warmly, Aunt Jane said, "how do you do."

Alicia, with far less perfect etiquette, plunged forward to hug and exclaim and found herself near tears. Embarrassed and awkward and more than bit surprised at herself, Alicia pulled together, and tried for a more staid greeting. What would this most correct aunt think? Yet all that sort of worry disappeared as the two plunked down at the kitchen table and began to talk.

And talk.

Mum tried to move the whole little party off to the dining room. Suggested letting 'Aunt Jane get settled' several times, and had (sighing) given up and put the water on.

"You look exactly as I expected," "sound so like," "I can hardly wait to show you," scattered about in a conversation that made up for all the things one could not fit in letters. The fifty year age difference was as nothing. The tea, such an impossible affair at the start, came together without difficulty. Aunt Jane casually dressed the bread before cutting precise triangles. Somehow, her triangles came out all the same size. She left the setting the trays to Alicia. They sipped tea as they sampled their efforts and talked, one-to-the-dozen.

"You two might be long-lost sisters," Mum remarked, though no one paid her more mind than the odd nod. And thus their week began.

No doubt, Aunt Jane saw a good deal of the adults. Uncle Edmund called, as well as others 'on his side.' The folks took Aunt Jane to swell places for dinners. Alicia, looking back, recalled only their 'two of us' adventures.

"Is that your little grey cat poised along that stonewall?" Aunt Jane motioned out a window one morning.

"Yes. Missus Tabs." Alicia could barely make out the cat, tiptoeing atop the grey granite stones.

"Well, someone is up to something on the other side. She's as good as telling us."

"Perhaps she's hunting?"

"Hunting, cats usually flatten out, swish the tip of the tail. She looks to me more curious."

"She does." Alicia affirmed, though she'd hardly thought to study the attitude of a cat before. "I wonder what is happening on the other side of that wall."

Aunt Jane gave her a wink. A tiny, lady-like wink, one almost didn't notice. "I have had that same thought myself, so many times in my life. If one wonders why a certain creature, or a person, behaves in a certain way, suddenly, you are so much more aware of what is going on in the world around you." She leaned forward, intent. "If you are up to something yourself, you learn how to be still, so as not to give the game away."

Alicia giggled. "I'm not sure what I would be up to."

"When I was your age, which, as I say it, brings me back to my own dear Aunt Katherine, who could ride a great thoroughbred horse or drive a smart pair of hackneys as well as any man. Aunt Katherine used to say, 'when I was your age' and she always meant to convey proper courtesy or teach a point of etiquette. 'When I was your age, we were expected to dress for company, and sit down to talk civilly, and none of this gadding about the back garden or having a guest cut flowers with you!' I always was dragging company out back, myself," Aunt Jane confessed. "I was so very proud of my flower garden. I am not sure if Aunt Katherine thought it was improper or disapproved of my pride, now I think of it."

"I wouldn't mind going for a visit and touring someone's garden," Alicia offered. "In fact, I was wondering if you would want to go out to the back field here. We don't have a fancy flower garden, but I have my pony out in the deep grass by the pond, and it's all waterlilies just now."

Aunt Jane eased to her feet, announcing, "I can hardly imagine a better outing." Pale pink lilies were less captivating than Daisy, the pony, as it turned out.

"So many years, since the railway took over, really," Aunt Jane had murmured. "Oh, your Daisy makes me miss the wonderful horses we had in my youth. The livery had a wonderful bay I rode, for a good many years. She was a cracking mount.

In fact, it was an outing on her that caught my Jeffrey's attention. Lots of people kept ponies, when I was a girl. They always claimed for convenience, but outings then were such fun. We'd go bowling along the lanes in a two wheel gig and stop overlooking the sea for a picnic. Any fine day in July we might go, with hampers full of cold chicken and lemonade." Aunt Jane stroked the pony's long face as she spoke, her mind far, far away.

Alicia could hardly offer a ride, but thought, as a treat, to borrow a cart from a neighboring farmer. The following day, Daisy, decked out in a mish-mash of harness and hooked to an elderly, hastily cleaned, wicker governess cart, stood at the ready to take them on an old-time adventure.

Mum set to spoil it all. "Alicia, I don't think so. That pony hasn't been driven in years. Not safe."

"She's fine," Aunt Jane eased out the front door, and clutching the rail, down the front steps. "She's a good sensible type pony."

Aunt Jane's unsteadiness gave Alicia pause. Aunt's liveliness and agile mind impressed as they talked, but out here, as struggled to get down to the street, she became a frail old lady.

"We don't have to drive her," Alicia looked up at her mother. She didn't know what to do but could see they ought to call it off.

"Tut." Aunt stopped to adjust the chinstrap of the pony's bridle. "I can see Daisy's nature plain as plain. She's not concerned about hitching up. Someone trained her right, long ago, and she's a good sensible pony. She'll do fine."

It took ages to get Aunt up the little back-step into the governess cart.

Daisy stood like gold.

Mum worried, and... somehow... Alicia did not. For Aunt Jane was right. She was right about a good many things. She could suss-out a pony's nature as easily as a human's.

"Walk on," Aunt Jane directed. The pony stepped up. When Alicia fumbled with the reins, Aunt Jane claimed them and began to talk about driving in the old days. Lengthening and shortening the reins, and why one might carry a whip. She pointed out corners where the cart must swing wide and rough terrain where it might tip.

They toddled over fields and hills and down quiet lanes. Aunt brought along her favorite book, Frost's '*A Boy's Will*,' and read out lines, like leaves falling all careless into their day. Frost had no small measure of sense, and Aunt Jane urged Alicia to gather good sense, like so many leaves, as well.

It was then she shared her story of Smithy, "long on ambition, short on skill." As well as Aunt Katherine, "always proper, and wanting everyone to behave properly in their place." And Claire, "My cousin Claire, your Uncle Edmund's mother. Always been such fun, but never quite sensible. I kept myself out of trouble a time or two, by not being deceived by people."

"Deceived?"

"Never believe people are what they claim. If you know human nature, you can see how things will go."

"Like Smithy, who wanted what he wanted, and risked hurting others and getting himself into trouble. He was a certain type."

Aunt Jane gave her a long, slow look. "It seems you can judge human nature too, Alicia."

Alicia felt uncommonly pleased with herself. She might be no great shakes at sandwiches, but she grasped what really mattered. Or so she thought.

The end of the visit arrived impossibly quickly. The afternoon drives, in so few days, had become habit.

Alicia determined to make the last the best. "Today's should be a picnic drive." This time, she made the sandwiches before cutting the triangles. Aunt made a yellow cake with cream and strawberries and they packed two jars of lemonade.

"Shall we ask the others?"

Just us," said Aunt Jane. "It was you I came to see Alicia. My Aunt Katherine meant so much to me you see, that I wanted to be a proper aunt myself. I feel like I've handed on her sensibility."

Alicia could scarcely frame the words to admit she somehow felt that history a part of her own self. She'd never seen even so much as a picture of Aunt Jane's Aunt Katherine, but could see her plain as plain, in mind's eye. She couldn't find words back then, age fourteen, but aunt had covered both their thoughts, with "I always knew we were like souls."

Alicia carried that certain sensibility from centuries past with her now. It was not without weight however, and she understood, or began to understand as she grew older, what Aunt Jane had attempted to pass along.

Chapter 24 The First Night Artists' Celebration

EDEN? ALICIA GOODMAN frowned at the gallery's brief description in the exhibition brochure and then back up at the framed artwork. Surely, the landscape was a bit rough-hewn to suggest such sublime origins?

New Year's Eve, alone, in an art gallery. It beat sitting at home alone, thinking about the past. Maybe.

The glorious painting, '*Yosemite*,' swept the eye skyward, past peaks to a golden sky. Yet, the gallery description of 'Edenic' seemed to miss the mark. There might be something unearthly in the steep cliff faces, something heavenly in the light, "but it's all so very untamed," she said, to no one in particular.

"Indeed it is."

None other than Sergeant Perkins strode over, in street clothes every bit as crisp as his uniform. He stood before the painting and clasped his hands behind his back, almost at attention.

He needed to cultivate more of an air of art appreciation, if indeed art had brought him. He looked far too alert. She could easily believe an arrest was imminent.

"Art reveals so much of human nature," he said.

Making conversation? Alicia had no idea how to respond. Human nature? She'd utterly failed in figuring out that department, herself. She resisted the urge to ask, "Have I lead you to some other killer?" she buttoned her lip and turned her gaze back to the painting on the wall. As she studied the wild-looking landscape, opened her mouth to speak, but then closed it again.

Why was he here? Surely he'd accomplished his goal. Arbuthnot's murderess charged, another case closed.

Devastated didn't begin to describe how she felt. She'd made herself come out for a walk around town, simply because it was New Year's Eve. It would have been too depressing to stay in, but this felt little better.

Alicia ran her fingers up and down the purple cord they'd used to rope off the area in front of the painting.

She'd not seen the sergeant since Marigold's party. Truth to tell, she'd been avoiding everyone. The gossip mill would be working overtime. It was exactly the sort of scandal Marigold would have loved, if it hadn't been about herself.

Perkins leaned close to read the gallery placard. "Revealing."

"It's a landscape," she finally blurted. "I can't see anything unusual revealed there." In the intimate environs of the art gallery, Perkins seemed utterly alien.

Alicia edged nearer the painting, waved a hand and pointed out, "It's Albart Bracht's most famous subject, I think. A very common landscape."

"Indeed. I was named for him," Perkins replied.

Named for? What a ridiculously artsy link for so staid and stern and individual. She looked at him, wondering if she'd misunderstood.

At her look, he continued, "His works were my mother's favorite. She adored his sort of aggrandized realism, entwined with his lesser-known tragic love story. I should tour out west. See the famous landscapes for myself."

"Like you feel a connection to Bracht, himself?" Alicia caught herself in the midst of the suggestion. "It's a sort of theatrical idea..." oh, how to continue that comment? She couldn't actually say it seemed too theatrical an adventure for the very 'official' official before her. "Albart. Really? I thought it was Allen."

"Call me Al," he suggested.

"Like the song," she said, instantly. Oh, good grief!

Perkins – Al, laughed out loud. "I don't know about feeling any great connection," he motioned to the center of the painting. "But, I'd like to stand on that same promontory as the deer and look up the valley toward the sunset."

"Do you think this exact valley actually exists?" Alicia looked back at the dramatic painting. "I would have guessed some measure of artistic license."

"It does exist, if I can say so without sounding like a know-it-all. I've heard a good deal about the artist, you see." Perkins leaned toward the work. "He traveled west, once. Just once. They say the landscapes drew him, but there's a local saga about how he left here as a struggling, actually failing artist. A romance changed him; made his painting famous." Al trailed off. Tugged at his collar. "I didn't mean to rattle on. The romantic part of the tale was probably all a matter of later embellishment."

"I'd love to hear it." Alicia smiled, doubtful, but Al took up the tale like a true storyteller.

"It was 1860-ish when this unemployed artist took a temporary job out west, climbed aboard the California Express, and set off with no expectations."

Alicia could picture the scene; the black smoke rising from the coal-black locomotive, the crowd squeezing into seats in the long train cars. A whistle pierced the general hubbub of voices and directives, and they were away.

"So, a romance unfolds," Alicia whispered.

Bart lolled in his seat along with the gentle sway of the train. The Derward Company's secretary sat opposite, primly upright. Mr. Derward himself, along with his top scientist, rode the comfort of one of the train's coach cars.

Bart shot the gal a grin. "We lowly, low-pay workers shouldn't complain. At least the old man didn't send us west in a covered wagon."

"I am not complaining." In spite of her youth, the secretary had a sharp voice to match her sharply pointed face.

Bart slunk lower. Colorado, California – the west, all of it, had no special call. His wife and sons were back east, in a Massachusetts most firmly unimpressed with his artistic efforts. He'd failed to attract gallery interest, he'd failed to sell, to sell anything, and everyone, wife and relatives alike, now expected him to work. He'd plunged into this last-straw situation. At least it involved drawing; sketches of areas, maps, and documentation of landmarks. He'd send money home and be back himself, before summer's end.

'Paid at least' played on 'Paid the least' in his mind, but he stifled further complaints. Plainly, Dorothy Ayers, while not rating a seat with the gentlemen either, felt herself too important to talk to the temporary help.

He shut his eyes but could not sleep – already he'd dozed far too much. He had a vague idea that they must be west of Chicago, but where, precisely, escaped him. It hardly mattered as every town and everything really, looked the same. Except for Dorothy, of course, who might look entirely different with her hair loose. He guessed her severe style helped her assume an older, perhaps more professional air.

She did have the bluest eyes.

The train's steady chug slowed as a whistle announced another, platform, another crowd, another town. The stop, departure, climb or descent; it all reeled along to passage of days and nights in a strange dozing muddle.

He felt too long away from home already. His boy Josh would have rushed out early to fetch kindling for the morning fire. His younger brother, Isaac, had the 'job' of holding the door for him. The two would giggle as they set the kindling in the fireplace. At least, they always did. They'd make the shape of a face or animal with the sticks. In his dream, he pretended to be surprised, as he did every morning. Would Millie play along with them? Or would they have forgotten the game by the time he got home? Millie had little lightheartedness in her. She worried so, as if wolves always stood outside the door. Instead of wolves, he heard the boys' laughter. The laughter went on and on until it became an odd, insistent crinkling. He came to slowly, to straighten and stiffen against the consistent rocking of the train.

Miss Ayers snapped the map out wider, with a great deal more crinkling. She did not look up.

Bart stifled a sigh and pulled himself upright. Outside, a steep hill climbed straight up away from the train, suggesting the rails clung to a precipice. Geographical changes might be worth noting. Bart glanced to the far windows, but could see no details through the crowd of passengers seated along that side.

The secretary gave the map a further shake. "Would you care to look? It's not long now."

"Of course," he said. Best if Miss Prim gave a good report about him to the head office fellows. He accepted the map and followed her gesture to an area notable on the map only for its high elevation.

"This is the Sierra area and the several counties in California the company is considering purchasing. The timber is well established, the size of the trees is apparently incredible, but the scientist will look for other development opportunities, too."

"Dig up coal, that sort of thing," he guessed. The pursuit of practical value brought them west, nothing else.

"I've already checked for land claims, various towns for owned properties, but lines on a map are not a great help out there. It's not like there are structures. I can record locations on the map, but you will have to note where that is in an actual area. Your sketches of landmarks will be vital when we send out a crew after timber."

"Let's hope there are some natural landmarks for us to find." As he spoke, Bart had no idea why, but his gaze drifted right as the steep hillside gave way to nothingness. The train traversed a bridge, allowing them a view straight up a perfect valley. In the distance, row after row of mountains crowded in shoulder-to-shoulder.

The vision, framed in the window for the briefest of moments, might have been an oil painting. Awe filled him, as this nave of granite, glittering here and there with quartz, swept his gaze skyward, towards the glitter of angels standing amid swirls of orange and gold. He must paint that amazing, glittering gold.

"My stars," he gasped. He seized Dorothy's elbow and urged her from her seat. "Look, you must look, from this side." He nearly fell into the lap of the man next to him, so great was his discomposure. Yet he wanted her to see – must have someone else see – this moment that surely could not last.

She rewarded him with a gasp. Her hands flew to her mouth, and there they were, arm-in-arm, for some untold time, while heaven itself opened its golden gate and shone down on them.

It would not last, could not; but did, gaining only a more and more angelic gleam as they watched. They found themselves most surely hand-in-hand, swaying along with the train as if at a church revival.

The train gave a lurch, and turned them from this vision, this first vision. Within seconds, each remembered courtesy, and propriety, and stumbled back to their own seats. They nodded to each another and to other passengers amid many 'beg your pardons.'

Dorothy Ayer's complexion glowed pink, a most attractive hue.

Albart risked a grin. "That was something, though, wasn't it?" As if the view itself made up for her discomfiture.

She hid her tiny grin.

The old fellow who might well complain about his feet or the appropriation of his lap, chuckled. "Ah, it was quite a sight wasn't it? A sublime moment for a young couple to share."

Their eyes met. They both should have protested. Neither spoke.

It felt, to each, as if he had looked into their soul.

Miss Ayers hastily looked to the window.

Bart, scarcely less touched, managed "I do thank you for looking at...the vision."

It might have been no more than a moment, a strange, re-membered moment, if the golden light had not assured them into a whole different realm. The train, utterly unrelenting, chugged them further and further into this 'sublime' world, as the old fellow named it.

If they both then waited for the next heavenly vision, they were not disappointed.

As the train climbed, the great sweep of plain opened on the one side. Distant peaks, some no more than shadow, sprang up westward. Constantly, the train climbed into and among mountains. Great peaks stretched upward, thinner and thin-ner, to disappear into the clouds, while valleys opened up in be-tween. Great swaths of green faded into the fog around water-falls, while the blue of the sky shone with a great, radiant light.

Albart tried to share his notion of departure from the ordi-nary world. Although his listeners nodded, he knew he could express this idea better in paint. He could scarcely wait to begin sketching. Oh, he was supposed to be sketching landmarks, to go with maps. Ha. He'd capture the essential lines of these mountains to paint them later. He could already envision his first great western landscape. He'd set it right here, looking up the valley heavenward.

He scarcely noticed the details of their journey. They disembarked. Efficient Miss Ayers had arranged for them to be met by a tourist-style mountain wagon and they proceeded with the company-arranged itinerary.

"Can you imagine," he asked. "They offered me a job painting scrolls on this style wagon. Scrollwork."

Dorothy looked at the weathered vehicle, its trim faded, yet attesting to its creator's skill. "This decoration requires no little skill," she pointed out, perplexed. "I should like to learn this hand."

"I, who will paint the very heavens." Albart dismissed with the very idea with a snorted "scrollwork."

They set off to find and record their first assignment. The surveyors' directions, like the map, gave no hint of the vast beauty they would discover. They took one long drive after another, first out along the crest line in the one town, then along streams by grazing lands, always riding side-by-side, sharing the picturesque beauty around them.

Bart could only speak of it in artists' terms. The atmosphere or aura, illuminating the clouds, the sublime glimmering down between treetops. Miss Dorothy Ayers saw it all as part of a wonderful world they had themselves discovered. Oh, they drove the mountain wagon and great draft horse along roads and paths that had been long established. Yet, these were rarely used by New England standards. They met few on their travels, and often stood alone in what seemed utter wilderness.

They stole away to drive Yosemite Valley on their own. The narrow mountain wagon, made to suit half a dozen, thumped uncomfortably over the rough-cleared road. Their livery horse, of rugged draft, struggled over rock and root. Yet, the drive felt idyllic. The covered top kept them shaded, the huge springs eased the bumps, the wide seats, made to accommodate several, allowed them to pack plenty of food and comforts. It was all company expensed, though it became something of a home to them.

Yosemite.

They stood among the trees.

They found themselves alone among the 'excellent timber.'

She took his hand. "We can't...can't allow it. We'll not give them the information, we'll refuse to let them find it. We'll keep this place secret."

Bart took her hand in both of his. "They have the map. We followed their map. Others have already found this. People know."

She brought his hands close. "We'll tell them it's too beautiful to ruin."

He snorted.

Desperately, she cried, "make up a danger. A curse! Frighten the workmen away."

Bart, as always, thought of paint. "If only I can share the heavenly light. If only others could see this place, as you and I see it. Perhaps then."

Together, they gazed up and up through the orange needles seeped in golden light.

"Truly, the best of the luminists have never imagined such light," Bart whispered. "This light is mine, my own."

"And mine," for Miss Primness was not one to simper and set-back.

Bart laughed aloud. "It is! And I shall paint it, for you as much as for me. I will show people what it is here. Rapture be upon us, in this realm. It is a place of dream, a place finer."

They scrambled to order supplies and he took to painting by day, every day. She hurried set up the canvas, learned to do borders, and even learned to make certain colors from raw materials at hand. They camped by the mountain wagon, meant for tourists' rides, and days passed.

She spent many a happy hour practicing her own hand at painting twined ribbons of red and gold to decorate the mountain wagon. Little did she suspect how her efforts would one day impress!

"I could live right here," Dorothy said more than once, "In the foothills of these mountains."

The artist placed one hand upon her heart, there in the nave created by trees, and whispered his love, before God. They stood together.

Under that heavenly light, they stood as if together forever.

"Oh." Alicia clasped her hands together. She felt the wonder, standing before the painting 'Yosemite.' "So beautiful. Did they live there all their lives?

"Alas, they were not a young couple, although Albart forgot his real life for that one summer. He was a married man. They stayed together, while Albart searched out views, sketched and planned, did this first painting. Only until, I guess, he finally remembered those he'd left behind."

Alicia could imagine it clearly. It had been the first chill morning of fall. Albart woke, thinking of kindling a morning fire, and waited for his sons' giggles. Only, his sons were home with their mother, gentle-faced Millie. They were all waiting, with no idea of his current occupation.

Beside him, Dorothy dreamed rapturous visions inspired by this realm they shared, between heaven and Earth.

"But love cannot be measured against duty," he said, speaking the truism harsh and bitter. He set the fire, one piece of kindling at a time, picturing his boys again. Laughing and giggling, but then not, for they waited, now, for their father's return.

He walked out to town and the train station the same afternoon.

"So, Eden." Perkins nodded. "They say, once he got home, he set his easel by a westward-looking window, though all he could see was his neighbor's lilac tree. He looked out on a garden but painted these sorts of views. He never did manage fame, beyond locally."

"But Dorothy did manage." Alicia felt the woman's heartbreak, from more than a century gone.

"I suspect she was always far braver than he," Al Perkins nodded. "A lady of 1861 takes a job, far from home, unescorted? I think she survived. I don't know, for sure."

Alicia turned to the vast, sublime landscape painting before them. "So, this painting is all about human nature."

"His ambition, and how the right versus wrong of it captivated so many." Al smiled down at her. "You know a little something about human nature, I think."

"I know a little something about Dorothy. I remember the name. A young woman took over all the decorative painting at the largest coach builders west of Chicago. She signed her first name only, but with a little twist. 'DorotheA.' The last letter capital. No one has guessed it was for her surname. She's been known as DorotheA, all these years. It must have been Dorothy Ayers. She'd have wanted to be somewhat anonymous. To save her family's embarrassment. So we have a record of this wonderful carriage painter, but until now, no one knew who DoratheaA really was."

"A woman working in a wagon factory in the middle nineteenth century?" Al guessed.

Alicia nodded. "She's remembered to this day. Her decorative painting was extraordinary."

"A better ending, for certain," he smiled. "Although, I like the sort of romance where the two end up together."

They gazed at one another, beneath the sublime work *'Yosemite.'*

'Oh ho,' Alicia scarcely had the chance to think, 'I wonder what Aunt Jane would think of my police sergeant?'

Sergeant Perkins, Al, tapped his watch. "Thirty seconds 'til midnight, Alicia. Will you share the countdown with me?"

Acknowledgments

Thank you to my Critique Partner, Vala Kaye -
www.valakaye.com
Also thank you to fab photographer Lisa Cenis –
www.shootthathorse.com
Nancy's stories - www.nlindleygauthier.wordpress.com
Nancy's reviews - www.longandshortreviews.com
A huge thank-you to my helpful readers and to ever-patient
Kent, too.

The Bonus Story

Heartbreak Cove

By Nancy Lindley-Gauthier
A Romantic short story by the author of
the historical novel: *TROUBLE COVE*
(Published by The Wild Rose Press)

CAPE BRETON ISLAND, 1917

"Come away from the water, Owen." Claire Digby tiptoed down the steep slope of granite and held out her hand. "Your Mum will skin me if I bring you back sopping wet."

Owen pried one more snail free, pretending he did not hear her, as he crouched perilously close to the incoming waves.

"Owen, come up here now!" Claire put her hands on her hips and stomped her foot, mimicking the gesture of her elder sister. If it took being cross to get him to behave, so be it. The ocean came back through the canyon of rocks at crazy speeds here and Claire knew the danger. Her nephew had scampered down the rocks a minute before faster than she could stop him.

251

Owen turned his cherubic face up to her and held out a shell. "For you, Aunty Claire."

"Oh, for me?" She couldn't help smiling. "An all-white one, is it?" She knelt on the warm granite in a pool of sunlight, all unaware of her distant admirer.

The silent man- a stranger to the two- stood alongside the lighthouse on the bluff above, as if transfixed by the view. He did not squint toward the grey horizon though, where the sky melted into the sea, nor glance at the foaming white water, arrayed in lacy threads around the rocks below.

The pretty girl with chestnut curls held him enthralled. She and the tot might have been a painting, as fine as any the stranger could ever claim to have seen.

Owen scooted across the grainy rock with his gift, and Claire, in the process of accepting the shell, captured her nephew and got him headed him back up toward the high-water mark.

They both had their backs to sea.

Neither saw the wave slam into the jagged rocks behind them, or felt the rush of water pour in between. The sudden swooshing sound sent Claire her only warning. She guessed, without looking, it was too late. Without hesitation, she seized little Owen and nigh onto tossed him up the rock face. Too late, too late.

Her admirer, one of the Cotton boys, sprinted down the wide ledge. He ought to have been hurrying along to collect up his traps before sunset...but he wasn't...all on account of her sweet smile.

He might have warned them, but had hesitated. Now, of course, he wished he'd spoke up. It mattered not now, for there they'd no time left to them. The swell of water rose fast.

"Owen!" Claire gave one last desperate shove as the frigid wave rolled up and lifted her. It stretched its great foaming paws to grasp Owen, even as it began to suck back. She shoved mightily against the terrible drag, but could feel it - could feel the sea try to claim her as its own.

All that was given her, in that one blessed moment of time, was the feeling of Owen being jerked away from her grasp and hauled up. Somehow, he had been saved.

It would have to be enough. Her whole life lived to rescue Owen. She'd no time for more. She flailed because she could not help flailing, but couldn't win. Way up above, the crumbling tower overlooking Heartbreak Cove would become her marker. Maybe one day they'd say her ghost roamed the headlands?

She slammed hard against a boulder as the frigid water swirled her body like so much flotsam.

Her dress caught tight around her waist and she was jerked back, quite abruptly, toward shore. The wave sucked back without her.

"Get right up to the top edge," a male voice commanded.

She could scarcely make sense of up or down, but clawed at the rock as the deep voice exhorted her. The topsy-turvy world steadied back to a familiar, sunlit sky over the brick-hard, grainy granite. She landed yards above the high-water line, gasping for air, Owen crying softly beside her.

"Foolish. Not paying attention." She berated herself as she draped her arms around him. "Owen, oh Owen."

Her words startled their rescuer. The lanky man, honestly more of a teenager, turned to her as sharp and quick as a gull. Claire braced for criticism.

"Darn unlucky." The deep voice hardly suited him. Without fuss, he hauled off his knit sweater and swaddled shivering little Owen in it.

Claire claimed the blame, if he wasn't going to go ahead and assign it. "My fault," she choked out.

"Happens," the fellow repeated. "No sense being upset about it."

"We might be dead," she blurted, "but for you." Poor little Owen, she kept thinking. Nearly killed because of his careless aunt. What would her sister say, never mind the rest of the family? She clutched the sodden sweater tight around Owen's shoulders.

Oh, horrors; the family. Her sister would never stop talking about this. All the family would know, then all the village. Claire would be called a fool and an incompetent and worse, and she wish she'd died right here at the foot of Heartbreak Tower.

Chills ran over her.

"Is your home back this way?" The fellow turned south toward the village and Claire managed to nod. He scooped up Owen for her and she stumbled in his wake. Her mind raced along ahead, hearing all them - all the village folk and her distant family members - all talking around dinner tables up and down the coast. She'd likely hear folks sneer at her in the street or look at her with disgust.

"How could I be so stupid?" She dragged along. Owen quieted as they walked, flopped against the chest of the stranger.

The young man walked in silence, but she'd not have guessed how his heart raced. She'd not have guessed he, who had run straight into the giant Atlantic wave to save them, now struggled to find the courage to ask her name.

"I've not thanked you." She almost blubbered out the words and took a quick, deep breath to try to calm herself. "I had no idea anyone was about."

"Truth is," the fellow admitted, "I go along about here regular, to fetch in my dad's lobster traps. I didn't see that one big curler coming, neither. Happens." The boy glanced over at her, but right quick, ducked his head. "There's a right deviltry in the ocean, I'd say."

Claire, nearly consumed by shame, felt a surge of surprise at his opinion. Hereabouts, the ocean was everything: admired and exploited, and the men who went to sea to fish or fight were the finest of all. "A right deviltry" hit her as an entirely new, if not wrong, idea.

They got home still sodden. There was nothing for it but the truth.

The talk was every bit as bad as she'd expected. Gwen's initial scolding seemed plenty, but then she ran next door to tell their Aunty Phyl. Probably five minutes later, the cousins down on the waterfront were talking about Claire's carelessness or shameful negligence or some such. Fool girl might have got poor dear Gwen's child killed. *Amazing Gwen put up with her,* they'd say.

Talk, talk, talk. Claire overheard some it and imagined even more. Gwen ghoulishly repeated plenty, too, as she made a great show of looking after both Owen and the new baby on her own. She might have a whole house to set to rights as well as two children, but her husband had gone to sea and her sister could not be relied upon.

"Poor, dear Gwen is having to manage on her own," rang here and there like a favorite chorus. Gwennie seized the mantle of sympathy and right nicely draped herself in it, until all and sundry spoke of the young mother who bore such tribulations with fortitude. She'd become the fine, long suffering sort.

Gwen set Claire emptying the dustbin and sweeping the walk, "if you think you can manage."

Claire felt the sting over and over. Not like she wasn't ashamed enough without reminders. She set to her chores of a morning, and ignored Aunt Phyl out there, saying "so sweet of you to keep her, Gwennie, when she's just more work for you," as if Claire stood there deaf as the post.

"As if I don't cook and clean like a servant to earn my way," she said finally, though no one heard. She kept out of the way.

Days after the wave, the talk kept her in. She hardly felt a moment of sunshine, what with hiding away.

Talk, talk, talk.

Claire felt her face burning if she had to so much as peep out the doorway. It was sheer chance, or perhaps, a measure of persistence, that her rescuer, her admirer, happened along at the one moment a week later that she set to sweep the front walk.

Claire knew the fellow's slouch at once, and she might have dove back at the sight of him, as he'd been first hand witness to her stupid carelessness, but she somehow could not let him wander on by without a word. She stepped out and raised a hand, but stopped short, surprised at his big grin.

"Miss Claire. This your house, then?"

"My sister's and her husband's. I'm up from Ingonish to visit." She didn't mention the new baby or helping about the house. Any villager would sneer at the claim. "You aren't from the village?"

"I work my dad's farm, down the way."

"Not a fisherman, not a sailor?"

He shrugged "We put in a few traps off the beach, come summers." He scuffed his feet, shot a sidelong look at the empty village road leading north, and took a deep breath. All at once, real quick, he spoke again. "Walking up now, if you'd like to join me?"

Claire stood stock-still on the threshold. After all this and here a fellow stood, asking her to walk out, with no doubt, none whatsoever, as to what he meant by it.

A couple of days ago, she'd have beamed and been flabbergasted and thrilled. She looked at him; he had fixed his gaze on the toe of his right boot as he waited. She took a long minute to study him up and down, from his heavy leather work boots to his hand-sewn trousers and cotton shirt. He'd a long jaw with the faintest shadow of stubble, and hair trimmed right straight and proper, by his mum, she guessed. More farmer than sailor, for certain.

A curtain twitched at Aunt Phyl's house next door. Claire felt her face flame.

"No. No, I can't. Not today." She drew back and shut the door right quick. Heavens above, the family and neighbors did not need more to talk about.

Embarrassed, she grabbed up her dust cloth and ducked into the front room. That day came back to her, too quick, like the wave. She recalled trying to get little Owen's attention and not minding the sea. He was always into something, that one. Owen needed keeping busy, every minute.

At the thought, she glanced around, and of course, here came Owen, teetering down the stairs.

"Take my hand, you adventurous one," she said and reached for his chubby fingers.

Gwen swept by her to snatch the boy off the step. "I'll thank you to leave him to me." She plonked the child in the middle of the front room and swept by, flipping her skirt away as if her sister smelled.

"If I'd left him to you, he might've rolled down the stairs," Claire said without thinking.

Gwennie flared up with a swift, "So, it's my fault, is it? Wait 'til I tell the aunts. They have plenty to say about you already."

"I have already apologized," Claire said. "I assure you, my apology, like my regret, is most heartfelt."

"And so it should be," her sister snapped. "You are nothing but a burden!"

"I guess you do think so," Claire shot back. "Since not once have you acknowledged how I've helped."

"You should be glad I allow you to stay. You put my child at risk."

"You have yourself been careless more than once. Some might have excused a mistake. There's been more than once I had to intervene or you'd have allowed this little bit to cry all night long in his crib."

"What do you know about it?" Gwen huffed. "What do you know about any of it?"

Claire pointed at the distant waves. "Here you sit, in this front window. I tell myself it's the most romantic thing ever, waiting and hoping for your sailor to return, but I see it now as nothing but pitiful self-indulgence."

Her sister rounded on her with a hand outstretched to slap, but Claire stepped nimbly back, though slammed her smallest toe into the sturdy oak leg of the rocking chair. "Ouch!"

"All your own doing," Gwen sneered. "Don't blame me."

"Don't blame you? You, who have such cause to complain? And complain and complain? You chose to be this weak, whiny worm. I was careless, and I am sorry for it. I am not sorry for you, though, not anymore."

"Get out."

Claire could hardly stop. "Talk about me all you want. Without me here, you will have to set your hands to work, or else all your neighbors will see what you are."

Gwen crumpled onto the chair, spinning to turn her back on her sister. "Go then."

Without a word, Claire marched for the door. She'd nothing; not her clothes nor her favorite book, not a bite to eat, nor a place to go. Still, going was the only choice. She hesitated as she left the garden gate, and she might well be forgiven for hesitating. Home was not too far south and she could always go home...or... she could turn for the north.

Suddenly set, Claire stormed out the front garden gate and straight up the narrow lane. Her imagination supplied the curtains twitching on both sides, so she kept her face set straight ahead.

She nearly blasted by the young man without even noticing him. He half raised his hand, hesitating. For an awkward moment, they stared at each another, until Claire blurted, "I'll walk with you."

Wordless, he held out the crook of his arm, as if they were really "walking out." He stepped along the lane with her on his arm until it became merely a path and still he carried on, perfectly proper, as if the entire village watched. They went up over the first little hill, overlooking the village and harbor.

Neither glanced at the view.

Claire kept her eyes fixed ahead, at the tip-top of the red and white tower up at Heartbreak Cove. She could imagine the *talk, talk, talk* behind her like the chatter of peepers in the deep green ferns.

"Heartbreak Cove," she muttered as they crossed the top edge of the rock. "So aptly named." It occurred to her she did not know this young man's name. Nor he, her's.

As if sharing her thought, he suddenly supplied his.

"I am Dan Cotton."

Her hand still tucked into the crook of his elbow, she felt his muscles tighten as he spoke.

"Claire Digby," she said. Then corrected, "just Claire, really."

Side by side, they looked down at the sloshing of water where she and Owen had lingered those moments too long.

"You must think me an idiot," she couldn't help saying, "with what happened that day and all. The village is talking of nothing else."

"No." He put one hand, most boldly, over the hand she had placed on his arm. "I guess I have never seen anyone braver."

"Braver?"

"Why, you pushed that child up, out of the waves, though it meant you fell back yourself. Only luck I managed to catch your dress, after." He blushed red, but battled on. "I am afraid I did tear it."

"You saved us both." It was all rather heartfelt and uncomfortable, and hardly polite conversation. Claire eased aside. This couldn't be the way newly-met friends talked when they "walked out." Folks sat around at shows, or met at the park. Surely they spoke of ...other things. She settled herself on a handy log and smoothed out her skirt tidily, as she cast around for more appropriate topics. She motioned to the view. "This must be the sight of many a heartbreak."

"Shipwrecks." Dan nodded. "It's why the beacon is here." He took a step nearer, then eased down onto the log next to her, folding his hands real careful, like he'd wandered into church.

Every bit as prim, Claire nodded to the tower. "I can see a face in that window, clear as day."

Startled, Dan stared up at the small panes overlooking the sea.

"I mean, I can imagine someone there. A new bride, waiting and waiting for her husband to return, anticipating his return, maybe forever. Perhaps her ghost wanders there still." Claire brought her hands to her heart as she stared, dramatically, out to sea.

Dan shot another doubtful look at the tower. "I guess I have seen that window a hundred times and never imagined anything like that. Sad thought, isn't it?"

Claire, about to expound on her theatrical vision, hesitated. "Sad?"

"Seems like a life together ought to be lots more romantic." He risked giving her a look. "You know, the old walking hand-in-hand kind of thing. Sharing the sunshine."

"It's not really the stuff they write stories about."

"I wish they would. Make a lot more sense than some poor soul pining all the time.'"

"Do you know, I never thought. Everyone imagines waiting for a sailor as the most dreamy, idyllic notion, but it is sad, isn't it?"

"Long absences." He reached over to pick one long strand of grass, hesitated, and stretched further to grasp one tiny violet just peeping from beneath the undergrowth. He held it out to her. "A beauty for a..." he couldn't quite get it out.

She grabbed the flower from his hand, perfectly sure her face was every bit as red as his. "Thank you." They both stared away east, as if transfixed by the wide expanse of sea.

The sun sank down into the gentle cushion of clouds as they strolled back. Dan Cotton carried half-a-dozen lobsters in a sack over his shoulder.

"I guess you've walked up and down this route half your life or more."

"Every summer since I was ten." Dan grinned. "Likely I always will."

She smiled down at the single flower in her hands.

"I'll call again." He didn't say it at all like a question.

"Wonderful." She touched his arm as they parted at her front gate.

Dan stood there, fiddling with the latch, not wanting to say good bye. Wishing the gal would turn around and say some further word.

Gwen flung the front door open and glared down the length of the walk.

Claire held out both hands to her sister. "Gwen, all this time, waiting for your handsome sailor. We all talk about it as if it's the most romantic notion in the world. I never once thought how awful sad you must be."

Gwen pressed both her hands over her mouth and sagged against the doorsill at her younger sister's words.

Dan Cotton, no longer the stranger, watched the two gals, so alike, laughing and crying together. Claire shot a smile back over her shoulder to him.

T'was near-enough like the sun coming out.

If you enjoyed this little romance, please do consider reading
Trouble Cove:

FAR FROM ALL THE ACTION of World War I, in a charming tourist's spot on Cape Breton Island, Elizabeth Eames has stumbled into the most wonderful man in the world.

She's landed herself in a world where wealth reigns supreme; where any eligible bachelor would meet her mother's aspirations. Of course, she's dead set on the one she's certain should not be mentioned in her letters home.

Actually, there's a lot she's not mentioning. Something is not-quite-right at the grand resort of Oceanside, but the possibility of trouble isn't about to make Elizabeth give up her one great chance at love.

www.nlindleygauthier.wordpress.com

Made in the USA
Lexington, KY
31 August 2018